MEMOIRS OF A TERRORIST

SUNY Series,
The Margins of Literature

Mihai I. Spariosu, Editor

Memoirs of a Terrorist

WITHDRAWN

A Novel by
Sally Patterson Tubach

STATE UNIVERSITY OF NEW YORK PRESS

Memoirs of a Terrorist is a work of fiction. Any resemblance to persons living or dead is purely coincidental. Any attempts to draw parallels to real persons could hinder the understanding of this work of the imagination.

Published by
State University of New York Press, Albany

For information, address the State University of New York Press, State University Plaza, Albany, NY 12246

Marketing by Dana E. Yanulavich

Library of Congress Cataloging-in-Publication Data
Tubach, Sally P. (Sally Patterson), 1946-
    Memoirs of a terrorist / Sally Patterson Tubach.
    p.   cm. — (SUNY series, the margins of literature)
    ISBN 0-7914-3005-7 (hard: alk. paper). — ISBN 0-7914-3006-5 (pbk.: alk. paper)
    1. Fathers and daughters—California—Fiction.   2. Women terrorists—Europe—Fiction.   3. Sexual violence—Fiction.
I. Title.   II. Series.
PS3570.U225M46   1996
813 '.54—dc20
                                                            95-39821
                                                            CIP

10 9 8 7 6 5 4 3 2 1

Table of Contents

Prologue in Hell

Dear Gordon,

　　When you read this, I will be dead. You are my last hope, but I know I can trust you to carry out my final wishes. We came a long way together since our days at Boston University—our moves west, our families, successful careers in business. But you never knew about the secret that lurked beneath the surface of my existence. The other day before I called you, I studied a class photo, yellowed with age, from our college days. We stood next to each other, grinning in the last row with our Red Sox' caps on our heads. Who could have guessed at that time that a deep crack would run through my life? It surfaced with the tragic death of my daughter, Megan.

　　As I write this, I have only a few months to live. Cancer is finally eating my guts, as Megan's death has eaten away my heart. All I have of importance, my old friend, are her writings. No one knew it, but Megan wrote about her life—stories, diary entries, reflections, miscellaneous fragments. If she had survived and her case had gone to trial, perhaps her writings would have been made public, brought forward as "evidence." As things turned out, I learned about them after her death and was able to obtain them from the legal authorities. For years I have combed through her words for clues, for a sign of her forgiveness, for a single positive word of understanding or reconciliation. Nothing.

　　During the last years of my marriage to Gina, she and I transcribed Megan's handwriting and spent untold hours poring over every detail of the resulting manuscript. We frantically looked for clues and scraps of evidence to prove Megan's innocence. We tried again and again to fathom the causes that led to her death. This was torture for me, because the deepest fault line remained an invisible abyss between husband and wife that prevented us from facing the truth together. Gina was not aware that for me, it was also a desperate search for redemption. She died three years ago, as you know, ignorant of the terrible secret I'm going to reveal to you.

Before I leave this world, you have agreed to visit me a last time so that I can entrust this entire manuscript to you—Megan's writings and my own commentaries interspersed throughout. You have promised to open it only after my nurse informs you of my death, and after you have finished it, to give copies to your friends in the publishing houses and the newspapers. That is all I ask you to do. Once they realize what you have handed them, the true story of my daughter will finally be known. I haven't had the courage to do this myself.

Megan has been dead for over seven years. To this day I am still unable to accept it—this perversion of time when a parent outlives a child. You took pity on us as our daughter's fate unfolded, that nightmare from which I never was allowed to wake up—her slow unraveling and her wild odyssey into the European nether world, from which she never returned whole. Paradoxical as it may sound, she indeed committed the crime of which she was accused, yet she was not guilty. You will be the first person to learn why this is so as you read this document. Her story remains in her own words. I do not violate it. I only fill in those blanks which she refused to write down, or rather, which she was not able to write down.

Now, finally, before it's too late, it's up to me to redeem Megan's memory. Only the truth can restore her name. It's all that matters to me. And I'm counting on you to finally disseminate it. No matter how you come to feel about me, Gordon, do it for Megan's sake. My life will be utterly valueless if this fails.

There is no need to read between the lines. Everything that matters is here in her writings and mine. Don't fail me, Gordon.

J. Arthur Lloyd
December 1, 1990

CHAPTER ONE

Growing Up

I should have known I would have a strange life when my father dragged home the body of a wrecked helicopter from an airport graveyard one summer day in 1953. He hauled the thing on a trailer pulled by a run-down truck. But then I was only three years old, and how should I know what a normal childhood was? Further back I have no memory.

We already had several abandoned vehicles behind our ivy-covered mansion, to the chagrin of our neighbors. Aside from these cars and trucks, our three-car garage full of motors, transmissions, axles, differentials, brake drums, and innumerable other spare parts, bore witness to my father's vehicular passion. I spent as much time as my mother permitted with my brothers playing among the parts and vehicles. But she tried to keep me busy inside the house, and hemmed me in with pink lace outfits and shiny patent leather shoes—attire wholly inappropriate for the precious few hours I eked out for myself in the male wonderland, a world just beyond my grasp.

The unexpected visit of our impeccably dressed neighbor, Mr. Marshall Glover III, signaled the beginning of the end of our Beverly Hills years. One evening Mr. Glover III rang our doorbell to complain about the presence of the helicopter shell in our affluent neighborhood and to demand its removal. During the ensuing squabble I slipped unnoticed out the back door and into the helicopter, which had come to rest in the area between our mansion and Mr. Glover's.

The cockpit was full of dials, switches, gauges, handles, levers and other magic objects, which I—lost to the world—pressed, switched, pulled and rotated. A sling made of canvas straps hung from the ceiling of the fuselage. I managed to pull myself up and settle into it. I was able to swing back and forth when I pushed my feet against the back of the co-pilot's seat. Then, with the mere flip of a mental switch, I was cruising above the nearby Pacific Ocean on a secret mission of my own making.

"Megan . . . MEGAN? MEGAN LLOYD, WHERE ARE YOU? DOVE SEI?" My mother's voice pierced my aerial reveries. Whenever she was upset she threw in some Italian. I heard other voices too, now nearby, now far away, but I didn't move, hoping they wouldn't find me. Eventually, footsteps approached, and my mother's head of thick black hair emerged in the gaping hole through which paratroopers had jumped. She surveyed the interior until she spied me. "Grazie a Dio!" The relief came first, then the anger. "Good grief, bambina! What *are* you doing all tangled up in that old parachute? I *knew* your father went too far with this helicopter. First the neighbors are angry, and now you get lost in it."

"I'm not lost," I insisted.

"Here Megan, let me get you out of that," she said, and extricated me from the parachute and from a ride more thrilling than ponies or tricycles or anything I'd yet experienced.

I was about to protest, but at that moment, she cried out, "I found her. She's in the helicopter!" Three more sets of footsteps approached on the run.

"Is she all right?" My two brothers and my father blurted out the question simultaneously, as they came to a halt and peered inside.

"She's all tangled up in this parachute. She could have been strangled. You get rid of this awful helicopter," she hissed at my father, or I'll never sleep with you again!"

✿ ✿ ✿

A year later we moved, helicopter, vehicles and all, into a deserted arm of Mandeville Canyon in the suburban west side of Los Angeles—I don't think it was just because of my parachute ride in the helicopter. By then I had quit worrying whether my mother slept with my father or not. My brothers and I all slept not only in separate beds, but in separate rooms in Beverly Hills. So why shouldn't *they* sleep apart? For some reason, only my parents shared one big bed and one bedroom at night. It was fun to crawl in with them once in a while and get lost in the sea of covers and bodies, but my mother never let me stay very long. She never got herself a separate bed either. Once, in the middle of the night when I woke up and wandered out to the cocktail salon, I saw her asleep in her bathrobe in an easy chair, a book spread out face down on her bosom. I tiptoed up close to find her mouth open and hear her snore. She and my father continued to eat together, along with the rest of us, so I figured if my mother preferred the big easy chair to their bed, it was all right with me.

My mother loved Beverly Hills, but my father hated it. He told her wealth created false values and that they'd be better off to raise the children farther away from society, in, say, a country environment—after all, their children were the most important things in their lives. Later on I learned that all three of us had been mistakes—or were at least, "unplanned." Not that they didn't seem to want us. It was just that my father had a greater love than the love for something as commonplace and easy to come by as children—a love for things mechanical, for the smooth functioning logic of the machine. His devotion was something only a particular type of mind at the dawn of the modern technological explosion could comprehend. He waxed absolutely poetic whenever someone did him the favor of asking, "How's the junkyard, Art?" His vocabulary stood ready—"the miracle of technology . . . the quality and artistry of precision parts . . . the intelligence, exquisite beauty and clean perfection inherent in fine design and craftsmanship." Yet there was another side to him. He was given to sudden and rambling reveries about the "starry night skies" that had been so much more brilliant in his youth before city lights and air pollution had dimmed them. He loved machines, but at the same time was often contemptuous of the civilization that had produced them. And then there were his cultured manners and classical music which, unlike his junkyard, he kept to himself.

My father had an inimical way of endearing himself to the rich and famous. Not only did he close the front door on Marshall Glover III the evening he dropped by to complain, but another legendary episode of family history was born shortly before we moved away from Beverly Hills. Several versions were told for years around our dinner table, but the version I remember went like this: the well-known sculptor, Marcel Corbin, also found occasion to relay his opinion of my father's helicopter over cocktails at the Beverly Hills Union Club, and in so doing dropped the word "eyesore." Thoroughly baffled, my father protested, "Eyesore, my foot! You, of all people, should know better. Has your aesthetic sense taken a vacation? That helicopter is one of the finest examples of quality American workmanship and utilitarianism. The stress calculations for its rotor are a hundred times more critical than the angles in your statues. Molding a bust is crude child's play compared to wiring the helicopter's vast and complex electrical system." My father left the meeting irritated and remained rankled by the conversation the rest of that infamous day. According to my mother, his last words before going to sleep had been, "that barbarian Frenchman!"

My parents called their new fifteen-acre arm of Mandeville Canyon a "rustic haven." I remember my father trying to convince my mother to make the move. She had no desire to leave our "lovely Beverly Hills villa," for some "dusty old canyon," while he argued that it would be good to own a "rustic haven." It would provide us with a silent hub in the midst of a growing metropolis, for enjoying art, classical music and mechanical pursuits. I remember him clearly during one of these discussions—an imposing man of Scandinavian descent on the veranda overlooking our enormous Roman-style swimming pool. He wore an ivory silk dressing gown and held a scotch in a Steuben crystal glass in one hand. The afternoon sunlight caught and turned his smooth blond hair and perfect, razor-thin moustache almost white. His parents had long ago anglicized their Norwegian name to "Lloyd," but for me my father embodied something of the far northern summers of continual daylight. At moments like this he seemed the incorporation of Apollonian radiance and reason. Inside our house, his appearance was always immaculate; only his eternally dirty fingernails gave away his mechanical passion.

As usual, my mother, elegant but brooding, languished and sighed in response to his comments in her cushioned patio chair, her southern emotions hidden behind dark eyes. My two brothers had inherited her dark hair and complexion, while I looked more like my father—light, blond and Scandinavian. My skin tanned to a deep brown during the warm summers, but no one could account for my green eyes. Now, as my father tried to win his point, he suddenly took off on a verbal flight of fancy, as if he were describing a piece of machinery: " . . . that rustic haven would provide us with an inviolate bit of paradise, an innocent refuge, pure and isolated from the world, in communion with itself alone." But I don't think he convinced my mother until he uttered the words, "We could build a new mansion on it." In the meantime, there was a little old cottage and a horse stable and corral already there, and we could live in it until the new abode was finished. The children could all enjoy the advantages of unpretentious, healthy outdoor living away from the effete snobs of Beverly Hills. We could turn up the console to allow his classical music to echo off the hills. And finally, there would be plenty of room out of the sight of snooty neighbors for his rare mechanical collection.

When we three kids saw the canyon for the first time, we were all on our father's side. A "rustic haven" was the same thing as kids' heaven. It meant you turned off the main paved road, and passed the metal "No Trespassing" sign with the bullet holes in it. Then you wound along a dusty dirt road next to a small gully and past gnarled oak trees that grew on hillsides full of wild chaparral, lizards, gophers, snakes and rumors of Indian relics. It meant hours and days of exploration, and fantastic games of hide and seek and blindman's buff in cool dark labyrinths of wild vegetation with narrow branching stream beds, and who knew what other treasures. The cottage was small, but that never bothered us three kids or my father, because we lived for the outdoors. In fact we all spread our wings. But with no room for it inside, my mother's washing machine was hooked up outside next to the back porch beside a long clothes line my father constructed for her between the porch and a laurel tree. He put her dryer in mothballs, saying that sun-dried fabrics were better for your skin. I could never understand why she didn't prefer doing the laundry outside, but one day as she hung up clothes, I overheard her say to my father, "I can't stand this healthy, rustic life. It was bad enough giving up the servants, but it's humiliating doing laundry outside." He countered that she should overcome her false snobbery now that they were free of Beverly Hills. Besides, no one could see her in the canyon except us, so how could it be humiliating? And she argued back, "What about low-flying airplanes?" and, "When are you starting on the new mansion you promised?" I don't think she adjusted as well as the rest of us to the changes. Eventually, she talked about the necessity of accepting one's fate in life.

Life in our rustic haven went on for a number of years without the promised new mansion, but not for lack of money. My father was simply too busy with his mechanical collection to take the trouble to get the project off the ground. To appease my mother he hid the ugliest objects in the stable that came with the canyon. The helicopter, his pride and joy, came to rest between the stable and an equipment shed. Around the other vehicles, my mother had vines and vegetation planted in an attempt to hide them from public scrutiny. My father argued that this was wasted effort, since no one could see his collection in the canyon, but my mother continued to worry about low-flying pilots and some sort of principle involved.

After my oldest brother, Jeff, mastered the electric saw and the art of hammering, he built himself an elaborate, two-room treehouse. My second brother, Chris, who wanted to raise snakes and sell their eggs for profit, built himself a large terrarium behind the house. The first fat snake he bought delivered herself of a clutch of 19 eggs, which, once hatched, yielded the same number of sleek wriggly silver babies that glinted in the sunshine. He fed the familial tangle with rodents caught in mousetraps and frogs he caught with his hands. He managed to sell a total of three snake eggs in two years to friends in his cub scout troop, who thought they were "boss."

Jeff's boy scout troop had its first camp-out in sleeping bags behind our house one weekend. Somehow, Chris's original mother snake, Marsha, now mature and sluggish at a full four feet in length, escaped from the terrarium in the night and terrorized one of the new scout members from 5 until 6 A.M. Sunday morning. She crawled onto his sleeping bag and stretched herself out for a sun bath in the early light of dawn. The brave scout, asleep on his back, was awakened by Marsha's impressive weight as she moved onto his abdomen. When he realized what had come to rest on him, his body froze and he stopped breathing. Without making a sound, he emptied his bladder and bowels into his sleeping bag, convinced he'd seen his last hours at the tender age of twelve, until the other scouts began to stir around 6 A.M. Their voices and motions sent Marsha on her way, and her presence in their midst, once noticed, created an uproar such as hadn't been heard since Indians danced in Mandeville Canyon.

After lengthy discussions between both parties' attorneys, the parents of the traumatized scout graciously declined to take legal action against my parents. And the brave young survivor earned two more merit badges than any other troop member that year. Jeff decided that his reputation had been ruined by association with Chris's negligence and idiotic hobby. One week after the unfortunate episode, Chris discovered his terrarium empty. After a frantic search he found all his snakes frozen solid in a grotesque Medusaesque knot in the deep freezer. As a result of the screaming brawl that ensued between my brothers, my father grounded them temporarily "for life." My mother ceased preparing frozen food for several months, but eventually my father announced that snake meat was a delicacy, and gradually our chicken dishes began to contain morsels which tasted more exotic than anything my mother had fixed before.

Some time after the snake episode died down, Jeff, by promising to wash and polish the Mercedes sedan once a week for the next century, persuaded my father to buy him a motorbike. Soon he had worn an enviable dirt bike track into two of the canyon hillsides far enough away from the cottage so that you couldn't see them, but close enough that you could hear a high-pitched, unmuffled whine buzzing away for hours on weekends—a noise which never bothered the rest of us, but which was "insufferably nerve-grating," according to my mother.

Looking back on it, I can see that my life took a turn for the better in the canyon. My mother quit dressing me in pink lace dresses and shiny patent leather shoes and got me some good things to wear—jeans, T-shirts and sneakers. I started to do more on my own. As soon as I could tie my own shoe laces, I would leave my bed at the crack of dawn on weekend mornings to be with my father and brothers. Jeff's and Chris's farming and reptile crazes were behind them, and they began to occupy themselves in and around the stables and the junkyard where they worked on vehicles along with my father. Jeff gradually added a sub-collection of scooters, motorbikes and motorcycles to my father's large-vehicle collection. My brothers didn't really like my presence there, but I wanted to be where the action was. As much as possible, I avoided the cottage, my mother and my grandmother, who had come to live with us. Since, according to my father, servants remained inappropriate to our new country lifestyle, the adult women spent their days making homemade pasta and tomato sauces, speaking Italian, listening to operas on the radio, rounding us up for meals, and washing clothes and dishes. Thank goodness they said I was too young to help. Probably they preferred their own company (occasionally, my mother dressed up, took her mother and the Mercedes sedan and spent a day on Rodeo Drive). But I also think they believed a light blond female was genetically incapable of learning to cook, so I fell through the cracks in their categories.

My father was different. By the time I was six, my regular presence in the junkyard was established. That's when he decided I should learn to do something useful, like grind valves. Jeff and Chris could already ride and repair motorbikes, and Jeff was overhauling the 1930 Chevrolet. My father was busy with one of his Duesenbergs when he gave me some grinding compound one morning and set me in front of

32 valves which were lined up in numbered holes drilled through a block of wood. He demonstrated how to twist them back and forth till the edges were smooth. I loved my work. When I finished the valves, he put a wire brush and a black rag in my hands and set me in front of a tub of cleaning solvent and a pile of dirty black engine parts. Then he showed me how to clean off the grease. When I was done, they looked like new and I looked like a chimney sweep.

One Saturday afternoon, when I bolted out of the cottage to head for the junkyard, I found my father and my brothers standing side by side watching something. It was Roxie, our small brown and white Collie who stood there glued to a strange dog who was propped up against her rear end with its paws on her back. Roxie tolerated this affront unperturbed, but it didn't seem right to me that this strange dog should lean on her like that. So I asked the assembled audience, "Shouldn't we try to unstick them?" Everybody ignored me in stony silence and continued to stare at the dogs until the stray mutt quit rocking back and forth and they separated on their own. That was all there was to it, but it left me with the uneasy feeling that Roxie had been somehow wronged while nobody had come to her rescue. Sometime later, rather vague in my mind, Roxie had a litter of puppies in the stable. She and my mother cared for the pups, and it wasn't until I was much older and wiser that I connected the two events in my mind.

During the next years, following my introduction to auto mechanics, I also became an expert in several other pursuits—naturalism, guerilla warfare and baseball. With my boyfriend from elementary school, Stevie Carpenter, who played first base in a little league baseball team, I learned to pitch, catch and bat. But when I decided to join his team, I was summarily turned down because of a reason beyond my comprehension—my sex. What sex had to do with the ability to catch, throw or bat a ball, I couldn't understand. I could bat and catch better than Stevie, and I threw at least equally well, but everyone told me that girls just didn't do that. I mean, I couldn't even apply to the Little League, because they didn't have application forms for girls. Period. No one would say why I couldn't use a boy's application form.

What was left were the boy scout activities, the long hide-and-seek afternoons, and all kinds of war games in the upper acres of the canyon—one enormous, jungle-like playground for me, my brothers and the scouts, who despite the snake terrorism weekend, continued to hold camp-outs on my parents' land. Often we got the neighborhood kids from down on the paved streets, who were lucky enough to be allowed to associate with us canyon kids, to join us. When there were enough of us, we divided up into two small armies and played hide-and-seek, and discover and ambush for hours. I loved to play the spy and was good at it. I could penetrate into the enemy's territory and learn their secret plans better than anyone else because I knew the terrain like the back of my hand. I had hiked several times with my brothers to the top of our long, narrow canyon and back. I had forded streams, straddled crevasses, slid down rock slides on my be-hind, climbed vertical surfaces clinging to roots, caught lizards and collected polliwogs. I knew the difference between a garter snake and a rattlesnake. I could spot a loose stone before I stepped on it. I knew which branch to hang onto, and I could start a campfire with one match and no paper every time—more than you could say for ninety-five percent of the boy scouts I knew. I had a sizeable rock collection which included a spectacular piece of peacock copper and a colorful piece of petrified wood from Arizona, and I could explain to you the differences between sedimentary and igneous stones. For our war games, I discovered and appropriated for myself the best trees for look-out points, the safe underbrush devoid of poison oak, the cave in the eroded bank and the concrete storm-drain pipe that everybody else was afraid to enter. *My* dough biscuits on sticks were good, I knew, better than any of the scouts', whose skills hardly impressed me.

But I was envious just the same. I couldn't join the Boy Scouts any more than I could join the Little League, my outdoor skills notwithstanding. All the while, the boys accumulated sharp-looking merit badges on their sashes and moved up from rank to rank. Instead, I had to to join the Brownies and Girl Scouts and content myself with learning various household arts and crafts, activities for which I ex-hibited no talent.

✧ ✧ ✧

Once, while I was still Brownie age, my family was invited by a scientist and his wife to join them for a weekend near Palm Springs to explore some of the canyons and caves which formed the San Andreas earthquake fault. I was enthralled with the prospect. Canyons away from home. Would they be better or different from our canyon? New territory offered an opportunity to prove my skills on different turf.

We arrived in the prearranged trailer park about noon with our Mercedes sedan and Airstream trailer and located the Carlsons in their trailer. Towards evening we drove out into the desert where Dr. Carlson took all of us—men, women and children—on a short walk through some of the small canyons and caves which were part of the large earthquake fault. I was awed by this new piece of wilderness, but the pace was a little slow for my taste. That is, my mother and Mrs. Carlson slowed us down (at least they left grandmother back at the trailer). No matter. The next day was the big, all-day hike, and that evening I caught a real live tarantula in an old tin can. I broke one of her legs accidentally as I pushed her with a stick into the can. My father transferred her to a jar of alcohol to better preserve her, but not before he gassed her to death, with a quick spray of butane from a canister in the trailer.

That night in the desert I could hardly sleep. Cozy in my trailer bunk above Chris, I tossed and turned and thought of Amaryllis in her jar, and how I'd found and captured her, and how we'd go hiking the next day—caves, dirt trails, the company of boys and men. During the night I woke up several times, always hoping it would be light. Finally, I couldn't help myself and fell into a deep sleep. I dreamed about a silver lizard who made its abode in an abandoned Duesenberg carburetor in the desert, and lived off dough biscuits it dug out of tarantula holes. The tarantulas fought against this thievery by snapping at the lizard with black pincers, but the lizard was faster and succeeded in knocking all the stolen biscuits into his carburetor home with his tail. At one point the lizard shot biscuits towards the saguaro cactus next to me. To get a better look at this struggle to the death, I jumped into the air and rose slowly off the ground. I flapped my arms like a bird to increase momentum and rose higher and higher until I hovered safely over the arid battles that were played out far below.

When I opened my eyes, I was alone in the trailer. The sun was high in the sky, so it had to be late in the morning. The sheets and blankets on Chris's bunk were jumbled up and he was gone, as was everybody else. Sensing something afoul, I scrambled down, pulled on my jeans, T-shirt and sneakers and ran over to the Carlson's trailer which was parked next to ours. The Carlson's jeep was gone. I burst into their trailer and my heart sank. There sat Mrs. Carlson, my mother and grandmother at their breakfast table drinking coffee. "Where *is* everybody?" I cried frantically.

"Why, *we're* here," my mother answered with a slight touch of annoyance, "and your father and brothers have gone with Dr. Carlson to explore the earthquake fault." My nine-year-old world collapsed. Betrayed. But by whom? The men or the women?

"But why did they go without *me*?"

"Well bambina, you were so sound asleep nobody wanted to wake you," my grandmother offered.

I knew and they knew, this was a lame excuse, if not a dirty lie, so I waited for more. "And . . . well . . . ," my mother hesitated but felt obliged to continue. "It was going to be an all-day hike, and it's probably too difficult and tiring for you, Megan." Another lame excuse. I stared her down and waited for something more plausible. "And . . . well Megan, you know they are all men except for you, and what if you had to go to the bathroom? Why, you would have no privacy!"

Suddenly her voice gained conviction. I was thunderstruck. So *what* if I had to go to the bathroom? *I* could find a big rock to hide behind without stepping on a reptile. But my mother grew taciturn, and her argument suggested a realm of mystery I had no right to question.

I held my tongue, but I suffered all day long in the presence of the women. Even when they took me to the swimming pool, I felt cheated. And I didn't want to hear the stories the men told when we all sat around dinner that evening. I excused myself early and went back to the trailer to contemplate Amaryllis. I decided I preferred her dead. I would have been uneasy with a live tarantula in my room, because anything living might possibly escape, and then what? A ray from the setting sun shone through her jar, and I watched the thousands of flecks of indeterminate nature—dust and hair as well as bits and pieces of her body—in a state of suspension, signaling the beginning of the process of physical deterioration, of her gradual diffusion into component parts.

✿ ✿ ✿

Back home in our canyon I was still pretty much master of my own world, and at school I found that Amaryllis created the biggest sensation by far in show-and-tell in both fourth and fifth grades. However, in sixth grade Otto Fredericks brought his tonsils and adenoids in an oblong vial of green formaldehyde to show-and-tell. I realized from the gasps of my schoolmates that Amaryllis would take second place to this gauche display, and I decided it was below her dignity to be shown in the same company. I discreetly left her jar in my lunch pail, and when Miss Bailey asked me what I had brought, I apologized for having forgotten to bring what I had intended, but promised to remember it for next time. Fortunately, Miss Bailey forgot to ask me next time, and I retired Amaryllis from public life. She continued to occupy the place of honor, however, on my dresser for another year. Eventually, hairs and pieces of her limbs grew thicker on the bottom of her jar than on her body. When I told my father about it, he said he'd take care of it. The next day Amaryllis was gone. I asked no questions.

When Stevie Carpenter and I were eleven years old, we developed a new game he called "King of the Mountain." We used our favorite honeysuckle-covered bank near the dead oak tree. We'd face each other at the top, and at the signal, try to shove or wrestle the other one down to the bottom while retaining one's own position at the top. Anything was allowed—except pulling hair or other dirty tactics. Strength and physical contact were everything, and we were pretty evenly matched. Part of the time I was able to force him down and scramble back to the top before he caught my foot or a leg to pull me back, and part of the time he would announce his sovereignty from above while I extricated myself from the bushes and readied myself for the next onslaught. The rest of the time we both rolled down to the bottom together in a tangle of arms and legs. Panting, we tried to hold each other down while we looked for an opportunity to make our own get-away for another ascent. This went on for hours and we never tired of it. We didn't keep score, and I grew to like it better than batting practice.

When Stevie and I turned twelve we both had to join the Presbyterian youth group in Brentwood. We went miniature-golfing, had picnics at the beach, sang in the youth choir, and eventually had parties where we had to dance with members of the opposite sex. At the first dance, he chose fat Janet Macintosh for his partner. I was sore at him for months and finally told him that I'd always thought his baseball playing stank.

* * *

About that time my father finally got around to building the new mansion he had promised my mother. The old cabin was torn down and his vehicle collection reduced to the items he could store in a new barn out of sight of what came to be called our new home. That "new home" wrecked our canyon idyll. It had another large Roman swimming pool like the one in Beverly Hills. A huge redwood deck and fence surrounded it, and eventually a hedge of red bougainvillaea covered the fence. My brothers and I had separate bedrooms again. My mother had her very own washing and ironing room. But with the mansion, servants returned and she didn't have to bother anymore with washing and ironing.

The house was too big, with too many rooms, many of them empty, and long corridors. The kitchen was large and airy with a skylight. Everybody spent more time indoors. There was a wet-bar, an elaborate stereo system in the living room, a pool table in the glass-covered sun room at the far end of the house that my father and brothers often used. But no one would teach me how to play. There were three flagstone fireplaces. For a while we kids got our friends together and roasted marshmallows in the big one in the living room in memory of boy scout days. But soon my brothers grew tired of this, and I gave it up too when I was reduced to doing it by myself.

❀ ❀ ❀

I started puberty about the same time as my girlfriends, and I didn't really mind, because the good times I'd spent with the boys seemed to be over. I used sanitary napkins for the first couple of years, but then my more progressive girlfriends convinced me, with a tone of condescension, that tampons were far superior. I envied them, and wondered why I was so out of it, so I persuaded my mother to buy me some, and when my next period came around, tried to use one. But, alas, I couldn't figure it out. I reread the directions and tried to make sense out of the anatomical drawing to no avail as I struggled with the little cardboard tube in the bathroom. Waking her from a nap, I confided my dilemma to my mother. She said she'd tell me how babies were made in detail when I turned eighteen. Then she went back to sleep and we never talked about it again.

Determined to solve the tampon dilemma on my own, I saved the anatomical drawing and used it as a place mark in a book I began to read on the sly—*Sex in a Happy Marriage*, written in 1933 by a German doctor, Johan von Wilamowitz, M.D.—that had gathered dust in an obscure spot on my parents' bookshelves for at least as long as I was aware of its existence, and probably longer. The cover page contained an inscription in my grandmother's handwriting to my mother: "May you avoid all the problems I had," dated November 29, 1935, my parents' wedding day. I studied this volume line by line from cover to cover. I especially pondered the sentences and paragraphs which were underlined or commented upon in my mother's hand, although they seemed to deal primarily with issues of hygiene.

At a favorable opportunity, after everyone had gone to bed one night, I set out to explore my intimate parts with my hands, convinced from my studies that I too must have the anatomy capable of holding a tampon, even a penis, according to the marriage book. Besides that, I was supposed to have a clitoris, too, about which the marriage book was a little vague, except to say it was very sensitive to the touch. In an immature way, it might or might not have something to do with "climaxes" and "orgasms," the culmination of sexual bliss in a happy marriage. Orgasms, moreover, were something which perhaps even some women occasionally enjoyed as a result of intercourse with their husbands (I couldn't tell whether Dr. von Wilamowitz approved of this for women or not, but he made clear that they definitely enjoyed it very much in a vicarious sort of way when their husbands had climaxes). I didn't really understand these new terms. I was mainly interested in how to use a tampon.

After some careful checking, I located what was what, according to the anatomical guide from the tampon box. Reassured, I explored myself with my hands. Continually cross-checking with my reference texts, I became satisfied that things were normal and focused my explorations on the clitoris.

Much to my surprise, the little spot was not only sensitive to the touch, as Dr. Wilamowitz had predicted, it hardened and felt good. The more attention I gave it, the better it felt, and I didn't see any reason to stop. I began to wonder if I could approximate marital bliss in this way all by myself.

When my manipulations reached a frantic pace and my leg muscles tensed, a strong wave of euphoria spread out from the miraculous spot and vibrated throughout my entire body, making me want to cry out and gasp for breath. After a moment's pause, I resumed rubbing, cautiously at first, and then more rapidly until another wave swept through my body that set my head turning from side to side from shear pleasure. I let that one subside and decided to try a third time. No sweat. Another electric arc to heaven for a few blissful moments. And again. Were these orgasms?

I interrupted my experiment to reread the relevant pages of Dr. von Wilamowitz. He confirmed to my satisfaction that these *were* the orgasms meant to bring bliss in a marriage, and I decided that in some important way I had become a woman. As the physical intensity subsided and I grew sleepy, I remembered that I'd had similar sensations riding horseback as a little girl.

✿   ✿   ✿

Dear Gordon,

How strange to see the days of my daughter's childhood through her own eyes. The things she recalls, the things she does not and the things that seem humorous, distorted, criss-crossed, mixed in with other events as time seems to overtake itself. Or perhaps it is my own biased recall, the warped prism of my own mind. I was totally unaware of her early interest in male competition and sex, for example.

I reread this chapter of our family life together many times. With all of its lack of conventionality—canyon, tarantula, junkyard—I have to admit it was a world all of my own reality around which everything else revolved. But isn't it fair to conclude that she enjoyed a relatively happy childhood? The simple ebb and flow of emotions, the little tragedies. What looms large in a child's mind constitutes a mere trifle in the everyday routine of the adult world—the incident with the dogs or her hiding in the helicopter fuselage. No mention of the many times she fell asleep on my lap while I listened to classical music. No trace of memory in her about the time she went under in the swimming pool at the age of six. I stood frozen at the edge, transfixed until she slowly turned towards me, her green eyes wide open. Then I dove in fully dressed and pulled her out.

But after that came the moment when time itself stood still, paralyzed. If it had not been for that moment, life would have taken an entirely different direction, for her and for me. That slight slippage on the surface of reality, that mere wing flap of a butterfly that is said to put into motion great meteorological events—storms and hurricanes. It was an event unique in my life, of a different order and magnitude altogether, that changed everything. For many years I wanted to believe it wasn't really me on that day, but an imposter of myself, usurping my place. My mind tried to flee from the incident, to wrap itself up in a cocoon, to find excuses for my crime against nature, Gordon. It is a living torture for me to bring this story to the surface now, this monster I have hidden for twenty-five years. But this is my last chance to let it out.

As close as I can determine, it took place within two years of the point at which she cuts off this narrative of her early life. I will try to recount it now as accurately as possible.

It was a warm, summer Sunday afternoon in 1965. Megan was fifteen and I was fifty-five. We were the only ones at home. Megan was sunbathing and listening to a transistor radio on the large lawn in the back, between the house and the pool. She had blossomed from a daredevil tomboy into a self-absorbed young female, and she wore a scant yellow bathing suit—the first two-piece suit her mother allowed her to own. I had finished some work outdoors and decided to take the rest of the afternoon off. I went into the house, showered and put on my robe. In the living room I put on a recording of Schubert's Die schöne

Müllerin *and sat down on the easy chair to enjoy the sad tale of unrequited love between the young apprentice lad and the miller's beautiful daughter. By the third side, I grew drowsy and would have fallen asleep had it not been for the sudden sound of rock and roll that came from Megan's room at the other end of the house. It startled and annoyed me. I got up and looked out the window and saw that she was no longer on the lawn outside. I walked down the corridor to the bedroom wing and found the door to her room ajar. Her plastic radio lay on the pillow next to her head and the sounds of some teenage crooner clashed with the voice of Dietrich Fischer-Dieskau coming from the living room. Her head was turned away from the door and she didn't notice my presence. She lay there bathed in the sunlight that streamed in through the windows. Perhaps she thought I was asleep listening to the Schubert. She wore only the yellow bikini top, and she lay on her back and seemed to be fondling her own body. The sun stood still for me, as if eternity had crash landed and put a halt to time. Her sheer beauty, so familiar to me, but suddenly transformed and unearthly. The perfect young skin, the long blond hair swirled around her head and shoulders on the pillow. The fresh passion that flowed out of her to overwhelm me. She was unaware of the world around her.*

But something bothered me. That insipid rock and roll on her radio. Megan never did exhibit any talent, interest or taste in good music, and she didn't realize how her poor musical choice clashed so jarringly with her own exquisite sensuality. The Schubert was just coming to my favorite song in the cycle—"Die liebe Farbe"[1]—and the disturbing noise was going to spoil the unimaginable beauty of the scene.

I don't know who was more lost to reality—she or I—as I silently pushed the door open and entered her room. She seemed not to hear me as I approached her bed to eliminate the loathsome noise emanating from the ugly box on her pillow. As I leaned down to pick it up with my left hand, my robe opened inadvertently at my waist. As I straightened up and switched off her radio Megan whirled around to face me, surprised. She gasped as she saw my hand try to cover my crotch and she quickly covered herself with her right hand. She was Botticelli's Venus rising out of the seashell, with her blond hair—or was it the hair of Medusa?—streaming in the sunlight and summer air. "Who are you?" she asked, startled. She squinted as if she were blinded by the

---

[1] The favorite color.

sunlight and her pupils had not yet adjusted to the darker side of the room as she tried to focus on me. Then she realized it was her father and demanded, "What are you doing?" But I felt no need to reply, because at that moment Schubert answered from a distance, "In Grün will ich mich kleiden, in grüne Tränenweiden"[2]

She was flushed and breathing fast. Her green eyes were wide with surprise. Again she demanded, "What are you doing?" in a louder voice and began to prop herself up on one elbow. Again the song's refrain seemed like the perfect answer—"Mein Schatz hat's Grün so gern . . ."[3]—in a major key, and then in a minor key as I told her, "Nothing. I won't hurt you." I dropped her radio on the floor beside the bed and pushed her shoulder back down onto the mattress.

I kissed her on the forehead as I swiftly lowered myself onto her, saying "My beautiful daughter, my beautiful Megan." As I forced her, she began to cry out, "No! Don't! Stop it!" I had to cover her mouth with my hand to silence her as I was drawn into the vortex, and all I heard over my own pounding heart was, "Das Wild, das ich jage, das ist der Tod."[4] I never listened to that particular song cycle again. Yet two lines of its enigmatic German text seemed to seal her fate and mine. They have haunted me day and night, as if those foreign words trailed our lives along in their wake, in a direction all their own: "Grabt mir ein Grab im Wasen, deckt mich mit grünen Rasen. . . . ."[5] Was it her grave or mine, or was it a grave prepared for both of us? Untold times I've asked myself why I didn't just step away from that moment before it overtook me.

It was a moment of infernal bliss. It lasted no time at all, and it came to an abrupt end, as if time turned itself back on with a vengeance. When I removed my hand from her mouth, she began to yell out hideously, and I became angry. No one could have heard her, and yet it was unsettling. I had to make her stop. I slapped her once on the cheek and then realized I didn't dare do anything that would leave a mark. She cried out even louder at this and began to hit me on the chest. I grabbed the belt from my robe which had slipped half-way off her bed and yanked it out of its loops. My first impulse was to whip her behind, but I feared she might be able to get away if I tried to turn her

---

[2] I mean to dress in green, in weeping willow branches.
[3] My sweetheart likes green so.
[4] The beast I stalk is death.
[5] Dig me a grave in the meadow and cover me with green grass.

over. She had no chance with my weight on top of her, but as her hysteria grew and her screams became louder, the only alternative was to use the tie differently.

With much flailing of arms I managed to string it around her neck and tighten it enough that she could no longer speak. I tried to calm her down. I told her over and over how beautiful she was, that I loved her, I didn't want to hurt her, and that I hadn't hurt her. She continued to struggle and throw her head from side to side. I realized I'd have to use harsher measures. I stopped trying to persuade her of my harmless intentions. I switched on the voice of the father. "Megan, " I said sternly, as if she were a naughty five-year old, "you're going to stop this right now. Hold still and listen to me!" She kept on jerking and her eyes rolled back and forth. I tightened the tie around her neck to cut off her breath entirely, just long enough to get her to listen to reason. She stopped and now her eyes fixed on me. I said, "Megan, stop it this instant! You know you've been a bad girl, but I'm going to forgive you. You are never to say anything to anyone about this, because if you do, I will kill you."

I relaxed the tie around her neck, and she gasped for breath. I sat up at the side of the bed and picked up the robe. I stood up, put it on, pulled the belt back through the loopholes and tied it shut. Megan had pulled the bedspread over herself and was rubbing her neck with her hands. "Make your bed, take a shower and get dressed," I ordered her. "And remember, not a word—ever!"

Then something extraordinary happened. She let the spread slide off her body. Slowly and deliberately she stood up and turned toward me. I must have torn the top of her bathing suit off in my madness, for she was fully naked now. Standing there, very erect, she faced me like a marble statue and stared at me for a long moment from the other side of her bed, or rather through me, with an expression I had never seen on her face before, and which I could not describe in words, then or now. She said nothing to me, absolutely nothing—neither protest nor assent. She did not cry. Her eyes were blank. Something convinced me that she would obey my terrible order, and you will see that in the strict sense of the word she did.

CHAPTER TWO

Berkeley, USA

Dear Gordon,

I'm sure you remember the running debate I had with Gina over Megan's higher education. Her brothers both attended good schools—Harvard and MIT—where they received solid training in science and engineering. As productive members of our technological elite, their place in society was secured.

I also wanted to send Megan to a top school academically, but I assumed she might be attracted to subjects that were more intuitive, perhaps less intellectually rigorous. And she didn't really know what she wanted to study. She thought she ought to get a "broad liberal education." Berkeley seemed the logical choice for that—not too far from home, but far enough away that she could make her own way. You see, incredible as it may seem, I still believed that I, of all people, had her best interests at heart. After my "encounter" with her, I swore to myself that it would never be repeated.

Gina was less interested in academic standards than in appearances, so she proposed that Megan should attend that light-weight finishing school, Pepperdine University in Malibu, that had recently opened. She saw no need to send Megan as far away from home as northern California, and she never gave up the idea of grooming our daughter for an upper crust life. She hoped the combination of the "right training" and her Scandinavian beauty would turn Megan into the old-world grande dame that she herself might have been if her family had never left their vineyards in Tuscany. We argued the pros and

21

cons for hours and it frustrated me the way Gina confused her aristocratic European notions of cultivation with the life style of the nouveau riche *of southern California.*

Of course, we never really got to the bottom of what we were fighting about. I couldn't discuss my internal struggles with my wife. At times I worried that Megan's life had changed radically since the event of a few years back. But the other, more aggressive voice in me argued that it hadn't been so significant after all. There had been no repercussions to date. Although Megan cooled to me, she never confronted me with it or even referred to it again. I came to hope that the ravages of time would gradually whittle away at this isolated transgression and reduce its size and importance until it finally disappeared from memory altogether. The agitated waters of the mind would thus become as calm as the surface of Crater Lake, and it would cease to matter that for a brief moment long ago the lake had been formed by the violent eruption of a volcano.

✢ ✢ ✢

Göttingen, October 22, 1970

Today I received notice that Berkeley's put me on academic probation. If my grades don't improve this semester, they may terminate my student status and send me home from my junior year abroad. It's been about ten weeks since I left Berkeley for this quaint, godforsaken German burg, and I'm beginning to wonder what the hell I'm doing here and what the hell I'm doing in general.

My Berkeley English professors claimed that writing serves a therapeutic, cathartic purpose. English professors are supposed to be members of the intellectual elite, so maybe they know something I don't know. Anyway, on the principle that it can't hurt to write things down, and if it doesn't hurt, it might help, I'll make a stab at it and see if it does me any good. I have my doubts, however, since what you write isn't necessarily honest—you always choose what to put in and what to leave out.

Anyway, Berkeley really began for me when Stevie Carpenter, my oldest friend in the world from Mandeville Canyon, picked me up in his battered VW bug and drove us up Highway One to Berkeley. It was one of those spectacular, sunny days, and I was furious with him for taking those hairpin turns too fast and almost running us off the road several times and over those high cliffs. At one point he spun out over the center line, crossed in front of oncoming traffic and came to a dusty halt at the shoulder of the highway next to the steep cliff. In my mind we plunged right on over the edge, his poor old vw tumbling and smashing against the boulders as we fell and crashed into the sea. My own vision is what made me mad. At one point, I thought, our heads would be smashed by a blow which would put an end to our horror and kill us, or at least knock us out, before we drowned in the ocean below. Or so I hoped. I mean, I was too young to die, and I didn't want to die *that* death, conscious of falling and totally out of control. That occurred south of Big Sur, and I insisted on driving the rest of the way to Berkeley.

We arrived after dark, and coming up Telegraph Avenue, passing the bookstores—Shakespeare and Company, Moe's, Cody's—the open cafés, restaurants, and the students, the *swarms* of students, hundreds, maybe thousands of them on the street that warm, summer night, I felt like I'd arrived in utopia. I was eager to start my life.

At the end of the second quarter of my second year, I picked up my grades—all "A's." I decided to attend a meeting of the Sexual Freedom League to celebrate my academic success and to expand my horizons. My roommate, Gayle, had been prodding me to come along. It wasn't that I was scared. I had lost my virginity after the homecoming game my senior year in high school with Craig Swanson in the back of his parent's Mustang convertible on a bluff overlooking the ocean (he put the top up). It wasn't bad, but I didn't have an orgasm, like I'd always had from self-masturbation. In fact, Craig and I did it eight more times during the summer before he left for San Diego State and I moved to Berkeley, so I felt like a pretty experienced woman. Yet, I thought there ought to be more to sex than just getting it on with somebody like Craig. He never asked me whether I climaxed or not, and after he took me home, I'd stimulate myself in bed until I came a dozen times.

My first year at Berkeley I went on the pill, because all the girls I knew were on the pill, and on the hopes I'd find some Berkeley student smarter and more experienced than Craig who would introduce me to sex à la *Kama Sutra* or something equally exotic. I really didn't have an excuse when Gayle argued that the Sexual Freedom League meetings were all about communal, nonexclusive love in opposition to the monogamous, bourgeois practice of marital sex with its exclusivity and its reactionary, repressive side effects.

I attended my first meeting with Gayle in the living room of the League's President, a heavy-set, dark-haired graduate student in anthropology named Cary. First off people smoked pot and listened to sitar music till everybody was there. One couple dropped acid in a far corner of the room, but I noticed later that they never even took off their clothes during the event. Then we sat in lotus position on mats on the floor and introduced ourselves. Cary explained that the purpose of the League was to liberate sexuality from its repressive, reactionary, monogamous, bourgeois prison and to get people of all races, creeds and nationalities involved in a shared, life-enhancing, consciousness-raising expression of love for one's fellow man.

Gradually, people started moving closer together. It was usually a man who would begin to touch the closest woman and take off her clothes. That established the group pressure for everybody else to join in—like being the only clothed person at a nude beach—so pretty soon everybody in the room was writhing around and making love on the mats on the floor. There seemed to be a few extra women who had to undress themselves, and since nobody did it with them, they ended up fondling other men or women. In fact, a strange woman kissed me while a blond man with a long pony tail gave it to me, and the funny thing is that her gentle kisses really occupied my attention and I can still remember them, even though two other guys also had intercourse with me before the end of the meeting.

I tried to keep one eye on the rest of the crowd. Most of the men started coming after they had done it with three or four different women for maybe ten minutes each. At that point there was a lot of moaning for quite a while, and you couldn't tell which women were really climaxing because they seemed to be competing for attention with the volume of their moans. In about an hour it was over. The couple high on LSD sat in a lotus position, rocked back and forth and uttered exclamations like, "groovy," "too much" and "far out, man!"

I attended several more meetings of the Sexual Freedom League, but I never climaxed from having sex with these men. After one of these meetings that Gayle hadn't attended, a guy I'd never seen there before, and with whom I had not had sex, left with me and asked to walk me home. His name was Thomas Drake, and he walked me to my apartment on Regent Street in south Berkeley and asked me what I thought about the philosophy of the Sexual Freedom League. I can't remember my answer, but he said that authentic sexual freedom was only possible after political and economic emancipation had been obtained for all suppressed and oppressed peoples, races and religions from exploitation by the establishment and the military/industrial complex, and that (finally) I should come to a meeting of the Students for a Democratic Society the following week.

I met Thomas at the SDS meeting in the Student Union building as arranged. While most of the people at the Sexual Freedom League had been younger, from, say, eighteen to twenty-six years old, this crowd had a number of older people, including some professors. It was a long, disorganized meeting, but I felt like important things were being said and planned—for instance, that Communists were people too, so that the U.S. involvement in Viet Nam was morally wrong. Perhaps troop trains could be stopped by blockades of bodies. People were getting killed, after all. Young, ignorant farm boys were being drafted and used as cannon fodder in an obscure country they had never heard of before the war, by old men and politicians sitting safe and sound in Washington, D.C. or even in the UC Berkeley administration. I knew this was true because my brother Chris was in a Marine reserve battalion which was maybe going to be called up and sent over there. In the end he wasn't, but he could have been, and he could have come back in a body bag like Roger Jacobson, one of the kids from Mandeville Canyon. My family was pretty upset about it—both Roger's fate and Chris's prospects.

A professor of sociology, Jack Bilsky, got up and gave a rousing speech about revolutionary consciousness. He didn't even mention sex. He only talked politics. Even though he was way over thirty, I got the feeling listening to him that here was a deep-thinking leader, a man of moral integrity and profound intellectual depth. He gave us details about the march to Liberation Park planned for the following week and urged everyone to be there, to put their bodies on the line for peace and freedom.

During that week I spent hours and hours in the SDS office and on campus distributing fliers, making phone calls, meeting with people and manning the table in Sproul Plaza in preparation for the march. I missed all my classes and one midterm examination. But our work paid off—at least that's what it looked like at the outset. On the morning of the march, thousands of people gathered in Sproul Plaza to march down Telegraph Avenue and up Haste to occupy the park. The bulldozers were there and a chain link fence already surrounded two corners of the big vacant lot. As the marchers surged into the park, the bulldozers were forced to a halt. It didn't take more than our presence to convince the construction workers to stop working. They stood around awkwardly, and we celebrated our success with speeches over the bullhorns, with chants, political songs and much hugging of friends and strangers. But as the afternoon wore on, most of the workers left

in disgust while the frustrated foremen telephoned university authorities from their trailer, who in turn called the police.

Professor Bilsky, with his bald head, grey moustache and wispy
goatee, wire-rimmed Bertolt Brecht glasses and paisley shirt, looked
very much the distinguished senior hippy leader. He gave what I
thought was the most impressive talk I'd ever heard about institutional
violence, the evils of the establishment, and the necessity of putting
one's life on the line for the revolution. Later on, when the police came
and ordered everybody to leave, based on the grounds that we were
trespassing and disturbing the peace, nobody did. When they moved
in on the crowd and the teargas, rocks and billy clubs started flying,
Professor Bilsky was nowhere to be seen.

The riot was on. The chain link fence came down and was
trampled underfoot. Forty-six people were arrested while the rest
fled. Ninety-nine people were injured, including two policemen, and
the bulldozers and construction trailer were trashed. I wasn't hurt or
arrested, but I was excited and upset at the same time by the chaos
and the police brutality. The following week, when I asked what had
happened to Professor Bilsky during the riot, one of the SDS leaders
told me he had left for an important engagement an hour or so before the police had arrived. I excused him with the rationale that the
revolution couldn't afford to lose such an important brain to a police billy club.

The following week I heard the term "sexual politics" for the first
time, and it started me thinking about the SDS and the Sexual Freedom League in a new way. I mean, it occurred to me that there must
be a connection between these things, and that if a university education was going to mean anything to me, it probably would have to do
with coming to understand sex, politics and their relationship to each
other. It also bothered me that nowhere in Berkeley had anybody been
talking about reproduction, because even if most of the students were
still too young and financially dependent to plan to reproduce, it would
have to be obvious to any thinking person that a major function of sex
was reproduction. Therefore, politics, governments and decisions of
war and peace should be made with the goal of producing and raising
children in a safe, nurturing environment. This, to my mind, had to be
the ultimate goal of human life, and it would follow that sex and politics were there to serve this goal. I thought of my mother and my
grandmother and believed that somehow they would have had better
lives if ideas like this had been operative in their days.

Having come to this breakthrough insight, I decided to sign up for Professor Bilsky's "Introduction to American Sociology" course for the spring quarter which was about to begin, and to write a paper on my new theory. I was sure he was the man to understand this notion of reproduction and nurturing as a necessary complement to contemporary revolutionary consciousness raising, and he would be able to advise me how to integrate it into an effective form of political activism.

I visited Professor Bilsky two weeks later during his office hours. I was nervous, of course. It was the first time I'd gone to talk with a professor directly, let alone one so brilliant and distinguished. He had published, after all, one of the definitive sociological studies on institutional oppression. I was pleased when he seemed to remember me from the SDS meetings and encouraged when he asked me about my political involvement. I told him about my interest in the Sexual Freedom League and my theory of combining a new kind of sexual and political liberation in a vision of a peace-loving and humane society, safe for mothers and children. He approved my paper topic and gave me some titles to check out in the library. He asked me to come back the following week as soon as I'd had a chance to do some reading, and we would discuss my paper in more detail over coffee or lunch. He said my idea was intriguing.

During the week I practically lived in the library. I skipped the SDS and Sexual Freedom League meetings and devoured all the articles and books on sexual politics I could get my hands on. My head was buzzing with ideas for a peace-loving society when I met Professor Bilsky at the Café Mediterranean the following week. He insisted on paying for my coffee and watched me with such intensity as I talked that I began to hope that this illustrious professor was moved by the logic, if not the brilliance, of my ideas. He told me he thought I had an authentic revolutionary frame of mind and that I should come to his office again the following week to delve more deeply into the matter. It would have to be following his graduate seminar on Thursday at 6 PM, and he was concerned whether or not it would disturb my dinner hour. I said it would be fine.

On the weekend, I again skipped the Sexual Freedom League meeting. I couldn't sleep well, and my mind raced day and night as I plotted my utopia. Gradually, a vision formed in my head: perhaps the true sexual revolution would begin with a meeting of like minds who would couple out of a sense of revolutionary responsibility, as a metaphor for wholeness that involved body, intellect and politics. Intercourse would be informed by a spirit of generosity in which bodies were freely given as a symbol of the love and sacrifice which were integral to the new society. Men of the establishment could be emancipated from their dominant and violent tendencies if my model would work. The more I thought about it, the more I believed that Professor Bilsky would understand my ideas and perhaps even agree with me.

I arrived at the appointed time at Professor Bilsky's seventh floor office in Barrows Hall. The building was relatively empty and the janitors had already come and gone. I walked down the corridor of closed and locked doors and knocked at his office, afraid it would be locked and empty. But I heard a voice say, "Come in," so I entered. The overhead lights were off, and Professor Bilsky looked up slowly from a paper he was reading in the early evening light that came through his window with its view of Wheeler Hall and the Campanile tower. "Hello," he said, and gave me a long, intense look. "Sit down."

As the door shut I felt suddenly awkward, as if I could never impress this learned man with my sophomoric theories, and I wavered in my resolve. If I blushed, he didn't notice it, or at least, he didn't show that he did, and he asked in a rather hoarse voice how I was.

"All right," I answered, and didn't know how to go on. An uncomfortable pause ensued, and then he asked, "Well, how's the project going?" I gained courage and started out by saying I'd read all the books and articles he'd recommended, except for the ones that were checked out or missing from the library. But I was wondering what the pertinence of the article by Ingmar Bateman on upwardly mobile immigrants was to my topic. He obviously knew the article and replied it was a classic study on the ethnic impact on urbanization, and wasn't I impressed by it? I was, but I again asked about its relevance to the theory we had discussed at the café. At this he paused, glanced out the window, cleared his throat and lit up a cigarette. He said that a budding undergraduate sociologist shouldn't try to specialize too early in her academic career; a good sociologist should have a broad background in issues also tangential to her specific area of expertise. I reasoned that he knew a lot more than I did, and I would do well to be guided by him. I promised to read more in this area and try to broaden my overall knowledge.

He asked whether or not I wanted to become a sociologist and said I had an obvious talent for the field. Feeling more confident, I explained that I was debating between English, political science and sociology. I was interested in writing or journalism as a career and was also very curious about how the world functioned and how to improve it. "A perfect combination." He smiled warmly and leaned forward. "You can combine your two gifts."

"But you haven't seen anything I've written yet. I'm still working on my research paper."

"Ah, but I can recognize a good writer from just talking to one. You can already articulate your thoughts in a way I normally expect only at the graduate level. That's a prerequisite for good writing, you know. Would you like a glass of wine? I happen to have a bottle from the reception yesterday for our visiting professor from London. Did you hear his talk?"

"No," I said.

"Oh, what a pity," he said and his face fell. He lowered the bottle of red wine he had pulled from his bottom desk drawer back down.

"I mean, 'no, I didn't hear the speaker,'" I said.

"Oh, good, that means you *would* like a glass of wine?"

"Uh, yes, I guess so."

"It's a very good cabernet from the Napa Valley," he said, sticking the corkscrew into the cork and twisting it round and round. "Do you ever go up there? It's really quite beautiful."

"No, I've never been. I've heard it's nice."

Two ceramic wine glasses also emerged from the bottom drawer, and he carefully poured them two thirds full, held one out to me and raised his for a toast. I raised mine too, and he began to say, "Here's to . . ." but then he stopped and said that no, it wasn't right, we'd have to toast properly. He came around to the other side of the desk where I sat, indicated I should stand and raised his glass again. I followed suit, but felt ill-at-ease to be physically so close to so much learning. He crooked his right hand holding the glass through my elbow, bent his forearm back and tilted the glass towards his lips. I did the same, and then he said, "Here's to good faculty-student relationships."

We both drank, our arms hooked so that as my elbow almost touched his chest, his elbow brushed against my right nipple. This did nothing for me, but I could see that he noticed my breasts through my sweater. Thus, I surmised that he was not merely a man of disembodied intellect, and I gained the courage to explain to him my theory of holistic sexual politics. I launched in immediately as our arms returned to our own bodies, and he didn't move from the spot, so I could hear him breathe while I expounded. He listened intently, taking several sips of wine, and I finished with the idea that a day in the Napa Valley might be the ideal place to carry out a test of my ideas. I had concluded that to have sex with an unattractive man who was, however, politically engaged in the right causes, would put my theories to the test. He replied immediately, "Yes, yes, yes, yes, yes!" quite emphatically. I was surprised at the ease of my success.

"A brilliant notion," he went on. "I've never had such a precocious and intellectually innovative undergraduate student. We must absolutely execute the experiment, and then you must write it up—not as a research paper, of course, but there are radical journals in abundance, and I have connections, so that you can be sure you'll get it published. We'd have to change the names, of course. Absolutely brilliant."

Satisfied with the meeting with Professor Bilsky, I was ready to put down my glass and go home. It was already getting dark, and I wasn't really into alcohol. But he hurried to fill up both our glasses and made another toast in the same way, and this time his elbow pressed continually against my breast as he said that he, of course, now, was obligated, as my teacher, to get me started off on the right track, so to speak. I noticed that his granny glasses had slid halfway down his nose as he peered over them and told me he would grant me full control over the actual execution of the main experiment, but, he said, some preliminaries were in order, if I agreed. He had to get used to the idea; to achieve the desired integrative effect, we ought to create more balance in this preliminary phase. After all, so far, we had only had a meeting of minds, and our bodies also needed to prepare for the wholeness of the actual encounter.

That seemed logical to me, so I didn't protest when he began to kiss and fondle me with growing intensity. I could feel that he had an erection, and by his heavy breathing that reeked of stale cigarettes, I judged that he was quite turned on physically. My nipples were not erect, neither was I wet, so I reasoned that to make a mini-test of my theory I would concentrate on and visualize the concepts of holistic sexual politics while he touched me. I squeezed my eyes shut and whispered "peace" in his ear, as his hands moved down from my breasts to my thighs. He said, "Open your zipper." And I said, "Yes, you may touch my core as an expression of political solidarity."

He fumbled with my zipper and whipped it down so violently that it got caught in my pubic hair. He shoved his hand through it and his fingers rubbed my vaginal lips roughly as I said, "Love and revolution," hoping he would get the point and be touched by my words. When his fingers couldn't reach my opening, he dropped to his knees and ripped my jeans down to the floor. I said, "Make love, not war," and opened my eyes as he buried his face in my light blond bush. I noticed a red pimple on the top of his bald head. "Please slow down," I said. "Couldn't you tell me in your own words what moves you about me or my ideas?" Silence, as he carried on. "At least say something—'brotherhood of man' or 'liberation for all'—please!"

"Yes, yes, yes, yes, yes!" he said. Then he stood up and said "Squeeze my dick!" He grabbed my hand and pressed it against his organ through his pants. Then he said, "No, in the flesh," and unzipped his fly, pulled out his hard little penis and stuck it into my hand. "Shake it," he said, "hard!"

I said, "Peace, brother, change the system" and fondled it gently. "Our bodies are our noblest gifts to each other," I said, still unable to feel turned on. He rammed two of his fingers up into my vagina, and started moving them in and out.

"Holy shit," he said, "I've got to fuck you," and he suddenly pushed me backwards down onto his desk.

"Wait a minute, these are just preliminaries, I said, "and I think you're concentrating too much on the physical side of things. You're not saying anything liberating!"

"Oh, yes I am! I'm *thinking* about it. But I have to *talk* dirty," he said as he leaned over me and shoved his hard little rod into me.

"Oh fuck," he groaned, "It's a matter of liberating the language from all reactionary repressive forms. It's a principle of free speech."

He just about shoved my knees out of their sockets with the weight of his body, because my jeans were still wrapped around my feet and I couldn't shake them off. Now he started to screw me hard in and out and at the same time he moaned, "Fuck! Shit! Screw you, slut!"

He pounded me so that my shoulder blades almost went through the desk and my head was getting bruised.

"Stop it, you're hurting me," I said. "This is *not* what I mean!"

"I *know* what you mean. Trust me. I'm *thinking* exactly the way you are. Believe me." His glasses were sitting on the end of his nose now, and he continued pounding away furiously, his curses growing more vehement so that he salivated and practically sprayed the fuck-epithets down on my face till I couldn't stand it anymore.

I grabbed his neck with both hands and started choking him as hard as I could. There was nothing else to do because the weight of his body crushed me on the desk. He made no move to stop me, in fact, he continued to ram me faster and faster for what seemed a very long time as his face turned red and his eyes began to bulge. I yelled, "Stop it!" over and over, but as he made no move in self defense, and as his face turned purple, I feared I was actually going to strangle him.

As the clock on the Campanile chimed out 7 PM, he exploded in a wild jerking climax, knocking his forehead so hard against mine that I eased up my grasp around his neck. He sprayed out a hideous groan of conquest, gasped for breath, grabbed my right hand and slammed my knuckles to the desk with such force I thought he had smashed them. He panted and choked, sweat rolling down his face as his normal color returned. I gasped over and over that that wasn't what I had meant.

Finally, when he'd calmed down a little, he said, "Fantastic! Unique! Genial! It was absolutely perfect. I'm sure you're on to something important, innovative."

I started to say, "What the fuck?" but he interrupted me with a long, intense kiss on the lips which only served to confuse the hell out of me. Slowly, he stood up, zipped up his pants and said, "That was absolutely the most marvelously liberating encounter I've ever had. You have a remarkable sense for both timing and analysis." Pulling me up and pulling up my pants for me and patting me appreciatively on the butt, he said, "but we will have to reexamine our premise and refine our techniques for the future, and we have an enormous amount to discuss—same time next week, all right? You come by, for sure." Somehow, he managed to gather me up and send me packing before I could react.

I had a bad weekend, and I didn't want to wait a whole week to talk to Professor Bilsky again. On Monday I went by his office in Barrows Hall several times, but he was never there and the door was always locked when I tried it. Tuesday, I couldn't return until the afternoon because of a midterm exam in my American Poetry class (I bombed that test), but I knew he had office hours between 3 and 4 PM. At 3:55 I knocked at his door, and since no one answered, I tried the knob. To my surprise, the door opened right up. The light was off, but there sat Professor Bilsky on the edge of his desk next to an open bottle of wine holding one of his ceramic glasses up to a young, brown-haired woman. Startled, he lowered his glass and said, "Office hours are over for today." I said, "Excuse me, I thought . . . ," but he came over and closed the door, forcing me to step backwards into the hallway.

I didn't return to Professor Bilsky's sociology class. I abandoned my research project on holistic sexual politics and threw away all my notes on the subject. I didn't bother to take the final exam either. But I wrote a paper just for Professor Bilsky's benefit in which I took my revenge not only on him, but also on academic language and research, in general. I did some library work on human sexuality, because if the experience with that dick taught me anything, it was that I didn't understand it.

I noticed that women hardly played a role in most of the works I checked out, and when they did, a lot of nonsense had been written about them and passed on by famous authorities as scientific "truths"—like the belief that the uterus wandered around the female body and caused hysteria. Or Sigmund Freud's claim that women (not *men*, of course!) had two different types of orgasm—"mature" and "immature." Incredible!

Anyway, I was so angry at Bilsky that I decided to turn things upside down in my paper and to look at history from a woman's point of view. In part of my paper I treated history as if it had always been written by and about women, and only recently had they discovered men as "objects worthy of study." In this way I was free to distort the male version of things using their own erudite, academic discourse, to ridicule male roles, to make all kinds of outrageous claims and to pass them off as "truths." In short, I treated men the way they have always treated women for their own ends. I called my paper "A Short History of Sex and Society" and asked one of the other students in the sociology class to turn it in for me. I enjoyed writing it, but I wonder if Professor Prickface ever read the paper, and, if he did, whether or not he got the point.

❈   ❈   ❈

A SHORT HISTORY OF SEX AND SOCIETY

by

Megan Lloyd

It's queer how out of touch with truth women
are. They live in a world of their own, and there
had never been anything like it, and never can
be.

Joseph Conrad

INTRODUCTION

For practical purposes, sexual reproduction did not take place prior to Aristotle's famous dictum about sperm in the fourth century B.C.—namely that sperm, a distillate of the vital nutrients which fed the body, produced both males and females. Our venerable Platonic philosopher further declared that the latter sex was only created when unfavorable cold and wet conditions prevailed in the uterus, with the sobering result that for a long time females were born into the world as mutilated and imperfect males. The enormity of Aristotle's contribution can now be appreciated, with historical hindsight, when we consider that before Greek antiquity the question as to why reproduction occurred at all had remained shrouded in mystery.

Weather, and temperature in particular, continued to play an important role in gender differentiation on into the time of Aristotle's compatriot, the illustrious physician Galen (AD c130–200). Galen noted in a medical treatise that chronic lack of heat starting in early years had deleterious effects on male development, causing normal adult men to revert to a state of physical undifferentiation. Although such deterioration never resulted in the drastic changes obtained by the "sex change operation" of a much later era, still many educated contemporary Greeks were familiar with the syndrome and able to detect the subtle yet observable signs of reduced male heat in the gestures and voices of the unfortunately afflicted.

At about the same time and in relative geographical proximity to Galen, Jewish sages in the Middle East made a surprising discovery about the origins of the first man and woman on the planet— namely that they had foregone the recently established rules of sexual reproduction, produced as they were, in the first case, by a spirit, and in the latter, directly out of the newly created man's rib. Unfortunately, documentation was lacking to show to which epoch the first couple (Adam and Eve, last names unknown) belonged— Mesolithic or Pleistocene, for example, thus confusing historical and prehistorical chronologies to the present day. Be that as it may, Adam and Eve got on with the business of sexual reproduction with a fury and populated the whole earth, with one other notable exception which took place around the beginning of the first century AD. In this case (discovered by ancient Near Eastern cultural historians), a married woman named Mary (last name also unknown) was impregnated (according to an angel) by a spirit (presumably the same one) and bore a son who spent his life wandering around the Mideast with a gang of male companions (several of whom virtually abandoned their wives and children) preaching an idiosyncratic doctrine for which he was highly ridiculed and eventually tortured to death. Since he never bothered to marry, his line died out. Thereafter, sexual reproduction has been the prevailing rule, but with new biological advances every few centuries.

During the Middle Ages St. Thomas Aquinas had the brilliant insight that male seed produced perfect men in the likeness of the semen's "active force," while women came into being as misbegotten men due to a defect either in the active force, some material indisposition or a prevailing moist south wind. In those days the sex of an embryo was decided much earlier than in modern times (nowadays male embryos cannot be distinguished from female embryos until about the sixth to twelfth week of gestation, see below), so that the soul could enter the previously "unformed" or "inanimate" male embryo as early as 40 days following conception. The ensoulment of the female embryo did not occur until 80 days post-conception, thereby allowing a greater temporal window during which a female embryo could be aborted without violating ecclesiastical laws relating to homicide.

By the seventeenth century sexual reproduction had evolved (due to the invention of the microscope) to the point that women began to produce eggs (and eject them during orgasm) that joined with male semen to create both sexes. Albeit, scientists remained unsure for a period of time whether the sperm merely incited the egg to do all the work, or whether the egg only fed the tiny homunculus ("little man") which was contained in complete miniature in each and every sperm polliwog, so to speak. A further question remained as to whether or not females were formed by the left or right ventricle of the uterus. However, with the advent of postmortem dissections, women abruptly stopped having ventricles. Moreover, up until this time, the female uterus had, due to the unruly and insatiable animal spirits it acquired during Greek antiquity, wandered in a highly erratic fashion throughout the female body, choking the intestines, squeezing together the liver, diaphragm, lungs and heart, causing loss of breath, speech, and sleep, encouraging sluggishness, prostration, vertigo, headaches, pains in the side of the nose, and generally wreaking havoc with normal sensibilities—symptoms of the gender-specific disease, "hysteria." Thus, for a number of centuries the female was rendered especially prone to confounded judgment, licentious behavior and untrustworthiness unless availed of sufficient outlets in the form of numerous pregnancies or frequent sexual activity, or until her uterus dried up and ceased its meanderings in advanced years.

Noteworthy is the fact that Victorian English ova remained passive and sluggish and contributed only uninteresting traits to the growing personalities they helped produce. Contemporary English sperm, on the other hand, was quick and agile, providing offspring with energetic and progressive traits throughout the nineteenth century.

Sexual reproduction has evolved dramatically during the course of the twentieth century, as the role of the female has finally gained ascendancy. The womb of the modern woman no longer wanders, but remains stable in one location throughout her lifetime. Hence, hysteria, like consumption or polio, has become a disease of the past. Nowadays, all embryos are conceived and remain female in the earliest stage. Furthermore, full-fledged female structures, indeed, whole women develop autonomously from this point on without the help of hormonal differentiation. On the other hand, men come into being, if at all, by the action of fetal androgens between the sixth week and third month *in utero* of pregnancy if the fetus has a Y chromosome (which may constitute a defective X chromosome, perhaps a late mutant in evolutionary history). Otherwise, all fetuses are conceived female and automatically turn into women. For the next six months pre-partem the male grows a larger hypothalamus but smaller corpus callosum and a small although proportionately over-large penis and scrotum; otherwise he behaves just like the female fetus until the doctors, nurses and parents get hold of him immediately following birth.

MALE DEVELOPMENT

Aside from social conditioning, the human male differentiates himself physically from the female beginning in puberty. During adolescence, his breasts remain flat (unless he's extremely obese), neither does he menstruate. Rather, a number of remarkable things happen: 1) hair begins to grow out of his face. Once he starts shaving this initially downy-soft "peach fuzz," it becomes coarse and unsightly. This initiates a daily shaving ritual which lasts throughout his lifetime and robs him—if he attains a normal life expectancy and if he shaves with average speed—of 78,840 minutes of his precious time, unless, of course, he grows a full-face beard and moustache; and 2) he loses control of his voice. His feminine soprano turns involuntarily into tenor, or in extreme cases, bass, and fluctuates in a wild, uncontrollable manner at unpredictable moments, rendering him unfit for polite society for months, if not years; and 3) his scrotum drops noticeably away from his body thereby exposing his testicles to untold perils for the rest of his life; in the rare instance where they don't drop, he's in big trouble.

The Male's Role in Reproduction

The male plays a minor role in reproduction. From the time of arousal it takes about six minutes for the average male to ejaculate semen, and if a female egg allows one of his sperm entry, the woman develops, bears and raises the resulting child for the next 18 years and nine months. During this period, the male is of no use to anybody, and in western societies he tries to hide this fact by a number of strategies: installing plumbing in buildings, marketing nondisposable styrofoam cups, suing physicians for malpractice, or designing population-decimating weapons that might elevate the value of his role in reproduction. Barring that, he thinks up religions which allow him to dominate the conversation, wear long robes, flowing skirts, and elaborately embroidered hats, and to live together in the company of other men, as in prehistoric and biblical times. He claims it was a male god who created the world, the universe and its first inhabitants, and that God's son, (cf. above) like a homunculus, didn't need a female egg to be conceived and that, in general, women aren't welcome in the divine company of Father, Son and Holy Ghost. He puts a lot of time, thought and money into perpetuating these ideas and coercing people into believing them.

In primitive societies he develops rituals called "couvade" which allow him to pretend that it is he who passes through the womb into the world in imitation of the birth process.

Unlike the adult female, whose erogenous zones and sexual organs are multifold and whose responsiveness is nigh inexhaustible, adult male sexuality focuses chiefly on the penis, homolog of the clitoris, a vulnerable and pendulous protuberance in which virtually all sexual feelings are located, to the extent that the brain is of minimal importance in satisfying the male sexual drive. Unlike the multi-orgasmic female, the average male can only enjoy one rather brief orgasm per sexual encounter.

THE MALE IN HISTORY AND POLITICS

Since the onset of historical times, men have busied themselves in a variety of ways while women have played the dominant roles in reproduction, childraising, household engineering and factory work. The first interesting things men did took place in the early Christian era and the Middle Ages when they began to leave their wives and children to go on pilgrimages to faraway places, like Rome, Jerusalem and Santiago de Compostella. On the way, they suffered many hardships and took up with other women and helped create other children. For a couple of centuries, especially the twelfth and thirteenth, they took crosses and weapons on these pilgrimages called "crusades" and went on to farther away places like Constantinople and Syria. En route they took up with other women and impregnated as many as they could. When they reached their destinations, they killed as many of the local men as they could and impregnated as many of the widows and daughters as they could of the men they killed.

Just about the time that the crusades lost their attractiveness, men invented the Inquisition, which allowed them to pry into the intimate lives and beliefs of almost everybody, and to pick out as many heretics and witches as they wanted to interrogate, torture and kill. For amusement, they burned particularly lots of women at the stake (somewhere between 30,000 and nine million), but by the late eighteenth century they finally stopped this practice when it looked like the supply might run out.

Starting around the sixteenth century, men built ships and sailed out over the oceans, discovered that the world was more or less round and that the Incas in South America had a lot more gold than the Spaniards did. Then they killed as many Incas as possible, took their gold back to Europe and claimed the New World as their own.

After that, men discovered that industrialization was best served by modern warfare, so they got busy on the First and Second World Wars. During WWI they dug trenches at Verdun and killed each other in the mud. During WWII they built ovens at Auschwitz and gassed and burned people, but saved a lot of their shoes, glasses, and hair for useful purposes, like mattress stuffing. Right after that war, they sent women back home from the factories to relish the Joys of Motherhood once again and the Post-war Prosperity created by the Economic Miracle. While they persuaded women to buy shampoo that cured split ends, men got busy and split the atom.

THE MALE IN THE HOUSEHOLD

The male's relationship to the household represents another ancient unsolved mystery surrounding this intriguing and enigmatic creature. Despite his proven ability to fly complicated jet airplanes, to operate and repair even more complicated computers, and to write lengthy annotated tomes on Old Norse Philology, the male distinguishes himself by his singular incapacity to change toilet paper rolls, read recipes or cook. To be sure, a few exceptional males have succeeded in learning to boil water. He is further unable to see dust, bathtub rings or dirty dishes, to wrap packages, tie ribbon into bows or to write thank-you notes. He can learn to wash and dry dishes, especially during the hours his wife takes off from her domestic duties to give birth, though he is incapable of learning in which cupboard they belong. He is further unable to recognize laundry detergent or to feel joy over sparkling glasses and toilet bowls, clean vinyl floor coverings or white collars. On the positive side, he possesses one talent of inestimable value in the kitchen—his ability to open too-tight lids on jars. He can also start fires in barbecues and mow lawns.

MALE PUBLIC BEHAVIOR

Three things distinguish male behavior in public:

1) The male seated on a bus bench designed for two adults takes up the entire space by spreading his legs wide apart, ensuring that small children or frail old females who hold their knees together can share this space only if they are practiced in the art of sitting on one buttock.

2) Unlike adult females, adult males spit in public. Both females and males spit in the privacy of their bathrooms, especially when they brush their teeth or clear their throats. A few females spit in private, in their showers or in their toilets, when the need arises. Both sexes have been known to spit in the face of a despicable enemy as a sign of great courage—an act which invariably precipitates a hard slap in the face or dreadful kick in the stomach, if not a thorough beating. However, as a daily occurrence, only the male spits in public—on streets, sidewalks, bicycle paths, and occasionally but less frequently on wooden decks. He prefers concrete or asphalt to grass, and dry warm weather over a cold blustery rainstorm (some professional male athletes spit through their teeth for TV cameras). For greatest satisfaction, he precedes the expectoration with a loud throat-clearing, and laces his saliva to the greatest possible extent with mucus. Joggers and children at play are well-advised to avoid these hazardous blobs much as a careful motorcyclist would an oil slick on wet pavement.

3) In social conversation, men know what they want and what to say. A man knows that a Volvo is better than an Audi, that the red wines of St. Julien are better than those of St. Estèphe, that the gross national deficit will bring about a depression within five years, that Ashkenazy is a better technician than Brendel, that *La Forza del Destino* is more satisfying than *Rigoletto*, that despite its shortcomings, *Der Spiegel* is ultimately more informative than *Die Zeit*, that Washington is friendlier than Chicago, that soccer is preferable to

basketball, that scallops are tastier than shrimp, that acupuncture is
less effective than narcotics, that turnips are healthier than rutaba-
gas, and that orange is prettier than pink. Women are unsure of these
things. In contrast to what women say, what men say is interesting.
If a man tells a joke, it's funny and everybody laughs. If a woman tells
the same joke, people smile and change the subject.

✿   ✿   ✿

*Gordon: now you have read the only "official" written document
Megan saved from her Berkeley days—later on she mentions burning
everything else before she went to Germany. You can imagine my relief to realize she did not address our incestuous episode directly, in
this paper or in her diaries (if she had, I would have had to censor
Megan's writings before Gina saw them), but also the pain I felt when
I first read about my daughter's struggles over the meaning of sexuality and politics. I wished in retrospect that she had not been attracted
to topics so "close to home." I wanted to believe her interests were just
a sign of the times that swept her along with all the others . . . or perhaps that her sense of justice about an unjust war made a contribution.
I did not want to believe that she was trying to make sense of the pieces
of a life I had possibly derailed. I thought that it was her perception of
the broader, more pervasive violence in society that motivated her
moral outrage, her actions, and her naive belief in utopian solutions.
But then why the hard, uncompromising, almost absolutistic voice
about men in this sardonic "research paper?" Something about its
smooth, satirical surface sent chills down my spine. Her thoughts faced
me like a hard polished mirror, and when I wanted to get behind it,
what stared back at me was my own uncomprehending, tortured face.
    At any rate, on the original paper, which I have in my possession,
the hypocritical Professor Bilsky had the gall not only to give her an
"F," but also to write some comments (in light of the disaster with him,
her idealism was touching, no—pathetic—wasn't it? How she tried to
develop a positive view of human contacts, linking up sex, reproduction and the nurturing of children). But Bilsky must have thought better of it, because he crossed his comments out with a black marking
pen, rendering them illegible.
    I called Bilsky not long after Gina's death. So he would feel free
to talk about Megan, I disguised myself as "George Cooke," an editor
interested in the possibility of publishing the stories of his infamous ex-
student posthumously. Well, despite the fact that he had his way with
her, he hardly remembered her. He claimed he remembered neither*

her paper, nor his grade or illegible comments. As an excuse he said he had taught thousands of students during his career, and he even boasted that one of his lecture courses was attended by over 400 students. For whatever it's worth, Professor Bilsky is (as I write this) a tenured senior professor at Yale University. If the venerable professor comes to suffer any repercussions in the wake of new publicity about the Megan Lloyd case, so be it. And if he harbors a perverse pride in being the inspiration for this excruciating piece of satire written by my daughter, may he roast in hell.

◦ ◦ ◦

Göttingen, October 26, 1970

This weekend my new friend, Shelley Burney, took me to Berlin. Shelley's an older American graduate student in Political Science. By older, I mean 32. At 25 she married a divorced businessman in Sacramento, California and tried to raise his two sons (her stepsons), but it turned out badly for her, so she got divorced and went back to graduate school at UC, Davis. She came over here when they started allowing graduate students to work on their doctoral dissertations abroad, and she just stayed on. She's writing a thesis on international corporations and local foreign economies, and she's employed by the university to tutor students like me in our German lecture classes and seminars, and to give us our grades.

Anyway, Berlin was a strange experience—I mean, these unbelievable border crossings and the wall that slices straight through the city. We drove there in her Volkswagen camper bus, and at the border they made us wait for hours while they searched our luggage and the entire vehicle. They even put mirrors underneath it to check if anybody was hiding there, of all crazy ideas—how could somebody hide *under* a car?

When we finally made it to West Berlin, we left Shelley's bus near this small hotel where we stayed over night, and we walked through Checkpoint Charlie and wandered around East Berlin all day, but we had to be back on the other side by midnight. But today, I really want to go back and finish writing about Berkeley. So I'll pick it up again. I haven't been able to get that Bilsky incident out of my mind, not to mention the helicopters, the teargas, the bloody bodies, all of which keep coming back and plaguing me in my dreams. Maybe I can write it all out of my system.

After I realized that Bilsky's actions were nothing but an assault on my body, I lost a lot of sleep. I started keeping all the doors and windows to our apartment locked tight every night and even during the days. Every noise—a gust of wind, a creak in the building, a rattle in the pipes—woke me with a start, fear sweating out of my pores. Gayle tried to be protective, but gradually my paranoia got to her too. She bought whistles and cans of mace for both of us, and we taught ourselves how to use them. Then she had the idea to sign us up for a karate class. I took to those classes with an intensity and passion that surprised even me. It was as if those martial skills were more important than politics. I began to wonder whether or not freedom actually began not with sharing the body, but with defending it. Sometimes I have crazy ideas.

Gayle decided she wanted to go study in France for a year with the junior year abroad program of the University of California, and her parents agreed. You could do this and not lose any credit toward graduation. Her father had already spoken with people in the administration—he's a wealthy alumnus and a generous contributor—and Gayle had the grades and the prerequisites in French. So she'd be going to Bordeaux, and she wanted me to apply for the program in Germany, here in Göttingen. I had the two years of German required, and she already knew there were still a few places open. She even brought me an application and helped me type it. She said we both needed to get away and we could meet during the European vacations and travel together. I guess she had a point, so I turned in the application, but I wasn't sure I'd make it. My grades had been good until they averaged in that disastrous semester, but I obviously wasn't headed for the honor roll. If I wasn't accepted, I'd have to rethink my future altogether. But for several weeks I more or less forgot about it, because the Liberation Park issue heated up again.

I avoided the SDS meetings, because I didn't want to run into Professor Bilsky. But I still believed in the Liberation Park cause, so I joined one of the groups calling for a student strike, mass demonstrations and a second march to the park. We went around disrupting classes. We'd enter classrooms and lecture halls and march through carrying strike placards and chanting slogans like, "Shut it down!" "Revolution now!" "All power to the people!" and "March the park!"

I felt bad when we picketed my American poetry class in Wheeler Hall because of the instructor, Mr. Dickerson. He was a guest lecturer and a poet who seemed pretty progressive and stood for "the true, the good and the beautiful." He took refuge in Plato whenever he felt under pressure from the young hotheads in his classes. Normally, he was very patient and puffed slowly on an aromatic pipe of fine tobacco while he listened to students interpret the assigned poetry. He believed that the study of literature had the power to instill humanistic values in people, to tame the beast in man, so to speak. Besides, he liked my writing and gave me "A's" on my papers at the beginning of the semester. I counted on his class to help my grade point average. But I couldn't back out of the marches because I'd look hypocritical with my fellow demonstrators. I tried not to meet Mr. Dickerson's eyes as we marched through his class, where my usual chair was empty, but I'm sure he recognized me anyway, and I don't know what he thought. I couldn't afford to worry about it, because there were bigger issues involved, like the principle and the second March the Park on Saturday. We had long planning sessions about every conceivable contingency, from the speakers' list to crowd monitoring. I actually enjoyed this attention to detail knowing that the various preparations were all focused to achieve a worthwhile political objective. It seemed like everything might still come together—both private and public aspirations and commitments. I felt a kind of singularity of purpose and a confidence that things would go well. But it turned out to be all words, words, words; actions without consequences.

It was a clear day following a rain. The crowd gathered in Sproul Plaza was optimistic and excited. Everybody believed that love and peace would overthrow the establishment and change the world. I still sort of believed it, even after what happened in Professor Bilsky's office. The leaders gave instructions over bullhorns discouraging vandalism or violence. We would, however, occupy the park again in an act of civil disobedience—technically we would be trespassing on university property—but we felt that ultimately it was the people who owned the university, so we had a perfect moral right to be there and to have a say in how the land was developed. The decision from the leadership was not to resist arrest if it came to that.

Despite our peaceful intentions, by 4 PM the Berkeley police had been reinforced by the notoriously brutal Oakland cops. But it wasn't until they started moving in on us and throwing tear gas at the hundreds, maybe thousands of us who were sitting around the park, talking, smoking pot, planting trees and flowers and grooving to guitar music and songs, that it turned ugly. Within five minutes of their charge, the police had turned peace, love and flowers into a riotous hell of gas, screams, billy clubs, smashed foreheads, blood, rocks and panicked chaos. A lot of demonstrators called them "pigs." Maybe two steps away from me a blond guy with a long braid was knocked unconscious. I went to help him and saw the blood running down his forehead over his closed eyes. I screamed at the pig in his blue jump suit with the club in his hand, ready to whack me too. "Why are you doing this? What have you done? For God's sake, try peace! Aren't you a Christian?" and I don't know what other arguments, trying to control my own impulse to swear at him and call him a pig or throw a rock at him. He hesitated when he faced me, but I couldn't even tell whether or not he saw me, because his helmet had a dark, shiny, opaque visor and a built-in gas mask. For an instant I saw myself reflected in it, distorted out of shape.

The next moment he turned away and started chasing a curly haired hippy with a bandana around his forehead. I was about to lean down to the bleeding, unconscious figure with the braid, when two more swinging blue meanies approached, and an arm grabbed me from behind and started pulling me away. "Come on, beat it, they're gonna kill you!"

Whoever it was started pulling me so hard, I had no choice but to run, too. In a sideways glance, I saw it was Thomas Drake, the student who had gotten me interested in sds in the first place. We were a few steps ahead of the cops, and Thomas fought a path through the fleeing bodies out towards Dwight Way and up the street. Tear gas canisters were exploding all around, so that it was hard to see, hell to breathe and almost impossible to run.

Eventually, we managed to gain a couple blocks' distance from the park and slowed down to a walk. Lots of the demonstrators were walking along. Some cried and everybody coughed, wheezed and rubbed their eyes. We stopped in front of a house where people were washing off their faces and eyes with a garden hose, and we could hear sirens from all directions rushing towards the park. Soon, helicopters were whirring over Berkeley.

When we could breathe again Thomas said, "It was pretty hairy at the park, wasn't it?"

I said, "Why did you grab me like that?"

He said, "I thought they were gonna bash your head in."

"They wouldn't hit me," I said, annoyed. "Did you see that cop turn away when I talked to him? You have to reason with these guys.

You have to talk to them and convince them they're on the wrong side! How are you going to change things if you don't talk to them?"

Thomas said, "Well, it just didn't seem to me to be the best time to talk."

"Well, who are *you* to decide that for *me*?" I said. "And besides, did you see that guy on the ground? He could have gotten trampled or killed. What's gonna happen to *him*?

"Well, *you* could have gotten trampled or killed right along with him. And then there would be two of you. What good would *that* do?"

We went back and forth like this for a while and continued to wander around south side to see what would develop, talking to people and listening to the TV news in the evening in somebody's open commune on Hillegass Street which became a kind of unofficial students' riot headquarters. By the evening, on the governor's orders, National Guard troops started rolling into Berkeley in military convoys and bivouacking in Liberation Park. By the time Thomas walked me home to my apartment on Regent street, two blocks from the park, the street was cordoned off by soldiers who demanded to see identification that proved I lived there before we could enter the block. A curfew for the entire city was in force, and they warned us both to get off the street immediately or face arrest. One of them, carrying a rifle with a bayonet, escorted us to the door of my apartment.

There was no choice but to let Thomas in. I introduced him to Gayle, who'd been in the library all day and had missed most of the upheaval, and we decided he could sleep in a sleeping bag on the floor of my bedroom. We talked until late and went to sleep about 2 AM, exhausted from the day's events. But I was awake again soon. Thomas snored and my mind raced.

At about 4 AM, Thomas noticed me staring out the window. He crawled out of the sleeping bag in his underwear and asked whether I wanted to talk or something. He put his arm around me, and I felt calmer and comforted, so after a while I asked him whether we could lie in bed together, not for sex, but for warmth. We both crawled into my narrow bed under the poster of Jean-Paul Belmondo with a cigarette dangling precariously from his thick lips. We lay on our sides like cupped spoons, my back to his front. He put an arm around my waist, and I held his hand in mine. I think he smelled good to me and his body warmth put me to sleep. I slept until 10:30 AM the following morning when I woke up in the same position with Thomas still holding me. He said he hadn't slept the rest of the night.

Thomas left after a late breakfast, and I didn't see him again for several days. In the meantime, the curfew in the city of Berkeley remained in effect and the National Guard occupied the park as well as both ends of our street. We got to know one of the soldiers who "guarded" our block—a twenty-year old truck driver from Fresno named Alfie who chewed gum and loved country music. After he'd been there three days, he asked if he could take a shower in our apartment. We asked him whether he'd get in trouble for leaving his post. He said "fuck it," and we said "OK," so he came upstairs and set his helmet and his rifle with the bayonet against the wall outside the bathroom. He took a long shower singing country songs about infidelity all the while. I had this uncanny feeling that while he was in there naked, the power relationships were suddenly turned upside down, and that at any rate, he had left himself awfully vulnerable. After all, he was supposed to keep *us* in check, wasn't he?

That night I dreamt of opposing cavalry troops who charged at each other across a meadow shooting flowers out of their rifles. Tens of thousands of flowers exploded with ear-shattering booms like fireworks and were pulverized in mid air. Petals rained down on the battlefield leaving an enormous colorful mess, but no one was killed or even wounded, and the troops left the scene in disgust.

The next day I walked to Mr. Dickerson's poetry class feeling elated by my strange dream. But halfway through the hour in Wheeler Hall, we heard screams and the sound of people running. We all rushed from our desks to the third floor windows overlooking the main library to see a large crowd of panicked students trying to escape a battalion of blue meanies in full battle gear. They appeared to be firing guns into the crowd. At the same time a military helicopter swooped down out of nowhere with a terrible noise and started dropping tear gas bombs into the battle zone. We closed the windows and stuffed jackets and sweaters into the cracks to keep the gas from seeping into the room. A few of the students in our class wanted to leave, but Mr. Dickerson pointed out we were probably safer to stay inside the building. The riot seemed to be moving down the hill past Wheeler Hall in the direction of the bay.

A few of the girls in the room started to cry. I stayed near the window to watch the battle down below as best I could through the rising clouds of tear gas. Two of the guys and a black girl in our class volunteered to go down to the second and first floors and close as many doors and windows as possible. Within a few minutes after they left, despite the roar of the helicopter hovering above us, we heard shots ring out below, and then screams erupted from the crowd. It was impossible to see through the gas where the screams came from and whether or not anyone was hit. But then we heard the heavy doors banged open downstairs, and the agonized cries of several people as they burst into the building and started running through the corridors and up the stairs.

There were about eight of us left in the room, and Mr. Dickerson said we should turn off the lights, close the door, put the chairs in order and gather quietly near the wall in the corner so that anyone, (like police running past the room) would think it empty if they didn't actually take the trouble to look inside. We did this and huddled together for a long time. One of the boys shook and started to cry now as we heard windows being broken. "What if the helicopter drops a real bomb?" someone asked. Everybody looked grim, and nobody answered. We couldn't predict how bad it would get.

It seemed like an eternity, but eventually the sounds outside quieted down. Either the riot was over, or it had moved on. The helicopter moved away, but periodically the ominous sound of rotors moved in and out of audible range. When the running and screaming in the halls subsided, we gathered our things and ventured out into the corridor to look for our classmates or to leave. The riot never got as far as our third floor classroom, but as three of us descended the stairway in the northwest corner of the building, we came upon the body of Stefanie, the black girl in our writing class who had gone down to shut doors and windows. She was slumped on the landing, blood oozing out of her side. Horrified, we turned her on her back to see if she was breathing. She wasn't. For a moment, no one moved. Then somebody said, "Hurry, call an ambulance! Call the police!" "The police?" somebody else said, "Are you kidding??"

Nevertheless, somebody ran off, and without really thinking about it, I started loosening her blouse and her belt, in the hopes it would help her breathe. "Here, hold her head up a little," I said to a classmate who stood next to me. He knelt down and did it. I picked up her limp arm and tried to feel her pulse at the wrist. I couldn't feel anything. Then I thought to press the jugular vein on her neck under her jaw. Her body was warm to the touch, and I thought I felt a weak pulse. I said to the guy holding her head and shaking like a leaf, "No, put it

down. We've got to try artificial respiration . . . yeah, hold her forehead back a little, and support her neck. That's it."

I thought that was the position to use. On my knees now, next to
her head, I opened her mouth, took a deep breath, placed my mouth
over hers and exhaled forcefully into her. Immediately her chest rose.
As it subsided, I heard air come out and thought it had already worked
and she was breathing. But then I realized she didn't repeat it on her
own and I had to keep trying. I blew my breath into her mouth in the
same way several times, and I could see her chest rise and fall, giving
me hope. But I had no idea how fast or often I should do this. I was
aware of other students gathering around, yelling things about police,
ambulances and telephoning, all trying to do something useful. Suddenly a voice in the crowd yelled, "Megan!" I glanced up between
breaths to see Thomas pushing his way through the crowd, but I
didn't stop my artificial respiration. A couple of breaths after this, as I
was about to blow into her again, my mouth suddenly filled with a
thick, warm fluid. As I pulled away, blood flowed and bubbled up out
of Stefanie's mouth and my breath rattled out of her lungs for the last
time. Her eyes rolled back in her head and her body went limp. Urine
seeped through the crotch of her pants.

Some of the bystanders looked away and some began to weep. I
stared at Stefanie's face while I choked on the blood in my mouth. As
I coughed, more blood dropped off my lips onto her face and the floor.
Thomas pulled me up and wiped my mouth with his shirt tails. He put
his arms around me and held me away from the body. I trembled and
shook against his chest and got more streaks of blood on his light blue
shirt. "I knew you had a class in Wheeler Hall," he said. "Are you OK?"

Göttingen, November 16, 1970

It was a good thing they selected me for this program before my
spring quarter grades came out. I was so overcome by the experiences
in Wheeler Hall and at Liberation Park that Gayle had to push me to
get my shit together enough to come here. It wasn't hard to persuade
my parents. My mother thought I never should have gone to Berkeley
in the first place; any place in the world would be better than that
hotbed of subversive, communist radicalism. She kept saying, you'll be
safer on the streets in Germany.

I hoped that was true, but I also had some different reasons for
wanting to leave. I was having a harder and harder time making sense

of anything—politics, the war in Viet Nam, love, sex, the point of a "higher" education and political activism, not to mention the meaning of life. Craig Swanson, who had never been a great student, had, in the meantime, dropped out of San Diego State, been drafted, sent to Viet Nam and returned in a body bag in thirteen weeks flat—this my mother told me when I called to tell her about Göttingen. She said maybe I should write his parents a condolence letter. Given the circumstances, I figured a change of scene (in this case, country) might be good for me in my attempts to pull myself together.

The night before I left Berkeley, I was burning my old lecture notes when Thomas dropped in and asked whether or not he could sleep with me—just once, he said. I agreed, thinking that the pill I was on deserved something better than the Sexual Freedom League or the disaster with Professor Bilsky. Strange, that I had never thought of sex with him before.

✿ ✿ ✿

Dear Gordon,

You can see how my good intentions came to nothing. Even if it meant that she had to live farther away from home, I truly believed that the rough and tumble life of Berkeley might provide Megan with new, real options. And please believe me when I assure you again that I also wanted to compensate for my transgression. I thought that by doing so consistently, by sacrificing any selfish desires I might have had in respect to my daughter from then on, fate would somehow forgive me, and the cosmic statute of limitations, so to speak, would run out.

But those bastards up north made me regret that my choice of a university won out. They talked about utopia but took their students for a ride. God, how I admired her guts as I read about the turmoil at Berkeley and how time and again she put her life on the line. She was out there protecting others, or trying to. When she came home for Thanksgiving or Christmas, she never really opened up to us about her campus life, in spite of many political discussions around the dinner table. All I remember is that she used to correct Gina's pronunciation of "Vietnam" ("Veet Nam" with two syllables, she used to say). Little did we know how much she was involved. If we had, I'm sure I would have taken her right out of school. If this strikes you as ludicrous, Gordon, remember that I wanted to make up for the fact that no one had protected her from me.

For years I have returned over and over again to her manuscript, even after Gina's death. I never stopped looking for an excuse, a bit of consolation, some hope. Something I would have paid any price for was not to be found in any of her writings—a reversal of time. Oh, how I wish she could sit on my lap as a little girl again. How differently things could have turned out, if only someone had forewarned me of what lurked inside me or even, barring that, had prevented me from being home in the languid indifference of the heat on that summer afternoon. Could it be, to paraphrase Shakespeare, that the mere place itself made me desperate, the location deprived my brain of reason and drove me mad, in the same way that the cliff he stood on seemed to urge Hamlet to jump into the ocean below? These were some of my early, confused speculations.

CHAPTER THREE

Göttingen, Germany

Göttingen, November 30, 1970

Last week I helped Shelley replace the plugs and points on her old camper bus. We got the parts and a timing light in the automotive department at Karstadt's. Then we borrowed some tools from her landlord. The entire time we worked on the bus in front of the building, his wife leaned out the window and watched us. She carefully examined each tool on all sides when we returned them. She even called her husband to double check that we hadn't damaged them.

I usually spend time with Shelley after her Poli Sci tutorial Wednesday afternoons. We go for coffee somewhere or a *Bratwurst mit Pommes Frites* for dinner or to her apartment for some *Abendessen*, which usually consists of bread, cheese, more wurst and beer. We talk till late into the night about all kinds of things. She asked me about my experiences in Berkeley. I've felt safe in telling her things. She invited me to a meeting with some German activist students. She said visitors could only come by invitation, but that it was OK, because she was a member. She thought I'd be interested because Germans took a different view of political actions, and I would learn something.

So we went to this meeting together, and it didn't start till 10 PM. We knocked at a badly scuffed up wooden door at the top of four flights of stairs in an old, lopsided building that still had *Fachwerk* beams on the outside. From inside a German male voice asked, "*Wer ist's?*" and Shelley answered, "Shelley."

51

You could hear the door being unlatched, and then it opened into a large, dimly lit, smokey room filled with a straggly assortment of long-haired, chain-smoking types. The tall, dark-haired guy at the door said, *"Grüß Dich,"* to Shelley and kissed her on both cheeks. *"Wie geht's*, Arnold?" she said to him, and then, *"Das ist* Megan."

Arnold shook my hand, kissed me on both cheeks, said *"Toll, daß du gekommen bist."* Shelley led me into the group of about fifteen people sitting and lying on chairs, sofas and mattresses on the floor. The walls were covered with posters of Lenin and Mao Tse-Tung and bookshelves held the complete works of their writings, hardbound. Several people shook my hand without rising, and then Shelley and I settled into some empty space on one of the mattresses. We interrupted a woman who had been speaking, and she began again. She had long dark hair toned with henna red, a pointed nose on a fine, beautiful face, and she spoke, between puffs on a slim, brown cigar in such long, complicated German sentences, that I could barely follow what she said. She went on and on while the others listened, drank red wine and smoked. I thought I surely wouldn't understand anything if I started to drink. But I didn't want to be viewed as an American puritan who couldn't even speak German very well, so I took the wine. Nobody smoked pot or dropped acid.

Periodically, people got up and disappeared to the bathroom and returned. I kept thinking somebody should empty the overflowing ashtrays, but nobody did, and the ashes and butts spilled out onto the tables and floor. Even the bedspreads got burned, but nobody seemed to care about that either. Unlike the loose, somewhat disorganized SDS meetings in Berkeley, this one was orderly and strict, not that views weren't expressed with fervor. But there was a definite pecking order of speakers, and people listened and rarely interrupted. Once someone had the floor he had the right to speak as long as he wanted, and that's why the meetings went on so long. A speaker could choose whether or not to answer questions or admit interruptions at all, and a strange kind of rigid discipline characterized the procedures, while the content of the discussions roved all over the map. The general subject at that first meeting had to do with defining appropriate modes of political activism within the confines of the university, given the oppression of the working class by multinational corporations in the working world at large. Occasionally, a name I knew from my studies at Berkeley would fall—Adorno, Marcuse, Karl Liebknecht—but the discussion was so abstract I didn't feel I could contribute anything.

Nor was I asked. Shelley didn't say anything that first evening, although she told me on the way home that she often held the floor as long as any German. She also told me that this wasn't the only group of its kind. There were others like it in Göttingen and in the other university cities throughout West Germany.

When we left at about 2:30 AM, I was almost delirious from the wine and from concentrating so long. I felt both sleepy and high, like I'd experienced something important. But if someone had paid me a million dollars the next day, when I was sober, I wouldn't have been able to tell them what that important something was. Anyway, what I do remember is an older man from the meeting who walked part of the way home with us. That is, he was returning to his hotel, and the next day he was going back to Munich where he lived. He walked a couple of blocks with us before we said goodnight and turned the corner in another direction. Shelley told me he was Jewish. It was the first German Jew I'd met in Germany, and then she told me this improbable story that seemed to be saying something about the formal precision of a system that doled out "justice" and violence with the same conviction and thoroughness.

His name was Moses and he was born in Munich, the son of a Jewish physician. He had a twin brother named David. Moses had been a holy terror to his parents as he grew up—disobedient, irreverent, rebellious, a terrible student—while David had been their pride and joy. A hard-working technical draftsman, he was everything a good son should be. In 1939, after their mother had died and when both brothers were twenty years old, Moses broke into a neighbor's house and stole the silverware. He was arrested and his case went to trial. The trial lasted four days, and on the final day, his father died of a heart attack. Moses was found guilty and sentenced to seven years hard labor by the Munich court.

As timing would have it, the day after his trial ended and Moses was waiting in jail to be sent to prison, his brother David was routed out of their house in the middle of the night, before their father was even buried, and sent to the concentration camp at Dachau, where he was gassed to death. Moses, however, was sent to a normal German prison near Munich where he was to pay his debt to society before he would be sent to a concentration camp.

For five years, Moses worked in the prison garden doing heavy work—digging, chopping wood, hauling and the like. In May 1945, however, the war ended and the Allied forces liberated him as one of the few Jewish survivors they found in Germany. Without much trouble, Moses was able to convince the Allies, who had already liberated the concentration camps, that the charges against him had been trumped up because he was Jewish. Freed, Moses learned of his brother's fate and discovered that the family house had survived the bombings. He moved back in and lived at first on financial assistance from relatives abroad. Later he started a locksmith's business in Munich which eventually flourished. At fifty, Moses still lived alone in the family house.

January 11, 1971

The weather's miserable. I never knew weather could be so fucking cold. The first snow fell on January third, and I didn't know what it was when it started falling out of the sky. It looked like ashes, so I asked a few people where the big fire was. They didn't understand me since I didn't seem to be joking, but eventually, as it accumulated on the ground, I figured it out. It seems stupid, but there's a first time for every experience you have, and after a few days of it I've already had enough for a lifetime.

One bright spot in the cold, dark winter was Shelley's birthday last week—her thirty-third. That seemed pretty momentous to me, so we organized a little party with some of her students and some of her political friends. We had a pretty good time. We ate and drank and got a little high, and we danced. I baked her an American style cake with a Betty Crocker mix one of the American students got from the PX in Kassel, because his brother's a G.I. stationed there. And we lit the candles and sang "Happy Birthday," and it was all pretty corny, but fun. I gave her a wool scarf and I wrote her a fairy tale about her marriage and her stepchildren, but I turned everything upside down so that the kids were evil and exploitative and the stepmother was oppressed and as good as Cinderella. She liked it and said she'd save it.

March 16, 1971

I thought coming here would be a good idea and would help me straighten out my head, but Christ, I feel like I'm more lost than ever. My German's improved a lot, thanks to the Peyote group—that's what the political radicals call themselves, a secret name. I don't know why they named themselves after an Indian hallucinogenic drug, since they're so serious and sober in their outlook. Anyway, I've become an accepted regular and we've been meeting more frequently and longer and sometimes in smaller cells, so I've really been speaking lots of German with Germans. But what conversations! I'm fascinated by their ability to invent ever more violent "activist strategies" with ever more abstract language. But it's gotten scary, because they've been leaning more and more towards the notion of a "decisive, liberating act" as a means to political change. Finally, at the general meeting last night, the decision to assassinate a wealthy industrialist or a government official was announced. It was not just the idea of this group, but apparently other branches of a wider organization I knew nothing about were also involved. And I don't mean they decided who to "execute," as they called it, but only at this point that the concept of a political assassination would fulfill a "rational objective." Every time I tried to criticize this idea or make a point contrary to theirs, they knocked me down and called me a confused, impulsive anarchist. I probably shouldn't even write this down, but I can burn it later, after I've sorted things out. Why do these goddamn Germans come up with these goddamn absolutistic answers all the time? I mean with the high level of abstraction of their discussions—and they talk endlessly, and I mean *endlessly*—I never thought they would end up with such a concrete conclusion. Well, that's dialectics for you. No psychology here. Then they turn right around and refer to it, not as "murder" or "assassination," but as *"die revolutionäre Tat,"* for Chrissake.

When they finally did vote, it was unanimous, except for me who abstained. That was OK, since I was the newest member, but I couldn't convince them it was a hair-brained idea, and when I tried, they shot back that proclaiming free love in the streets and sticking flowers down rifle barrels hadn't stopped violence in Berkeley, Viet Nam or anywhere else, so what did I know? They reasoned that the enormous, incalculable violence of the establishment against workers, minorities, oppressed races, classes and underdeveloped countries was so great that the murder of one of its figureheads, while insignificant *per se* in comparison, would still send a powerful symbolic message to the world that the struggle was beginning. When I argued that murder wasn't just symbolic, they claimed I didn't understand the nature of contradictions.

We argued for hours, for days and weeks leading up to this, but this was their conclusion. Period. It wasn't just the moral question that bothered me, but I ultimately couldn't see what practical difference it would make, I mean in changing the political/economic power structure. I feared that the earnestness of our views and actions would probably have no relation to their impact on the rest of the world—which could easily turn out to be close to zero. It also seemed to me that the plan could get the perpetrators into a hell of a lot of trouble.

I couldn't sleep all night for tossing and turning while conversations about politics and violence churned endlessly in my brain. Violence—is it ever justified?

Today I didn't get out of bed until almost noon. I felt lousy. I drank some tea and looked out the window at the rain. I skipped my morning classes. I went back to bed and slept without dreaming.

It was late afternoon when I woke up. Both the weather and my head had cleared. I realized I was tired of this scene with the German radicals and needed a change. I wanted to be someone else. I wanted to make a move—not just any move, but a move out and up. I took a long bath, dried my hair with my electric hand dryer and pinned it in a bun to my head. I opened the small bottle of French perfume my mother had given me as a bon voyage present. I dabbed it behind my knees, in my navel, underneath my breasts, on my wrists and on my neck. I kicked my usual old jeans, ratty parka and dirty running shoes into the corner and opened up the closet. I put on my green wool dress, black silk nylons and leather boots. I added some makeup, jewelry, my green silk scarf, suede coat and called a taxi. I didn't want Shelley or anybody from the Peyote group or any of the American students to see me. I had the taxi drive me downtown to the best café and pastry shop, "Kron und Lanz," and let me out directly in front of it. I went straight in and demanded an upstairs table overlooking the main street. I ordered an entire meal of three of their most expensive pastries, coffee *mit Schlag* and French cognac. I opened a copy of the *Frankfurter Allgemeine* and pretended to make notes with a pen in the financial section, so that the waiters would think I had some business of importance. I didn't manage to absorb anything in the paper, but I ordered a second round of pastries, coffee and cognac and began to feel high. I caught someone's attention, and he asked to join me at my table.

Guido turned out to be an Italian pharmaceutical manufacturer from Rome on his way to Hamburg on business. He was stopping overnight in Göttingen to visit his younger brother who studied mathematics here at the university. He had thick dark hair, a dark complexion, eyes concealed behind horn-rimmed dark glasses and sensuous full lips—an absurdly beautiful male animal, rich, powerful, obviously in perfect tune with himself. He didn't even have to try to persuade me, because within an hour's conversation (his German was excellent, his English and my Italian adequate), I was overcome by an overwhelming animal lust. Body and soul reacted in complete synchronicity. In fact, I had never believed I had a soul until we undressed in his hotel room and we ravaged each other's bodies with our hands, mouths and genitals in a way that I felt my skin was stripped away from some core that was born inside me for the first time during that hour. In the shower—darkness . . . water . . . steam. Flesh merging, melting. Lost contours, loss of breath. Earth, water, fire—fast running rivulets. Mouth cock tongue cunt lips thighs bellies. Soap, saliva, foam, necks, arms, backs, hips, legs. Probing thrusting hurting gasping. Splitting bodies, splitting wood, piercing, oozing, flowing sap. Womb warmth, free-floating before birth. Nervous systems lost in time and space, sloshing through primeval muds, rapacious for the hunt, pounding breath and life away—for pleasure, for relief, for forgetfulness. If only for an hour. If only for five minutes in a lifetime. If only for a few blinding seconds. . . .

He wore his thick, dark glasses the entire time, even in the shower, because he said he was terribly nearsighted. It didn't bother me. I came fifteen times as he pumped me later on the bed, and thought I would expire from sheer ecstasy. I had never felt anything like it.

June 22, 1971

I feel totally fucked up and freaked out. Guido has not called or written me, and I'm going to flunk out this semester for sure—except maybe for Shelley's course, I mean the one she tutors—because the Peyote group thing has really gotten intense, I should say serious, and even that's an absurd understatement. It's more like insane. We've been meeting more frequently and longer, and they have been discussing the possibility of knocking off a government official, not necessarily a corporate president. Government officials seem to be easier targets in some ways than corporate presidents who are more anonymous. A lot of people have dropped out of the group, but I keep going, partly because of Shelley and my political science education, and partly to improve my German (which has improved), and partly out of curiosity. Anyway, I haven't really taken their wild ideas that seriously;

or maybe they were just beyond my comprehension. I've kept think-ing that they were just playing around with the assassination thing and they'd eventually come up with some other clue to political action. Yet they convinced me that the Berkeley mode with its idealism and ide-ology of love, peace, nonviolent demonstrations and marches, wasn't going to work. So I thought if they knew what doesn't work, they must also know what does, or must be able to figure it out. I mean, they are a pretty brainy bunch and I've had the mistaken impression they would simply go on talking forever.

Well, last Thursday, they actually discussed names. Gabriele, the beauty with the henna hair, had made a long list of possibilities, and the pros and cons were discussed until 4 AM, at which point the group voted and narrowed it down to three finalists, two heads of big Ger-man corporations and the Federal Republic's Minister of Culture. I can't quite believe what's happening. Are they serious? Tonight, I'm begging off. I'll tell Shelley I'm sick with a fever and can't make it.

July 6, 1971

They did it. They actually did it. The media are full of it and the Germans have gone bonkers. Police are everywhere. Terrorist para-noia has taken over. I'm glad I quit going to those meetings when I did so I don't know any of the details—I mean, like who did it and how. So I can't be implicated. I mean, I don't even know if Shelley went along with it all the way or not. I guess she realized it was too hot for me to handle when I started making excuses for not coming, and she didn't pressure me. But she caught me on the street one day near the Wil-helmsplatz and told me in a low voice, after she looked around to make sure no one was in ear shot, "July fourth, Reichhardt."

I knew that Ludwig Reichhardt was the Minister of Culture, and that he was one of the "finalists." Sure enough, during the Fourth of July picnic arranged for the American students by the California study center on the banks of the Weser river, we got the news. Our German bus driver was listening to the radio in the bus while we fried *Bratwurst* and hamburgers in the drizzle, and he heard the an-nouncement of the assassination. Reichhardt and his chauffeur had been accosted at gun point, forced to drive to the woods outside of Bad Godesberg and then gunned down by machine-guns. The assassins had fled the scene in a Mercedes. The next day a group calling them-selves the "Red Liberators" claimed responsibility for the murder.

⁂ ⁂ ⁂

Patient friend,

Here Megan's diaries from Göttingen come to an abrupt end. Two years ago I made a number of long-distance phone calls to Shelley Burney, who continued to live in Göttingen as an aging, professional student. I asked her about the fairy tale Megan wrote for her, but she refused to send me a copy (she, too, thought I was a book editor interested in Megan's "story"). It was hard to engage myself in a broad ranging conversation with someone on the other side of the world, particularly someone I didn't know personally. She did, however, offer a couple of opinions—for one, that while Megan may have had some uncompromising ideals like a revolutionary, she could in no way be considered an activist. She was too passive and reactive for that. For another, that Megan—as far as I was able to understand Ms. Burney— did not share the terrorist's belief that violence is caused by systems, but rather by people, by individuals. I wish I could have talked to Ms. Burney in person, but the opportunity never materialized.

Ms. Burney consented to contact their former radical friends for me—Arnold Kohlhaas and Gabriele Kurz. She had not seen them in a long time. And she didn't get much out of them, as they seemed to still be under surveillance as potential terrorists and were themselves suspicious of everyone. Years of a siege mentality had thoroughly deformed them. Ms. Burney maintained that Megan had been a marginal figure among the larger circle of their acquaintances and friends in the sixties and seventies. She denied the existence of any kind of organized political group, certainly nothing like the "Peyote" gang that Megan described in her writings.

Interesting for me was that Ms. Burney was present at Megan's wedding. She remembered the unannounced arrival of Megan's friend, Thomas Drake, in Göttingen, one week after the assassination of Ludwig Reichhardt, the culture minister. She hitchhiked with them to Hannover and acted as their witness when Tom and Megan got married before a German judge on July twentieth. She was rather vague about the ceremony, and she was very sorry to see Megan go when she and Tom flew back to California on July twenty-ninth.

We were surprised to see our daughter return to California married, but happy she was back. We thought she was too young for marriage, but we liked Tom very much, as you know, and welcomed what seemed to represent a turn towards normalcy in Megan's life. Tom got along with Megan's brothers and became a positive addition to our family. He landed a well-paying job up north in a computer and electronics business in Walnut Creek, and Megan went to work as a legal secretary in the neighboring town of Lafayette. With some help from Tom's parents and us they were able to buy a condominium. The first time we visited them in their new home in Walnut Creek, I came away feeling greatly relieved and optimistic. I thought that Megan's zigzag course through life had now stabilized on the straight and narrow, with Tom as her rudder. It seemed that her past was behind her without leaving any discernible traces, and she had come full circle as an adult to embrace a predictable suburban way of life.

Several times I asked Megan if we could visit the campus in Berkeley together, but she always managed to come up with an excuse. It finally dawned on me that it was not just a matter of inconvenience for her, but a deep seated reluctance to look back, even for a moment. I saw it as a hopeful sign that she had learned to turn the pages of her life with a certain degree of firmness. If she could do this, then she could also leave entire chapters of her life behind forever.

Gina was concerned, but it mattered little to me that Megan had dropped out of college. She received failing grades or incompletes in all her second semester courses in Göttingen except for the course Shelley Burney tutored, and she was suspended from the University of California at Berkeley. She apparently never attempted to rectify her university record and I persuaded Gina that we shouldn't press her on the subject. After all, she was no longer our little girl, but an adult, a married woman who would define her own life.

CHAPTER FOUR

Scenes From a Marriage

I still remember dreaming about a ship that carried Aeneas away from our coast across calm blue water, and about a huge fire which interposed itself between the voyagers and us, who stayed behind, as the ship moved away toward the horizon. The sea was burning.

Christa Wolf

Dear Gordon,
    Except for the following documents, I found nothing at all Megan might have written about her life while she was married—a gap of over nine years since her Göttingen diaries. Before I read this, I assumed that during this period my daughter had settled into a normal, married life. I believed that suburbia and the predictable days, weeks, months and years with her husband in pleasant Walnut Creek had succeeded in draining the past out of her. We had all escaped fate, not because of luck or some supreme effort of the mind and spirit, but simply because of the overwhelming presence of daily life filled with its diversions, distractions and trivia.
    I puzzled for a long time over these scenes you are about to read. The more I poured over them, the further Megan seemed to get away from me. I checked out the date of that Malibu fire in the fall of 1980. I am certain that she never called to tell us she was in southern

California at the time, let alone anything about the events of that week-end—I would have remembered it if she had.

❊ ❊ ❊

THE MALIBU FIRE

The usual PSA flight from Oakland to southern California—Burbank instead of LAX this time, because it's closer for Danny and Carol to pick us up. After we lift off from the runway in a northerly direction, we make a sharp turn to the left towards San Francisco before starting south. I peer out the window on the right side of the plane, and the Campanile of the Berkeley campus comes into view through the late morning coastal fog. I have avoided this place for years, but it remains like an unresolved puzzle in my life. I turn to Thomas, who has ordered orange juice for both of us. We're in a good mood, ready for a weekend in Malibu. Time off from work and responsibilities. Good weather, beach, sand and the best Mai Tais we know. Danny tells hilarious off-color jokes.

From 20,000 feet we see a cloud of black smoke as we approach the Tehachapis. At the same time the pilot makes an announcement about the fire in the San Fernando Valley hills. He flies us through the smoke and slams into heavy turbulence over the brown, scrubby chaparral hills on our approach to the Burbank basin. My palms break out in a cold sweat. I always pretend I like flying until I hit rough air. Then I realize with new intensity that I'm imprisoned in a complex and incomprehensible machine zooming along at inhuman speeds in the sky above the earth, of all places, defying gravity and common sense. I can't help but recall my mother's story of her own mother and her mother's sisters lined up proudly on the runway of the Santa Monica airport one morning in 1937 to watch the uncle I never knew take off on his first solo flight. It was to be the culmination of the flying lessons for which he and his mother had sacrificed and saved during the Great Depression to enable him to start a career as a pilot. From the end of the runway, he waved at them out of the open cockpit of the little biplane. Then he accelerated down the runway and lifted into the air to their applause and cheers. They all heard the engine cut out before the nose suddenly dropped from its sharp upward angle. As the plane started to spiral towards the earth, the engine sputtered to life for an instant. Then the crash at the end of the runway and the ball of flames. I have several versions of the scene in my head. In one, a breeze blows the long skirts of the three Italian-American sisters as they hold onto their hats. In another, it's drizzling and they sit in Great Aunt Francesca's 1930's sedan and watch out the windows. In another, they are distracted by a large Goodyear blimp that comes into view towards the east and they don't see the crash until after it has happened.

It is the fall of 1980, and sitting in this jet, I tell myself that flying is safer than it used to be, but that I will nevertheless try to avoid it in the future. I hang onto my armrests and hope Thomas won't notice my white knuckles. He does, of course. He notices everything I do and feel. He's been a blanket to me, both protecting and suffocating.

I gain courage as we pass out of the turbulence and enter the landing pattern over Burbank, a town with few redeeming social qualities, if we're to believe Johnny Carson. No matter, we aren't staying there. On the ground I'm my confident self again, and Thomas his impatient self, especially as it becomes apparent there's no one here to pick us up. I can't find Danny and Carol's phone number.

We wander around the Burbank passenger terminal, inside and out. The rest of the passengers from our flight have long since vanished into the immensity of the greater Los Angeles metropolitan area. Suddenly, out of nowhere, Carol whips up to the curb in a big new metallic-grey Thunderbird. She honks, waves, jumps out, and hugs and kisses us. "God," she exclaims, out of breath, "I hope you haven't been waiting too long. When did you get here? They've closed Malibu Canyon Road because of a fire. I had to go all the way down the Coast Highway and out Sunset to the San Diego freeway. Hey, how are you guys? It's great to see you!" She hugs us again.

Something in Carol's voice recalls an emotion peculiar to a childhood spent in southern California. A big Malibu fire! The exhilaration of a disaster. Helter skelter panic and excitement. The arrival of evacuated friends from Malibu with their trailers and cars full of household valuables and horses. The anxiety of the adults was adventure to the kids. Particular moments were etched into my mind. "The Johnson's house has burned down. The fire was near the McKinnon's when we left. Georgette was still watering her roof as we drove past the Robinson's. We couldn't find Sissy and we're worried sick about her, but then cats are smart. She'll probably be OK." The feeling of being part of important events. The spectacle on TV, the clammy thrill of other people's devastation—a devastation that can come about as quickly as the spark from a motorcycle's exhaust, a carelessly tossed match or the look in someone's eyes.

Carol helps us pile our luggage into their new Thunderbird—a marvel, a luxury, a warm bath. We head toward the freeway feeling rich, free and sensual like our friends. Carol turns on the radio and we listen to the fire reports. It's spreading rapidly towards the ocean, fanned by strong Santa Ana winds.

Aside from the fire, the weather is gorgeous, if you like wind. Los Angeles sparkles like it must have for the Indians, the Spaniards and the first Anglo settlers, in that order, when they decided they had discovered paradise on earth. Carol drives fast because she's worried about Danny and their house at Paradise Cove. Thirty minutes later, north of Topanga on the Pacific Coast Highway, we see the huge cloud towering in the sky and fanning out like a giant grey flag. Police are setting up a roadblock as we reach the Malibu Colony. Carol avoids it. She turns off to the right and weaves through the Pepperdine campus. Then she floors the accelerator as she connects with the highway north of the roadblock. I remember that she once took a race-driving course.

Over the hill the entire sky has turned a murky brownish gray. We're one of the few passenger cars among the police and fire vehicles that now dominate the highway. As the sky darkens and reddens, the talk of beach and Mai Tais wanes. Carol tries not to show her nervousness as she hits 85 miles an hour. I'm convinced we're going in the wrong direction. Thomas tries to find something to joke about. Helicopters drone overhead. The disc jockey gives an update on the fire. Winds have driven it to the edge of the Coast Highway near Paradise Cove. It is not yet known whether arson played a role, but the authorities are investigating. Then he says that for the benefit of all those in the fire area, he's playing an "oldy but goody"—"Smoke Gets in Your Eyes"—ha, ha. My heart sinks.

We are one mile from the Paradise Cove turnoff. It would be senseless to ask her to turn around and leave this brown-reddish hell. The pitch of Carol's voice is about five tones higher than usual. The highway is empty as we turn down the Paradise Cove road. We can't see flames, but the sky has vanished. An eerie dense red blanket has replaced the air and threatens to smother us. The red deepens; it is almost palpable. Carol turns on the headlights. As we reach the guard's station at the bottom of the road, we see people running around. Some carry objects in their arms, others pull children. Animals scurry, and cars drive around aimlessly.

The guard recognizes Carol and waves her through. Carol yells at him, "What's going on?" A superfluous question. Obviously, the place is going up in a holocaust in a very few minutes, and we ought to grab Danny and split as fast as possible. But I keep my opinion to myself. The guard yells back, "The Cove has been evacuated, Mrs. Sawyer." A silent panic strikes me. The warm red glow begins to turn yellow. I wonder how much oxygen this smoke contains as we reach their house and burst in on Danny. He's standing in the living room in jogging shorts waiting for us with an open bottle of red wine and four glasses.

"God, how are you guys?" he says. He shakes Thomas' hand and punches him on the shoulder. Then he turns to me. "Hi, green eyes," he says and gives me a big kiss on my mouth. I'm stunned as he goes on, "Sit down, make yourselves comfortable, and we'll have this cabernet. It's a Beaulieu '76, private reserve. I've been airing it for over an hour."

I'm thunderstruck when Thomas says, "Yeah, that sounds like a good idea." Don't they notice, for god's sake, that the sky is falling outside?

Carol communicates her nervousness, thank goodness, in a high-pitched squeak, "But Dannykins, I just saw the Krugers driving down the hill pulling a trailer load of their stuff, and the guard says we have to evacuate the Cove."

"You know that guard's a moron," Danny replies. "Don't get uptight. I haven't heard any such order. I've been listening to the radio, and besides, they can't force anybody to evacuate, you know. Come on, the wine is perfect now." Danny starts to pour the wine, and Thomas excuses himself to go to the bathroom. When he comes back, I realize he's nervous too. He says, "You know, I closed your bathroom window. There's some ashes getting in your bathtub."

Suddenly we hear two shrill siren squeals and a male voice over a bullhorn. We carry our wine glasses outside to the porch in order to better hear the announcement. We can't see the patrol car through the murk, but we can hear what they're saying, "This is the California Highway Patrol. All Cove residents are ordered to evacuate immediately. Leave your houses immediately and proceed to the parking lot at the beach. This is your last warning."

"Last warning! Shit!" Danny exclaims under his breath and then carefully sets his wine glass down. For some reason we all wait for a cue from him, and when he says, "I'm afraid we'll have to break up the party," Thomas is the first to toss the wine out of his glass and dash into the house.

We explode into motion and action. We grab and throw things into their cars—desk drawers full of papers, arm loads of clothes, picture albums. In ten minutes the cars are loaded and we're ready to go. I suggest we meet at my brother's house in Brentwood whenever we can. Carol says, "You guys take the T-Bird. We'll follow you." I grab the keys she offers and push them into Thomas' hands and him into their Thunderbird. We yell, "See you later at Chris's house. Good luck."

We roll out into the smoke and wind our way down the hill. Trying to find the headlight switch, Thomas activates the windshield washer and wipers, the front and back defoggers, the heater fan, the air-conditioning, and all the power windows. At the bottom of the hill, the yellow-red smoke is so thick we can barely make out the human shapes in the parking lot near the beach restaurant. Then I realize there are hundreds of them milling around—people abandoning their cars in the lot and moving towards the ocean. The guardhouse is empty. We start up the hill towards the Coast Highway. Bright, dense smoke rolls onto the windshield like a thick fog. It's less than a quarter of a mile to the highway and our escape route to the south. I know this baby can travel. But the unearthly atmosphere tells me we won't make it. No one else is driving up this hill.

As we round the curve, a wall of flames a hundred feet in front of us is licking up the trees. I see something I've never seen before: wild animals—rabbits, gophers, mice and deer—all of them running for their lives ahead of the fire straight toward our Thunderbird, for Christ's sake! Right behind them, as if to shepherd them away from danger, a black and white highway patrol car emerges from the murk and bears down on us, pushing us like another lost animal back down the hill to the dead end at the beach.

"Oh shit!" I think. We are trapped by the Pacific Ocean with a tremendous fire burning down on us. Then I feel resentful. An hour ago we were winging our way through a brilliant day, aiming for a weekend of the southern California good life at the beach. Now we're in the middle of a disaster zone where we could die. Simple as that—quick as the opening of a switchblade.

I remember our suitcases in the trunk of the T-Bird, buried under piles of our friends' household goods. If the fire burns through the Cove, it will stop before the parking lot and at the edge of the sand. We park the Thunderbird in a lot between the bank and the sand. We can see flames at the top of this bank, but we are determined to turn off the headlights in order to spare the battery. We press, twist, pull and rotate every switch again till we get it. We even lock the car. I grab my purse—just in case I survive, it will make life afterwards simpler if I haven't lost my driver's license and credit cards.

Coughing, we hang onto each other as we move towards the crowds next to the restaurant. Soon we decide to take our fate into our own hands and head south, as close to the water as possible. If the smoke gets worse, we can dampen a shirt and breathe through it.

The sky above us is all motion—dark, majestic and ominous. But the horizon out at sea is calm and perfectly clear. The silhouette of a large ship floats at the juncture of sky and water, untouched by our frenzy and the smoke cloud on the distant shore. Farther south we see patches of blue sky through the smoke. The wind could shift at any time. It whips up the sand now and blasts our faces, hands and hair. I take my sunglasses out of my purse and push them tight against the bridge of my nose to protect my eyes. I remove my sandals, roll up my pant legs and walk on the hardest damp part of the sand, paved by the waves. The water is warm for early fall.

It's good to be on the move, but the odd assortment of stragglers who pass us in the other direction shake our confidence in our resolve to go south. A very pregnant woman, blond and tanned, leads a nervous horse down an embankment onto the beach with one hand, and a small child with the other. She looks around, uncertain which way to turn. We trudge on. Our moods switch according to the amount of light we can see ahead of us as massive billows of smoke open and close at random creating bizarre patterns of light and shadow on the coastline. Again, wind and sand blow so violently that we hold onto each other for several minutes. I think, "I don't want to die, not yet, and not here." When the gust subsides we look back and see two remote figures heading our way through the smoke. As they grow more distinct, we recognize them: Danny and Carol! I'll be damned if they didn't do the exact same thing as we did.

Danny sets a large briefcase down in the sand, and we hug each other. Then everybody talks at once. They couldn't drive out either. They feared the smoke above all, they don't trust crowds anymore than we do, and they figured to head south was their best chance. So great minds *do* work in similar ways!

They are health freaks, we are joggers. We're all in good shape. We trudge through sand for at least two more hours, maybe longer. Our mood fluctuates between hope and despair. I persuade Carol to tear up her Nike T-shirt, so we can wet pieces of it in the surf and breathe through them. It turns out to be a strong fabric, hard to rip, so the men have to do it. But they don't have the patience to make four pieces. They manage to remove one big piece. I notice Carol cringe at the loss of a favorite shirt, but she offers the piece to me, saying, "You take it, Megan." I douse it in ocean water and ring it out. I say, "It's big enough we can both use it if we walk together. Take this end." After five minutes she gives it all to me. I find it helps. I offer half of it to Thomas. Thomas is absorbed in thought and waves it off. Danny shows no interest in it. At least *I* feel better *with* it.

Half an hour later, as Thomas and I walk at some distance from Danny and Carol, he's angry at me for hogging the wet cloth. What the hell is this? It's big enough for everybody. Why doesn't he just tear off another piece? I move away from him and mentally try to compare other immoral acts I'd committed with this one, to see if he's justified in the reproach. I remember the time I was cruel to one of Roxie's puppies as a kid. There were three solid brown ones and one black and white one. When no one was around I singled out the black and white one, yelled at it and whacked its nose with my hand. Yelping, it leapt away from me and cowered at a safe distance wondering what it had done to evoke my wrath. Then I changed my tone and lovingly called it back and fondled it. The pup quivered with joy and gratitude and licked me all over as if the little ritual made it love me even more than if I'd never hit it in the first place. I repeated this experiment over a couple of weeks until its new owners took it away, and it never failed to work. I look back at Thomas through the smoke now and dislike him for precipitating this unpleasant recollection. I feel like a child again, tumbling down the hillside with an adversary, struggling to see who would come out on top.

The smoke and wind are particularly bad. The four of us huddle together next to the crashing surf. Carol says, in an outburst of honesty, "I want you guys to know that if we don't make it out of this, I love you guys, and we've had a lot of good times together, and I'm sorry." I'm touched by this. It would be a unique death, together with your husband and your good friends, to slowly lose consciousness next to the Pacific Ocean. Not cold, not lonely, simply wiped away by a random event, like a gust of wind that scatters the leaves on the ground. You could say some nice parting words. People would ask, "How did they die," and others would answer that their bodies were found lying arm-in-arm in the sand next to the waves. But I suddenly intuit that nothing's going to happen to us after all.

We go on. We stop talking to save our breath. Ahead the houses are built very close to the surf. The only way past them is over some craggy rocks against which the waves crash. We are no longer as careful as we should be, and suddenly it's too late to avoid the wave. It pulls me from my moorings with tremendous force and carries me out in the opposite direction into cool water. I feel my head surface and gasp a breath before the next one strikes. It pushes me down and tosses me around in somersaults. It shoves me against the base of the rocks. My right shoulder hits up against something solid, while the water churns all around me. As the wave recedes, I manage to brace my feet against the sand and push up with all my might towards the surface. I need air, my lungs hurt. I'm pulled back out, it seems like a long time. I swim frantically now to reach the surface, and I have to breathe out on the way up. When I feel my head emerge, I gasp and open my eyes. Through the blur I see the ship on the horizon just before another swell hits me and I swallow a mouthful of salt water. I'm pushed down again, and turned around. Choking and coughing, I only breathe water. My nostrils and sinuses fill up painfully as I lose my orientation and flail madly, thinking two things at the same time—Stefanie's lungs full of blood and the surprising warmth of the water. Then my head hits something and I'm gone.

The next thing I know I'm stretched on my back on the sand and my shoulder's killing me. Thomas, Carol and Danny kneel around me. I vomit water onto my chest. I sit up, cough, choke and feel wretched. But I'm alive.

There's no time to recover. They help me up and wipe off my blouse with some ocean water. Danny and Thomas' clothes are wet too, from pulling me out of the water. The fire is burning fiercely on the other side of the highway, and sparks and cinders have ignited the roof of one of the beach houses on the beach side, twenty-five yards from where we celebrate my return from the deep. A man is on the same roof with a hose, but the water pressure is so low he will soon lose his battle. The houses and the rocks form an impasse between us and the highway, so we are forced to climb one of the long wooden stairways to someone's back porch and excuse ourselves to the man watering his roof. He waves us on, "It's OK, go on through," while his children wait for his instructions. We advise them to leave, but our sense of urgency hasn't infected them.

Several cars head south on the alley which connects with the highway. Carol grips my arm to prop me up. I let her although it's not necessary. My shoulder and head are cut and scraped but my legs are OK. My clothes stick to me. My throat is sore and raspy. I want to comb my hair, then I realize my purse is gone. The men drop behind to pump people for information. It seems like we are heading right into a wall of fire, but if we can just get beyond it on the highway, they think we will be out of it. We trudge on, now joined by a growing motley crowd.

A highly-chromed Lincoln Continental pulls up and stops beside Carol and me. A grey-haired man and a beautiful dark young woman are in the front. Already seated in the back, Danny and Thomas open the back door and beckon us inside saying we've got a ride to the Colony.

We climb in and sit on our husbands' laps. We have to put our feet on top of Danny's briefcase which takes up half the floor space. Thomas asks him what's in it. He says, "I'll tell you later." A few minutes pass in silence. I'm thinking that we still have to get past the trial of fire on both sides of the highway. Thomas starts to whistle some inane melody. My glance tells him to shut up. He says, "Mozart . . . sorry," and our driver turns the radio on to a rock station as he slowly enters Highway 101. He hums along with his chosen music, as if to assert the audio rights to his own territory. I guess this station hasn't heard of the fire. The headlights barely penetrate the thick smoke enough to illuminate the dotted white line. He taps the fingers of his right hand on the steering wheel. Each bears one or more bejeweled rings. The windows are shut. We don't say anything. How long can six adults share this little bit of oxygen? What's the minimum amount of oxygen needed for the functioning of carburetors and spark plugs? We purr along.

The driver speaks up. "This is my third Malibu fire." "Really?" Danny says, mustering up a conversational tone. My attention fluctuates between fear of this dark passageway and their conversation. "Yeah," he says, "I lost a house each time."

"That's *terrible*," exclaims Carol, real sympathy in her voice. "We had to evacuate ours at the Cove a few hours ago, and we don't know what's happened to it." The driver doesn't comment at this but says, "My name's Frankie, and this is Ginger." Ginger says "Hi," and then "meow," or so it seems, and turns her head around.

About twenty years old, she has a beautiful dark face, but too much makeup. She cuddles a small grey kitten to her bosom. She asks us what to name the kitten. "I found her in front of Frankie's house, just before we left." I lean forward to touch the cat, and I see that Ginger wears a skimpy top, very short shorts and nothing on her feet. "How about 'Smokey?'" Carol suggests.

Suddenly the Lincoln passes as if through a wall into brilliant sunshine. We see the Pepperdine campus again, its sparkling modern buildings sprawled on the hillside to our left. All the muscles in my body go limp at once. I suddenly notice how tired I am.

Danny asks Frankie, "What do you do?" "I'm a lawyer" he answers. Slowly, he lights a cigarette. The four of us forget we hate smokers.

Frankie is about sixty-five. Partially bald, he wears a black and red checkered polyester suit with a shirt open halfway down his hairy chest, on which rests a large gold cross on a chain. Now the cigarette hangs from his lips and he has both hands on the wheel. I get a better look at the rings—heavy stones of uneven shape mounted on broad gold and silver bands. I ask him what his legal specialty is. "Conflagrations," he replies, tersely. I don't know how to take that. He asks our names. We tell him, and then we offer the information that Thomas and I just flew in for the weekend from northern California, and really don't belong here. But naturally, we are very grateful to him for the lift. "No problem," he says casually. "I'll take you to Charlie's pad at the Colony where you can rest and make phone calls, or whatever." Smokey meows weakly.

As we straggle into what must be a multimillion-dollar beach house, Frankie introduces all of us flawlessly by name to blond, stoned, fifty-fiveish Charlie, even telling Charlie where Thomas and I are from. I notice for the first time Frankie's feminine red velvet slippers. We apologize for our disheveled appearance as we enter, but Charlie doesn't mind. His house is already full of sand. Inside the hallway Charlie says, "Let's have a party. Everybody's here."

Everybody includes about four or five more Gingers—all around twenty years old, all pretty, all scantily dressed. The real Ginger holds onto Smokey, jealously repeating the kitten's new name. Charlie shows us to the living room and the back porch that extends onto an expansive white beach—the one where you might catch a glimpse of Bo Derek or Johnny Carson strolling on rare occasions. Here the world is enjoying an Indian summer. Swimmers frolic in the surf and sunbathers sleep on towels in the sand next to portable radios. The black cloud a few miles up the road seems utterly remote here, like a catastrophe on another continent. The ship on the horizon hasn't moved.

Charlie brings us beers, bread sticks and a basket full of bananas. Several times he repeats, "Let's have a party," in a vague tone.

We eat and drink gratefully. We are hungry. We try to call my brother Chris in Brentwood. No answer. But Danny reaches their friends in the valley. They will come and get us, but it will take an hour or two, depending on traffic and road blocks. Charlie doesn't mind if we stay. "No problem. Make yourselves at home. We could have a party."

We sit on the beach and talk. Frankie leaves and returns later with a woman in cowboy clothes who is worried about some horses up in the mountains. We meet the other Gingers, who are all "actresses" of indeterminate relationship to Charlie and Frankie. The real Ginger decides she likes us and lets us play with Smokey. We are happier when they leave us alone on the deck.

I have to go to the bathroom. I tell one of the starlets, who points down a hallway. In the hall I glance through the open door of a bedroom which contains an enormous fluffy round bed. Two more starlets are stretched out on it, naked and asleep in each other's arms, as if posing for an unseen painter.

In the bathroom I urinate for what seems like a heavenly five minutes and ask myself whether or not I might be hallucinating. I take my time as I wash my face, hands, and arms. I borrow a comb from the counter to get some of the sand out of my hair. When I blow my nose, the tissue is black from smoke. In the mirror my face is burned and my eyes are red. My throat still hurts and my lungs ache.

When I leave the bathroom, the bedroom door is still open. I pause and glance at the women on the bed. Sleeping animals, their sleek, tanned bodies are stunningly beautiful. Then I'm startled to notice stoned Charlie seated quietly in a wicker chair in a corner of the room. One of his hands is hidden in his crotch and he holds the index finger of his other hand in front of his lips to indicate to me not to disturb this delicate scene. He watches them dreamily, and a sensitivity in his gesture suggests the jealous protectiveness of a curator of fine art. I nod at him to communicate my complicity. But after a moment, I feel self-conscious and return to my own kind.

☼   ☼   ☼

Later that evening we dined in our same sandy clothes at a beach side restaurant near Topanga Canyon with Danny and Carol's friends from the San Fernando Valley. By midnight the highway patrol let us back into the still smoldering Paradise Cove. The fire had swept through. Power was out and fire trucks still scurried around to this flare-up and that one.

In the dark we walked through the smoking ruins of homes and trees, weird molten remains of cars and motorcycles, to find Danny and Carol's place still standing between two, now empty black lots which belonged to their neighbors. Only a fence and some trees on our friends' property had been singed. Excited residents told us the fire fighters had arrived just in time to save it. The fact that two houses on either side of it were already too far gone to bother with gave them time to attach their hoses and save Danny and Carol's place. The crowd caught at the Cove by the beach had survived.

We rinsed out the ash-dusted wine glasses, sank into the couch next to the coffee table and drank what was left of the bottle of cabernet sauvignon which had stood on the dining room table ever since our hasty departure. Thomas asked Danny what was so important in the briefcase he had carried around all day. Danny said, "Oh yeah. Just a minute." He got up and fetched the heavy case and set it down on the coffee table in front of us. He knelt down with one knee on the carpet, opened it up and proudly displayed two charcoal colored, long barreled revolvers, as if he were a salesman displaying his wares. He called them his life insurance and explained that if you owned guns you had to be responsible for them. He wouldn't have wanted his ammunition to explode and harm anyone if their house had burned down. Then he added with an ironic tone and a faint smile, "If you ever need to settle a score. . . ."

About 2 AM, Thomas and I curled up in the ash-filled guest bedroom and fell into a fitful sleep while Danny and Carol prowled around most of the night like the other homeowners, keeping watch over their charred property and exchanging stories. When I woke up the next morning, I didn't know where I was.

STUNG BY A WASP

Two weeks after our escape from the Malibu fire, we took our ten-speeds up to the Napa Valley and went riding on the Silverado Trail. It was a beautiful warm day, and the vines were various shades of red, orange and yellow. An occasional slow truckload of newly harvested grapes passed us on the highway. We stopped for lunch at Calistoga and an hour's soak in the mineral waters at the spa on Washington Street.

On the way back I felt enervated. I sweated as I peddled along about a hundred yards behind Thomas. Suddenly, an insect flew into my open mouth and landed on my uvula. At first I didn't know what it was. I stopped the bike and at the same time gagged and coughed in a frantic effort to expel it. A violent cough ejected the wasp, which brushed its stinger over my lower lip as it passed out of my mouth before landing on the earth, drenched in saliva. Injured and disoriented, it trembled and buzzed around in circles while my lip started to hurt and swell. If it had stung me in the throat, I might now be writhing around in the dirt instead of it, trying to suck air through the narrowing opening of my swelling larynx or esophagus.

It struck me that its chance trajectory into my open mouth at that particular spot, elevation, velocity, and instant in time had brought me close to death. If my teeth had been closed, it would not have happened. If I were an inch shorter or taller, it would not have happened. If I had not been biking, I might not have had the breath to spit out the insect.

High on adrenalin, I stomped on the enemy with my Adidas training shoe, jumped on my bike and streaked towards our car as fast as I could peddle. But I clenched my teeth tightly now and shut my lips. Moreover, I watched out for rattlesnakes, skunks that might dart into my path, falling trees and brush fires. I monitored the ground as best I could for earthquakes. Sweating, I arrived at the car, where Thomas was already putting his bike on the rack. I set mine against the car, got inside, slammed and locked the door. A nonsensical children's rhyme I knew from sixth grade ran through my head:

> Two Irishmen, two Irishmen
> were digging in a ditch.
> One called the other
> a dirty son-of-a—
> Peter Heimer had a goat
> and tied him to a rock,
> along came a bumble bee
> and stung him in the cock—
> tail, ginger ale, five cents a glass,
> if you don't like it,
> shove it up your as—
> k me no questions,
> I'll tell you no lies,
> or you'll get a pail of shit
> right between the eyes.

Thomas got in the car and I ordered him to drive home fast. "What's wrong?" he asked.

"I don't believe in God anymore," I answered.

         ❀ ❀ ❀

Dear Gordon,

I also tried to contact Danny Sawyer after Gina's death. I learned from former neighbors at Paradise Cove that he and Carol had divorced. She followed a spiritual guru to India, and he lived in a run-down trailer in Culver City. His neighbors advised me not to try to visit him, because he had developed a fascination for guns and a reputation for drunkenness. He never answered the phone calls I placed to his number, but I wrote and asked him questions about Megan, nevertheless. I hardly expected a reply, but my letter was returned to me with the following note scrawled on it: "What are you, some kind of CIA *agent? She had more balls than most of you goddamn pricks. Screw you, asshole!" At times I felt like getting back to him, to find out whether there was more to his liquor-sodden, abusive attack than met the eye. But in the end I decided it would have been a waste of time.*

CHAPTER FIVE

Dallas, Texas

> . . . the serpent spread its hind feet round both thighs, then stuck its tail between the sinner's legs, and up against his back the tail slid stiff. No ivy ever grew to any tree so tight entwined, as the way that hideous beast had woven in and out its limbs with his; and then both started melting like hot wax and, fusing, they began to mix their colors . . . so neither one seemed what he was before. . . .
>
> Dante, Inferno

My dear Gordon,

Here my daughter's life becomes ever more incomprehensible to me. You agreed to meet me for drinks at the Riviera Country Club two days after Megan's unexpected visit in 1982. I told you how she had arrived at our door unannounced, late that spring afternoon, and had stayed overnight before departing the next morning for points east. She dropped a bombshell on us with the news that she and Tom had divorced three weeks earlier, in Reno. It was a complete surprise; we had no warning that anything was wrong between them. When we asked her for an explanation, she said it was a mutual decision, but a private matter she didn't wish to discuss. And furthermore, we shouldn't try to reach Tom. He had moved out and didn't want to have any more contact with us.

We were terribly upset, shocked would be a better word, but she refused to communicate one significant thought or feeling about this drastic change in her life during that precipitous visit, and not one detail about her plans. I even felt angry, I must admit, because she treated us like a gas station stopover, with no real interest in communicating with us on a personal level. It was just lucky that we happened to be at home. What were her plans? She told us that she had quit her job and they had sold their condominium in Walnut Creek. She was on her way to a vacation; she needed a change of scene. I could barely contain myself. "A change of scene! Is that how you react to your divorce? To eleven years of marriage you're tossing out the window? Talk to us. Please, say something!"

She ignored my pleas, evaded all our questions and made no attempts to justify her actions. She refused to talk about the past—recent or distant—and seemed to focus instead on the trip she was about to take, fixed, even transfixed on a goal that we could not see or imagine. What could we do? I have since wondered why she bothered to come by at all.

She arrived with two suitcases in her blue Honda wearing faded jeans, cowboy boots, a black leather jacket, and dark sunglasses. Her hair was long and straight as in her student days at Berkeley. She helped Gina in the kitchen as she put together a meal, but her mother also failed to divine her daughter's feelings. Since Megan subverted all attempts at communication, we ended up watching television after dinner, in silence.

I tossed and turned all night, and the next morning Megan was up early wearing the same outfit, anxious to get moving. She wolfed down an English muffin and two cups of coffee. Then she packed her things. She wouldn't tell us where she was going, except to say East. How I longed to hold onto her, to make her stay, but she barely tolerated the hug I gave her before she threw a suitcase into the Honda's trunk, climbed into the driver's seat and turned on the ignition. Her sunglasses were on as she pulled out of the driveway, briefly turned to us and waved before disappearing down the gravel canyon road. I had the impression that she gunned the car to get away as quickly as possible. It was the last time I saw Megan in California, and the last time I saw her in her normal state. The last contact before inexorable events would crowd in on her, on me, on all of us. I stared at the driveway and what I could see of our private road before the *bend, until the last dust of her car settled. Later on I even walked down the road to trace her tire tracks, but they blended into the usual ruts in the gravel.*

❀ ❀ ❀

April 1982

On my own for the first time in years, I headed East and then Northeast out of the L.A. basin and reached the desert near Victorville. At Barstow I hooked up with Interstate 40. I could go forever now, so I drove and drove and stopped in motels overnight. I passed through Flagstaff, Albuquerque and Amarillo, Texas, on the old Route 66.

Redneck country. Miles and miles of highway, rolling tumbleweeds, flat distant horizons, wide skies. Scorching midday heat in dusty gas stations. Coffee boiled for hours on truck-stop hot plates. Eighteen-wheelers, pickup trucks with rifles in the back windows, constant air conditioning. On the radio endless country western songs about heartbreak. I had liquified all my assets, so I could move unhindered. For the first time in my adult life, I felt completely cut off from my past—mother with her social clubs and Italian hand-wringing; father; my brothers—Jeff, always ready for a practical joke, married for the third time, church-going Chris, an airline pilot; Berkeley with its classes, professors and politics; Thomas and his controlling ways; long days in suburbia with its clean houses and manicured lawns. Fleeting shadows ran through my mind like the cars that shot by in the opposite direction. Usually, a solitary vehicle would whoosh by, followed by a long moment of silence.

The blue sky was open and free of obstacles. On an empty stretch of two-laned road, I sped up to a hundred miles an hour. When the first car passed me in the opposite direction, I realized how easy it would be, with a slight turn of the wrist, to obliterate myself and the unsuspecting victim in a head-on collision. At one point I noticed that the highway, the telephone poles and the railroad tracks which paralleled my route all grew smaller and seemed to converge in one spot in the distance. Then I had the sensation that I was heading for the center of the earth, rather than the center of the United States.

I reached Oklahoma City towards evening of the third day. Unwilling to give in to my fatigue, I swung south onto highway 35 and drove the last 200 miles to the northern outskirts of Dallas, Texas, a place I'd never been. This might be a town to be in.

❊ ❊ ❊

I debated with myself whether or not to interrupt Megan's narrative here in order to insert my own thoughts. Believe me, Gordon, at times I came very close to applying the editor's pen to prepare an image of Megan more in line with my own wishful thinking, but that would have constituted an absurd distortion of reality. The events that overtook her—and me—had such an inevitable, compulsive direction to them that there was no use tinkering with them after the fact.

Megan suddenly put behind all things familiar to me—home, school, education abroad, a regulated life. After that last short visit with us in LA, she was free on her own, heading in some new, unknown direction. I tried to assuage my uneasiness about her departure by entertaining thoughts of my own mother and her stories about moving West a generation ago—her family's search for El Dorado, the golden dream, and how they made it. In those days the trip took weeks, the entire family and as many of their belongings as would fit, packed in the car. Highways were poor, motels scarce or nonexistent, gas stations few and far between. Strangers often tented together overnight and drove in small caravans during the day to provide protection in case of breakdowns. In short, it was an adventure. The people who undertook the westward journey were optimists. The country was large and open, and the promise of a better life and brighter destinies waited at the far coast.

My mother was a rugged individualist, a fiercely independent loner who was never lonely. In California her family established a successful hardware business in the central valley. As the oldest girl, she helped care for the younger children and worked regularly in the store from the age of ten on. As a young woman she taught school in a one-room schoolhouse for eight long years before marrying my father. I wanted so desperately to believe that Megan carried deep in herself a genetic blueprint of her grandmother's life and that her journey would take her in a positive new direction. Of course, the parallel didn't hold.

❊ ❊ ❊

Off of 35 East, south of Lewisville, I pulled up in front of the office of the Round Table Motor Inn, one of the few accommodations on this frontage road—which consisted solely of glittering neon motels, gas stations and so-called family restaurants—whose sign was still flashing "Vacancy." I stepped out of my dusty and bug-bespattered

Honda into an enveloping heat and stretched my legs. I rotated my arms in their sockets and my head from side to side while pressing the back of my neck with my hand. I felt alive and well. As I tilted my head back, I caught sight of a jet's white contrail leaping forward almost imperceptibly in the Texas sky. Sharp as the pin of a needle or the point of a stiletto, it split the sky at the seams, rending it in its wake. My brother Chris could be sitting in its cockpit.

In the chilly, air-conditioned restaurant an hour later, I sat down in a red velour booth under a bronzed plaster plaque which displayed two lances crisscrossed over a medieval knight's helmet. I ordered the "Jouster's Special"—fried chicken, gravy, mashed potatoes, peas and fruit cocktail. Afterwards I wanted a drink and wandered into the adjoining "King Arthur's Lounge" which emitted a red glow and some low music. I'd never been in a bar by myself, but I felt at ease since no one knew me. Everything was a new experience, and I didn't care what it all meant. I sat in a dark corner at one of the many round tables and asked the waiter to bring me a "Merlin's Magic," an enormous chilled goblet full of rum and some indistinguishable fruit punch with a long plastic sword stuck through a slice of kiwi fruit. Before the drink arrived, an innocent-looking, pretty-faced man in cowboy boots approached me. Ten gallon hat in hand, he had a sad air about him and asked if I minded some company. I took a good long look at him; it was the first man my mind had fully registered since my divorce from Thomas. I said I didn't mind. He sat down. At first he said nothing, but soon he began to talk, and as time went on he told me his life's story.

Andy was separated from his beautiful wife, Peggy, and his young son. He didn't know what had gone wrong with his marriage. "So, what else is new?" I thought. He loved Peggy, but she wanted to live alone in order "to find herself." They had everything they needed and much more. He drank and talked in a soft Texas drawl almost until midnight, in obvious need of a sympathetic ear. He wore a Rolex watch, a Pierre Cardin shirt, and his haircut must have cost $50. I felt sorry for him.

When I made motions to leave, he didn't protest, but his shoulders slumped. On a sudden impulse, I asked him if he wanted another drink in my room. He sighed gratefully and followed me outside into the warm night. He stopped next to a spectacular silver Corvette in the parking lot and said he wanted to make a brief phone call. He got inside and shut its doors so I couldn't hear what he said over the car's telephone, but I saw his face grow business-like and strained. When he emerged, the sadness returned. What kind of rare bird had I caught here? I began to regret my invitation to him. Moreover in my room, I realized I couldn't offer him a drink. Would he like instant coffee? He didn't care. He seemed dead tired and far away. He turned on the television and asked if I wanted to watch the rest of the "Tonight Show"? He couldn't quite face driving home yet to an empty apartment. He sat down on the edge of the bed with a sigh. We were perfect strangers to each other, and I was struck by the odd intimacy of this motel room. He was too drunk to take much notice of the settings, and I was sure I was no more to him than a listening post. But I was stuck with him now, so I decided to relax about it.

"OK," I said. "Sit back against the pillows. It's more comfortable." Andy propped the pillows against the headboard. Johnny Carson was playing "beat the band" with his audience back in Burbank. A woman from South Carolina won four free dinners for "She's more to be pitied than censored, for a man was the cause of it all. . . . " I confessed it was my long-standing ambition to beat the band with "Piccolomini," a song made up of only one word, repeated over and over ever faster to the same tune, but which accentuated different syllables each time around. I laughed at my own idea and began to demonstrate: "Piccolo*mi*ni, Pic*c*olo*mi*ni . . . Piccolo*mi*ni, Pic*c*o. . ., *lo*mini*pi*ccolo-*mi*nipic*c*olom*i*n*i*pic*o*l*o*mini *Pi* . . ."—until I heard Andy snore. His curly brown head rested on his chest, and he breathed heavily. I called his name and shook his shoulders, but he sank deeper into an alcoholic sleep. "Oh Christ!" I thought. "This is absurd." But then I reasoned that he was not only impossible to move, but also harmless in that state, and that I might as well leave him in peace.

I removed his shoes and socks, and, after a moment's hesitation, loosened his shirt and belt. As I pushed and shoved his youthful body under the sheets, I became aware of its indefinable scent. I watched the "Tonight Show" to the end and got ready for bed. I changed into my nightgown, pulled the bedspread off the bed and wrapped myself in it. I curled up in an armchair. After half an hour of discomfort, trying to conform my body to the armchair's shape, I knew I would never be able to sleep. Suddenly I began to feel resentful of this unknown man, this oversized doll, who lay on the bed I was paying for. How did I get into this? Maybe I was too used to having a man tell me what to do. After all, I had some problems of my own. Andy remained dead to the world. I threw off the bedspread and crawled into the queen-sized bed next to him.

He gave no sign and slept on as motionless as a rock at the bottom of a pond. I still couldn't fall asleep. I tried not to move more than necessary, and then only with great caution, avoiding his body, but at the same time aware of its fragrance.

Towards morning I finally fell into a deep sleep and dreamed I was a contestant on a TV show called "The Mating Game." I stood on a stage next to the emcee, an enormous man in a black tuxedo with foul teeth, who announced three different, but equally repelling "mates" whom I had to interview. The first was a pock-marked virgin from Solvang, the second a masochistic homosexual from San Francisco, and the third a transsexual with a synthetic penis named Francis.

I had to ask them questions which were written on a squashed wad of paper I held in one hand. I was blinded by spotlights, deafened by applause and raucous whistles, and incensed by the comments of the emcee who kept insisting I was a left-wing hippie whore from Berkeley who got my start on the streets during the student riots in the sixties by sleeping with every National Guardsman who was stationed there to keep the peace. "This whore is so dumb," he said, "that she did it with the soldier boys for free."

"No, that's not right," I tried to protest, "I'm a poet who keeps a conscientious diary of her daily activities. . . . . No, NO! That's not true either. You don't seem to understand. I'm not supposed to be on this program. I'm a Malibu fire survivor, and my real ambition is to desalinate the Pacific Ocean. No, no, NO! I don't mean THAT!" I realized I could neither control my speech nor move from that spot. The audience jeered wildly and threw spitballs onto the stage.

I had to start my questions, but I couldn't control what I asked. I really wanted to know the political leanings of these mates, their opinions on the armaments industry, the arms race and the Free Speech Movement. But the questions I actually uttered had to do with Freud's theories of vaginal versus clitoral orgasms and the role of menstrual blood in pornography.

Their answers were equally absurd and incomprehensible, mixing up references to Kinsey, Sappho and polymorphism. Two of them got into an argument over a recipe for making cunnilingus cake. One insisted you used a cup of olive oil and the other was equally adamant about sesame seed oil. They grew very angry, started a fist fight and knocked over the screen which had concealed them. As they rolled around on each other punching, kicking and tearing hair, each kept yelling at the other, "You insufferable jerk! You insufferable jerk!"

The audience went wild at this. It hooted and stamped and sent a veritable waterfall of spitballs onto the stage. The emcee commanded me to choose my mate. I looked at my crumpled paper for a clue, but couldn't decipher a thing. I looked back at the emcee for help, but he was sticking his tongue out at me. On its tip was a small bubble of saliva which grew larger and larger until it concealed his entire body and then burst with a flash.

I woke to the dim morning light visible through the gray slatted Venetian blinds and the chirp of a strange bird. Nightingale? Lark? "It is the lark that sings so out of tune,/ Straining harsh discords and unpleasing sharps. Some say the lark makes sweet division. . . . " Somewhere a big rig started revving up for its cross-country run. I was curled up on my left side. To my great surprise, Andy's body hugged me tightly from behind. His snoring was more disjointed than the night before. Something pushed against my rear. Andy must have undressed during the night. I must have slept more soundly than I thought. The pressure aroused a sensation I had rejected all the years that Thomas had pleaded with me to try it—"just once. I'll be gentle," he used to say. "If it hurts, I'll stop. Lots of people do it and enjoy it. There's nothing abnormal about it. You've read Masters and Johnson. What do you think all the gays do in San Francisco? Try to have an open mind. Maybe you'll like it if you're honest with yourself."

"The gays get their heads bashed in," I thought to myself, and postponed his wish again and again. "Maybe sometime, but not *this* time," I would tell him whenever he brought it up.

Now, here I was in bed with a stranger who had a telephone in his glitter-silver Corvette, and who would certainly wake up with a terrible hangover and be gone out of my life forever. I squirmed towards him to increase the pressure. Andy snorted and pushed his pelvis forward just enough so that the tip of his penis opened my sphincter ever so slightly. I pretended to sleep, in case he woke up at that moment. But his breathing resumed a steady rhythm. "Was it immoral to take advantage of an unconscious man?" I wondered. I thought about the story of the oral surgeon who had fondled and raped his anesthetized patients. But I relinquished the thought at the same moment I pushed my buttocks against the hard tip sinking inside me—a peculiar sensation which produced, nevertheless, a feeling of yearning. Suddenly Andy gave a hard push which sent a painful jolt up my back. He was awake.

He stretched his left arm around my body, and the way he touched me told me he understood something about women. But almost immediately, his intensity grew intolerable, and with another motion he exploded inside me.

After Andy's Corvette pulled out of the motel parking lot, I walked across the street to a pancake house for breakfast. I drove around Dallas all morning and decided to stay, despite my ignominious beginning. "I can always leave again," I told myself. I checked out apartment ads for several hours and returned to the motel in the late afternoon, where I took a swim and a nap. In the evening I decided to treat myself to the best dinner I could find, and made a reservation at "L'Etoile," after checking out restaurants in the Dallas yellow pages.

The maître d' ushered me to a corner table in a secluded section of the restaurant, which was located atop a downtown skyscraper. An oriental screen hid my table from a larger one next to it. "So Dallas, Texas is not without culture," I thought to myself as the maître d' in his black tuxedo removed the table setting of my nonexistent partner. The style was quasi-Parisian and the menu French. The abundant city lights sparkled below, and the large Texas sky glowed orange and red in the distance. Other guests arrived dressed in furs and tuxedos, for the most part. The waiter recommended the escargots, the *salade au chèvre chaud*, the *escalope du boeuf*, a red wine—St. Emilion, Château Pavie 1975—*et après, la mousse au chocolat avec Armagnac*. I said, "*D'accord*," and the waiter replied with a slight nod, "*Oui, madame.*"

The escargots were floating in butter and garlic. After the salad with its grilled chevre, coarse black pepper and a delicious vinaigrette, I went to the rest room. When I returned, the table behind the screen was occupied by two well-dressed gentlemen, probably in their fifties. Apparently, they didn't notice me, because I could hear their conversation through the partition between our tables.

One of them was saying to the other: "You fool, don't you understand a good deal when you see it? With Lillian out of the way, Shirley will crumble, and we'll be able to buy out the Marshall sister's video syndicate. The live peep shows alone net 60 million a year—*net*, you idiot. We'll have an edge on the porn market. It's the logical adjunct to our houses. How many slobs can afford them nowadays, and besides, the future is in video and telephone sex. You have to move with the times. Daddy always said, don't be afraid to diversify. Well, the time has come, and I've got the right John for the job. It will only confirm her reputation. Everyone believes she's a whore, and most of *them* come to a bad end, anyway. And the world thinks they deserve it. No one is going to worry very much about another dead slut."

The other voice was younger and softer, and the Texas drawl more pronounced. "Damn you, Carl," it said, "Murder is *not* our business. You know that's not what Daddy meant when he said to diversify. His business was a service. He kept his girls clean, and he protected them. He'd be ashamed of you. You can stuff that idea right now. We're competitive as it is. We've got the second biggest chain in Texas. There are other ways to grow. . . ."

"Damn it, Andy, where are your balls?

I was startled for a moment, thinking I'd heard the name, "Andy," but then I determined it was actually "Randy."

Carl's voice continued. "You haven't got an ounce of imagination in your gray matter. You think too fucking small. Why don't you go into gardening, or something that would suit your sensitive soul, if you can't take it in the business world? I don't want the Chandlers to be *second* biggest in Texas; with the Marshall syndicate we'll be first in the West. We're talking about Oklahoma, New Mexico, Arizona and southern California, too. Think of it—Los Angeles, man, LA! We're talking big time, Arab money. Now's not the time to squirm, Randy. We've got to move. And we need to stick together in this. I can use your charm and PR ability once we've got the syndicate. We'll expand, we'll become equal partners, the way Daddy really wanted it. Nobody will be able to stop us. Are you with me?"

The escalope was pink, tender and perfect. Even the carmelized carrots were delicious. But I was having trouble concentrating on my meal.

The younger voice rose in anger, "You dirty son of a bitch! You pervert Daddy's memory. You stop this ugly business right now, or you've lost your brother, too. What's wrong with you, Carl? You can't get along with your wife. Your own mother doesn't trust you. Is nothing sacred to you anymore? You're going to lose your whole family in the end, and maybe ruin it. Don't you give a damn?"

"You ask me what's sacred, well I'll tell you, you self-righteous prick. Money! That's what, and don't try to tell me Daddy didn't believe in that. Wealth is where it's at! Greater than you can imagine, because you haven't got an ounce of creativity beneath those pretty, thick curls and that thicker skull. What we can't do with that kind of money.

You just don't seem to understand the political power we'd have. *Political*—do you get it?"

"Stop it, you asshole! You're crazy. It will never work!"

The waiter went to their table, and when he looked at me, I waved him away with a gesture that indicated he should leave me alone. I refilled my own glass with the heavy French red wine and drank it down. I debated for a moment whether or not to go ahead with the chocolate mousse, but then I heard Carl's voice say, "It's too late, Randy. . . ."

I decided to sneak out before my two Texas neighbors noticed my presence. I emptied my wine glass and quietly rose and walked away, keeping out of their sight. At the entrance, I paid the maître d' in cash, informing him that I felt ill and had to leave.

The next morning I sat down to breakfast in the motel coffee shop with a newspaper in hand. I intended to comb the classified adds and go apartment hunting, but I was stopped by the headlines: "Brutal 'Sexecution' Murder of Marshall Sister. Powerful Chandler Family Implicated." The article couldn't resist reporting the gory details—the victim had been tied down, the barrel of a hand gun inserted into her vagina and the trigger pulled. I left the coffee shop without ordering breakfast and checked out of the motel.

In the afternoon I sold my Honda to a foreign car dealer in the town of Irving, between Dallas and Fort Worth. At 7:05 PM I boarded a plane for New York at Dallas International, and at 8:30 PM the following evening I got on another one at JFK. I sat at the window, and as the jet taxied away from the terminal and made a turn onto the end of the runaway, I caught a glimpse of two rows of landing lights stretching straight into infinity separated by a wide dark strip. I gripped the armrests tightly, and as the plane accelerated, one row of the same lights became a straight blur before it lifted off for Frankfurt, Germany.

✿　✿　✿

My friend:

It was so exceedingly difficult to track down Megan's motel room lover, that for a while I began to think that she had only made up this entire story about her trip to Texas. In the end, however, the man she described turned out to be a real and highly visible person, Andrew Tarkington, the Chief Executive Officer of a large Texas oil company. I used my alias with him too, and he agreed to meet me for lunch during one of my "business trips to Dallas" (Gina was still alive at this time, and I made up some excuse to explain this trip I took by myself).

He knew in the meantime, the story of the infamous Megan Lloyd—the media story.

It was a most bizarre experience to speak face-to-face with one of the men who had used my daughter. We had a long talk on the appointed day, and I appreciated his candor. I asked him to read her story about her visit to Dallas, and he admitted that the one-night stand took place during a difficult period in his marriage—between two consenting adults. But he denied sodomy was involved; it had been an uncomplicated, straightforward affair, and he had been perfectly awake. He had found Megan extremely attractive—slim, long blond hair, beautiful green eyes, somewhat boyish—and had often thought about her afterwards. He claimed that the parallels to the TV series, the Etoile restaurant and the "sexecution" murder had to be pure imagination. Indeed, my investigation in the Dallas area failed to turn up a restaurant similar to the one she described. And, back in Los Angeles, an exhaustive search through both national and local Texas newspapers at the UCLA microfilms library failed to unearth any of the characters or the sensational murder of the type she describes at that point in time (ultimately, of course, I've come to see that her sexual fantasies and fictions formed a logical attempt on the part of her unconscious to bring to the surface my own crime that she had successfully buried).

So I believed this Tarkington character's version of things. But it was a difficult encounter for me. I did not know whether to hit him, to shake his hand or to run away from him, because there were moments when I saw him more as a conspirator than a person from whom I wanted to glean information.

One more thing—he remembered that Megan had asked quite a number of detailed questions about the organization, management, and functioning of a large corporation—something she doesn't mention in her version of their meeting. I welcomed this new information because it indicated interests in her that had nothing to do with me. It allowed me to flirt for a while with the self-serving explanation that Megan had indeed been interested in political terrorism.

To this day I still cannot totally account for my eagerness to retrace all her steps, Gordon, including the dead ends. I mean to say that at first I was looking for answers, but later on, when I knew the answers, the search continued just the same. It became a compulsion. Perhaps I never gave up on the irrational hope that if I continued to trace the tracks she left behind, I could eventually recapture the fatal moments and magically turn things in a different direction.

CHAPTER SIX

Autobahn Dogfight

> A man must stand in fear of just those things
> that truly have the power to do us harm, of
> nothing else, for nothing else is fearsome.
>
> Dante

It was cloudy over the continent, and rain drizzled onto German asphalt as the jet touched down in a rough, two-bounce landing on the runway in Frankfurt am Main. I was very tired, but at least far away from Dallas, Texas and farther yet from California, from the Wild West and the New World. I hadn't been back to Europe since my student days.

After a long wait for the customs inspection, I loaded my suitcases onto a pushcart and went to look for a car rental agency. Announcements rang out over the loudspeaker in German, French and English, while travelers from all over the world surged through the giant halls. At the Hertz Rent-A-Car counter, I signed up for an Opel, my mind dazed from the flight. Jet lag is both tiring and exhilarating. Like sleepwalking wide awake, you go through the motions while part of you seems to stand next to yourself watching.

Ten minutes later, I turned the key in the ignition and drove, with some trepidation, out of the airport and onto the *Autobahn* where I was swept into the midst of its deadly game. I reached the Frankfurter Kreuz, then headed north towards Göttingen on the E4 via Kassel.

What I saw kicked my mind into automatic pilot, and I drifted into a nightmare world behind the steering wheel. . . .

I gave full throttle to my single-engine Ford-Opel rent-a-plane and lifted off at about 60 knots. At Tempo 100 (kilometers per hour, that is)—a recommendation of the airliner magazine—I found myself in the middle of a struggle for survival of the fittest race. Sleek, low-flying Daimler-Benz Messerschmitts were shooting past dangerously close to my port wing as I rolled along in the right air lane. So close, I could make out the faces of the pilots who turned their heads towards me for a *blitzschnell* second as they passed. Immediately, I realized that to them, I was the mysteriously cunning, slow-flying enemy, whose strategy lay in this deviant behavior. Their first shots must have gone astray due to the discrepancy between their super- and my sub-sonic speed—also perhaps to an infinitesimal hesitation, when they realized their enemy was a woman. Shocked and frightened, I resolved for the moment to maintain Tempo 100 to frustrate whatever their designs might be.

But then two Audi Stutzas appeared with wings bent as if they could flap. They were piloted by daredevils who presented a more immediate danger than the Daimler-Messerschmitts. They dove at my tail. In the last possible instant they swerved to miss me, and then only by a hair, so that their breakneck speed and proximity rocked my little Opel with their wake turbulence. They swooped out of sight briefly, but when I turned my head, they dove for me again with their landing lights aimed to blind me. Squinting and blinking, I kicked the right rudder and banked the wing to deflect them. Top speed in my Opel was two hundred knots—no match for the Stutzas. To slow down even more would be foolish. The dive-bombers would certainly crash into me. All I could do was hold tight to the controls and pray (but to whom?), and hope the more chivalrous officers, perhaps the Prussians among them, would take pity on a damsel in distress and spare her, perhaps miss her deliberately so as not to lose face with the *Luftwaffe*. But there were so many of them. Squadrons of hundreds swarmed by. I feared the law of averages was against me.

One thing gave me momentary hope, or at least satisfaction. I noticed that not infrequently the Nazi planes collided with each other and spiraled to earth after a hideous crash. Their smoldering wreckages dotted the rolling green landscape 2000 meters below. This was because the *Luftwaffe* consisted not only of small, aerodynamic death-defying Daimler-Messerschmitts and Audi Stutzas, but also of slower, less maneuverable Junker-Mannesmann flying tanks, Heinkel-Käss-bohrer troop transports, and Volkswagen-Porsche cargo planes, all of which shared the same narrow north-south air corridor. The larger slower craft kept a greater distance, but I could still see their pilots' faces. I was amazed to note that they were flown by old men and women, probably grandfathers and grandmothers, as well as handi-capped war casualties who lacked an occasional arm or hand or Lord knows what else, and also a number of boys, who appeared to be no more than fifteen or sixteen years old. Though their reaction time may have been superior to the tough young Messerschmitt pilots, these teenagers all had a look of panic about them, probably because they lacked the skill and experience of the hot-shot pilots, or, on the other hand, they feared death more than their elders whose feelings had dulled with years and sorrow. Their flying was the most erratic but the least threatening to me. I reckoned that the war could not go on much longer if the Fatherland had to draft the very young and very old.

Near the Giessen turnoff I noticed, with a twinge of hope, a large cloud bank which might conceal me from my enemies. At the moment what seemed to be a large troop transport was approaching. As it bore down inexorably, I saw it was a flying bulldozer which could easily scoop up my Opel or simply crush it with its treads. For the first time, I accelerated as a new escape tactic, but even when the Opel attained its top speed around 200 knots, the bulldozer continued to gain on me. As it slowly came abreast of my port side, I could make out the face of its pilot—tired, old, wizened, and nearly bald, with thick glasses, and hearing aids in both ears. Very pale, with coarse white hair sprouting out of his eyebrows, nose and ears, he looked sick and worried and much like the pictures of my own grandfather, only older. With no more than three meters to spare, I thought I was a goner. But suddenly, out of nowhere, a racing Messerschmitt roared up alongside the bulldozer. Just before we all entered the clouds, it accelerated and dove diago-nally towards me as if to say, "Out of my way, you old fart, she's mine."

I gained a few meters altitude as I jerked back the little Opel's stick in a desperate attempt to elude my pursuers. In fact, as I craned my neck back, I saw that the Messerschmitt had miscalculated his dive ever so slightly to his own detriment, cutting in too close to the bull-dozer, whose pilot, in his old age, had neither seen nor heard him un-til the Messerschmitt was positioned hopelessly in front of him. I glimpsed both the young pilot's rage and the old pilot's horror at the instant before impact, which exploded both aircraft in a tremendous ball of fire and smoke, shooting debris as well as bodies in all directions—for the bulldozer had been towing a trailer full of German soldiers. Due to the force of the crash, bodies and limbs shot like missiles past my plane, and one even grazed my landing gear before hurtling towards the ground. It sickened me to see that they were all elderly.

Inside the clouds, visibility was reduced to a blinding white zero. I eased back on the throttle to slow the Opel as much as possible. I knew the clouds would be filled with the same German squadron, none of which had decelerated at their sight. I would have to rely on my instincts and ears to avoid a collision. I decided to close my throttle and glide. At first I heard only the high pitch of the air rushing by my wings, but soon the first crash took place off my port side, perhaps 100 meters away. A terrible clash of metal, it was followed swiftly by the whine of a diving aircraft going into a spin. Then silence again. After a few minutes which seemed like years, I heard the characteristic sound of a Messerschmitt cross my path going the wrong way. Lord help *him*, I thought, and continued to peer into the terrible whiteness. Right after that I heard two heavies from above roaring down towards me at three o'clock. I nosed down a little more, hoping to lose enough altitude to avoid them. Luck was with me. When it sounded like they were about 200 meters in front of me, another explosion took place, followed by a great turbulence which I feared would shake my rental plane to pieces like a grass shack in a hurricane. I held on for dear life trying to ride out the bounces which sent me flying off the seat and nearly knocked my head against the roof of the plane.

Suddenly, patches of blue punctuated the otherwise total whiteness, and colors and shapes gradually re-formed as the clouds dissipated and the earth and sky took on their familiar contours. I found I had dropped to about 1000 meters and was gliding at a steep angle to the earth and towards a new cloud bank. Finally, I saw the ground. The landscape was smoldering with the wreckages from the conflict in the sky.

Now I thought to turn on the radio. Surprised, I realized I could still understand German, and the male voice that spoke was familiar to me. I knew it from all the World War II movies and documentaries I'd ever seen. It was the *Führer* himself in an official broadcast to the German nation. He was describing the very battle in which I was caught: "At this moment our brave German *Luftwaffe* is engaged in its most perilous aerial battle of the war to date in the center of the Fatherland. All available manpower and aircraft have been activated to pursue and destroy the most devious foe yet to threaten our great *Reich*. We will wipe the vermin from the German skies forever. No sacrifice is too great for the Fatherland. Already, the new secret Jewish-communist weapon, the insidious maintenance of Tempo 100, has succeeded in seriously hampering our glorious *Luftwaffe*. But our superior Aryan air technology will restore the inalienable National Socialist right of the German *Volk* to fly at supersonic speeds over against the decadent tendencies of inferior races to fly at seductively slow speeds. . . ."

He raved on and on interminably. I was both fascinated and repulsed by his ability to string so many idiotic phrases together with such unflagging, vehement enthusiasm. The shrillness of his voice competed with the static on the radio and made listening almost intolerable. But finally I got the feeling he was approaching the end. "Forward with me into the *Reich* of power, beauty and happiness and the joy of living! What expresses the joy of living better than the fastest possible dive and swoop over free German air space? No one will threaten our right to pursue this supreme happiness, particularly no foreign powers, who may have instigated pusillanimous speed limits. We will never forget our countless brave brothers and sisters who have made the supreme sacrifice on our *Autobahnen*, in order to keep them free for continuous race driving trials. Their high-speed deaths will not be in vain. It is they, who by their example and with their very lives, insist on and protect our precious right to press our feet ever downward on the gas pedal. Beware the liberal intellectuals who argue that a harmonious speed limit would facilitate traffic flow; they propose weakness and faintheartedness over the glories of speeding and tailgating with pride and power, a cherished need intimately linked with our national ego and great destiny. We are a strong, healthy nation, wherein the fittest survive. The German *Reich* will never be reduced to a land of snail colonies. Not for that did we build our *Autobahnen*, but to prove our manhood as a nation and a people to the rest of the world." Hitler's speech ended with the sounds of march music and enthusiastic crowds yelling "*Heil, heil, heil*" over and over, while his last strident words were, "All for one and one for all!"

"One against all," I thought. "Megan Lloyd against the *Reich*. Megan Lloyd against . . . what?" I came to with a start.

I continued on for another ten minutes, my mind a blank. Then I spied the rest stop near Kassel coming up, not far from my destination of Göttingen. "Jeeeesus!" I thought to myself. "Some case of jet lag." I turned off the *Autobahn* and rolled into a parking place in front of the restaurant. Here I'd been racing along with the Germans, battling at supersonic speeds with Mercedes, Porsches and BMW's. I loosened my tight grip on the wheel. Perspiring with fatigue, I nevertheless felt a twinge of arousal.

I entered the restaurant and ordered camomile tea. I took the cup to an outside table, since the weather was hazily clear in Hesse, and because I wanted to relax before attempting the last stretch of country road to Göttingen. The *Autobahn* below was visible from the terrace, but I didn't mind watching the continuing battle for survival unfold now from this safe distance. Most tables were full of drivers taking a break. I became aware of an American tourist family of four a couple of tables away, speechlessly watching the same spectacle, their gazes mesmerized by the *Autobahn*, their heads turning rapidly from right to left to right, as if watching a tennis match from the stands. They ignored the drinks on their table. Finally, as they collected themselves to go, the teenage son said to his father: "Just like at Indianapolis, isn't it Dad?"

✿ ✿ ✿

Gordon:

I debated whether or not to take this surrealist dog fight out of the manuscript, but I left it in because it reveals a part of Megan's personality that I never quite understood, even when she was a child. In school, she always chose scurrilous, bizarre topics whenever she could get away with it for her writing assignments. She sometimes talked at the dinner table about odd subjects all of her own invention. I once asked our psychologist friend, Jason Evans, about it, and he explained her interest in the outlandish as a strategy to survive in a family where the disparate elements present in our urban wilderness had to be reconciled—the greasy clothes and automotive parts with the crystal wine glasses and opera arias. In those days I disdained psychologists and their simplistic answers.

CHAPTER SEVEN

The Summer Solstice

The man that hath no music in himself,
Nor is not moved with concord of sweet sounds,
Is fit for treasons, stratagems and spoils;
The motions of his spirit are dull as night
And his affections dark as Erebus:
Let no such man be trusted.

Shakespeare

Dear Gordon,
The following stations of her life struck me at first as if they came
from an alien creature and another planet. I tried to convince myself
that the quantum leap that took place here undermined the very idea
of causality. I rejected the notion that sin, guilt and retribution drove
the world and reasoned that randomness determined human affairs
more than we think. Yet, no one will ever know how frantic and des-
perate I became as I followed my daughter's gradual undoing.

* * *

In Göttingen I looked up my old friend Shelley Burney. She lived
now with a German woman named Gisela at the end of town near
Geismar. The flat had two bedrooms, but a large bed in only one of
them. I slept on a couch in the living room. We talked for hours—that
is, Shelley and I did all the talking, and Gisela listened. She learned a
lot about me, although I never learned anything about her. Shelley
said, that's just the way she was.

Shelley and I went to visit Arnold and Gabriele. They had never been arrested for the terrorist murder of 1971, although they were rather thoroughly investigated. I couldn't learn either from Shelley or from them whether or not they had been directly involved in that assassination. They still lived in Arnold's same spacious and chaotic flat where we used to have the long meetings. They had a four-year old boy, and it seemed like we had all aged. The sixties had arrested Arnold's and Gabriele's notions of fashion. He still sported long disheveled hair, now with a touch of gray, bound to his head by a leather cord around the forehead, and she dyed her long black hair henna red. Her loose flowing dresses still concealed a beautifully proportioned body, despite motherhood, and her entire appearance was airy and ethereal. They were still enveloped in a cloud of cigarette smoke and surrounded by steadily heaping ashtrays. I thought that so much smoke was unconscionable with a small child in the house, but I didn't say anything. I did tell Gaby and Arnold a few things about my life during the last years, but I could not get myself to talk about the divorce from Thomas.

They still held discussion meetings, and Shelley and I attended a couple during the three weeks I stayed in Göttingen. Gisela came along and took copious notes but never opened her mouth. As in the past, glasses were continually full of French table wine, and I joined in drinking and talking until the small hours of the mornings with a bizarre assortment of students and acquaintances of vague professions who gathered there, floated in and out of the discussions, and crashed on the ash-covered floor. Just like the old days.

I got a headache and a smoker's cough after these meetings from the polluted indoor air. Suddenly, I'd had enough. On a Thursday morning at 5 AM when Shelley and Gisela were asleep, I slipped out of their apartment and made my way to the Göttingen train station, where I turned in my rental car and caught a train to Paris. I didn't want to drive that far on the German and French highways by myself. The first part of the trip was uneventful. Later that afternoon, the train stopped for three minutes at Compiègne, the last stop northeast of Paris, and the place where in 1918 and 1940 the German Reich (second and third editions) ceased firing at the French and Allied armies.

I stood up and pulled down the window. A few people got up and headed toward the exit. New passengers got on and walked down the corridor in search of empty compartments. I leaned out the window and watched the platform where people stood around waiting for different trains. A dark-haired man in a blue suit, a black briefcase in hand, waited not far from my window. About 45 years old, his hair was longish and disorderly, and his dark eyes darted back and forth. He looked more German to me than French. I averted his glance and looked instead at other happenings in the station. Three minutes passed on the station clock before a nearby conductor waved to another conductor at the head of the train and placed his foot on the steps of my car as the train began to move. Now I caught the glance of the man in the blue suit, or he caught mine. He was right in front of my window, maybe ten feet away. I held his eyes and studied his face. He spoke to me: "*Mit Ihnen möchte ich einmal gern schlafen.*"[1] Surprised, I furrowed my brow and blinked. The train picked up speed. I turned my head away and rested it on my forearm. The wind whipped my face. At the first curve, I looked back to see the blue suit fade out of sight. So he was German. I closed the window and sat down. I wondered if the woman in my compartment with the Feuchtwanger novel in her hand overheard what he had said. A man whom I would never see again, but an idea out of nowhere that I remembered.

In Paris I set up housekeeping on the Left Bank, near the Musée de Cluny, with its Roman remains of the ancient city of Lutece. After a few weeks I started to feel better. Perhaps if I stayed long enough my life would take on some shape. This was the city of all cities, after all. I walked its streets and discovered new worlds. I sat in cafés, sometimes for hours, and had the feeling it was time well spent—in the middle of western civilization and history. After reviewing my finances, I decided to give myself six months here and see what might emerge. For all the color on its surface, Parisian life had a well-ordered substructure—it had to support so many people. I hoped something of this deep structure would rub off on me and help organize my life.

You always run into someone you know in Paris, either in the Louvre or on the Champs Élysées. It was Alfredo Torelli, an old friend, more Thomas' than mine, who had been an exchange student at Berkeley—on the Champs Élysées, in a café. I had never taken much notice of him at Berkeley, and he recognized me first. Although he had attended a couple of SDS meetings way back then, he struck me as rather bourgeois and conventional, despite the rumor that he belonged to the Communist Party in Italy. He had always been low key

---

[1] I would like to sleep with you sometime.

and soft-spoken for an Italian. He seemed genuinely sorry to hear of
my divorce from Thomas. I was surprised to learn he played the flute
in the symphony orchestra of Florence. This profession seemed to me
to clash with his physique, which was dark, heavy and ponderous. In
the States you'd call him a stud and expect to see him on television
praising his mother and father and the Lord Jesus Christ right before
crushing every possible bone in the opposing right guard's body on the
line of scrimmage with the full force of all 250 pounds of his impenetrable, hard flesh. The thick neck and heavy shoulders gave the impression, however, that he'd have a hell of a hard time running because
of the brawn he'd have to transport.

   We talked over coffee and cognac. In Paris for a series of chamber concerts, he had a wife and young daughter in Florence. But I
could sense that the big, dark figure across from me also had sex on
his mind. He loved to tell stories and anecdotes in an understated
manner, and he mixed in a lot of Italian words and expressions that I
comprehended. I realized I still had a large passive vocabulary and a
rudimentary understanding of Italian from my mother and grandmother. I was charmed by him, and also appreciated the fact that he
was a good listener. I realized I was enjoying his company and invited
him to my apartment.

   For several days Alfredo and I divided our energies between my
bed and his evening concerts at the cavernous cathedral of St. Eu-
stache near Les Halles. The wildly enthusiastic Parisian audience
didn't seem to be bothered by the impossible acoustics of the church
in which the precision of the baroque music was lost as surely as if it
had been performed in an under-water echo chamber. I attended
these concerts as a favor to Alfredo, and the sensuality of the days we
spent together compensated for the eeriness of these sounds during
the evenings.

   When we weren't in bed or in the church, we ate oysters and other
fruits de mer in wonderful restaurants. When we were in bed, he filled
me with his abundant masculinity. I opened to it like an empty barn at
harvest time, ready to be stacked with fruit, grains and other good
products of the earth. I straddled his torso for hours while he caressed
my body with his slender, agile fingers, which seemed as if they should
belong to a different person altogether. With his hands he played me
as expertly as he did the flute. But when I stretched out on top of him
or when he lay on me, he squeezed the breath out of me with his bear
arms to which these sensitive, out-of-place hands were attached. I

gladly bore these pleasurable pains for four days with abandon.

I wondered what it was that had conditioned away any traces of intentional brutality in him—a brutality which could have been so easily inculcated in such a large specimen. Was it a gentle upbringing or perhaps a learned sensitivity? Was he a freak success in the process of civilization? He feared he appeared brutish and unattractive to women. I didn't know. But he seemed to me a kind of an evolutionary anomaly in the more feminine cultures of Italy and France. At any rate, he served a useful function for me at the moment. He made me feel like a free-roaming, wild animal. My interest in Parisian culture was momentarily reduced, but I didn't mind.

Our last night together he took his flute out of its case, and as we lay naked on my bed he played a melody by a composer with the peculiar name of Gluck. I think he called it the "Dance of the Spirits," and I suppose he played it for me because he thought it was beautiful. When he finished, a passerby outside the building below the window of my flat began to clap and called out *"Bravo, encore!"* I guess I was impressed by this anonymous enthusiasm, and for the first time believed that I too had enjoyed a piece of good music. Maybe that pied piper's melody was beckoning me to a better future in a better world.

But in my dreams that night I found myself on a paleolithic plain populated with historic and prehistoric horses, bears, mammoths and foxes, all of which threatened to pursue me. Panic-stricken, I fled to hide behind a clump of trees and rocks. Suddenly, out of a dust cloud, human shapes appeared and turned the animals on their heels in pursuit. Six men slung rocks and spears at the dispersing beasts and eventually struck down a strange little horse which they stoned and stabbed to death and flayed on the spot. My relief at escaping the animals turned to disgust and fascination as I watched the men pull the warm bloody flesh and entrails straight off the bones of the horse and stuff them into their mouths. They hissed and grunted as they ate, and blood smeared their faces with the protruding brows and jaw bones. Yet some of the sounds mixed with what seemed like articulate syllables that they understood in common. Six pairs of ancient eyes regarded me with suspicion and aggression. Some of the animals were returning stealthily, approaching dangerously close, attracted by the smell of blood. There was nowhere to go and I feared the animals, so I stuck closer to the men.

When they finished their gory repast, the men snarled and threw rocks at the lurking beasts who snarled back and waited impatiently for a turn at the remains. Black vultures swirled overhead while some of the men picked themselves up. Two of them urinated thick yellow streams onto the bloody carcass.

The leader of the band took a few steps towards me, hissed and growled some semi-articulate sounds and pounded his club on a tree trunk. I realized as he regarded me that I was naked, and pale as an albino in contrast to them. I wanted to hide, but the animals were stirring nearby. The men gathered behind the leader and grunted and gestured for me to follow. Soon I was straggling behind the dirty, bloody crew towards an unknown goal. My feet hurt from the rough terrain, but theirs were as thick as leather. They hunched over with heavy arms as they walked.

Eventually one of them fell back towards me. He had an erection, across which he rubbed his club. He growled at me and bared his teeth. I recoiled, but the leader noticed what he was doing and snarled at him. He fell back in line. At the next tree, however, the leader stopped, beat his club against the trunk and stared at me. The entire group produced strange noises and stamped their feet with increasing excitement so that the dust rose. The leader continued to beat the tree and the others hit their clubs on the ground. I froze in place. I tried to cover my crotch with my hands, but found that my arms were too short to reach it. All six moved closer to me, the leader first in line. I was powerless to resist, and he forced me onto the ground on my hands and knees and pushed himself into my depths. He grunted in antediluvian ecstasy and vibrated rapidly before shooting a hot stream of primitive genetic protein into me with snorts and groans of animal relief.

As soon as he collapsed, the rest of them were on me, growling and pushing at each other for a chance to mingle with a more advanced evolutionary line. One by one they had their way with me in the sand. The sixth one, the weakest and the youngest, now took his turn in the orifice overflowing with prehistoric sperm. He came immediately with a scream, and I woke up as an orgasm pulsed through me.

❊ ❊ ❊

For some reason Alfredo Torelli's visit evoked memories of my other Italian lover, Guido Bonatti, the businessman from my Göttingen days who had introduced himself to me so many years ago from behind dark glasses. Despite the intervening years, I could raise every detail of that hotel encounter to the surface of my consciousness with perfect clarity—the feels, the smells, the sounds. Guido's ubiquitous dark glasses, in the shower, in bed. It had been not just the best sex I'd ever had, but an experience of a different order and magnitude, something transcendent, like fate. None of it had ever left me. Rather, the experience had anchored itself firmly at the core of my being.

I decided to call Guido Bonatti at his pharmaceutical company in Rome. It was easy to obtain the main number through the international operator, but when I reached it, I was blocked by a rigid secretarial network that screened unsolicited calls to the corporate president. After three unsuccessful attempts during one week, I was stymied. At the same time Stevie Carpenter, my oldest friend in the world, announced his arrival in Paris.

After the breakup of his nine-year-long gay "marriage" to Ralph in their Castro district flat, Stevie had been shattered. Desperate, he phoned me in Paris. He had taken a leave of absence from his insurance job in San Francisco. He didn't know where to go or what to do, only that he absolutely had to get away. Could he stay a few weeks with his oldest friend, calm down, and get back his bearings? Nothing was sadder, he told me, than a lonely, aging gay.

After I forgave him for dancing with Janet Macintosh and he forgave me for insulting his baseball skills, Stevie and I went through puberty together as confidantes, sharing all our tales of woe and triumph. I knew of his failed attempts at heterosexual intimacy in high school, and he knew the details of my first relationship with Craig Swanson. Later on, he told me about his crushes on male teachers at Berkeley and then described in detail his first, full-blown homosexual affair with an accountant. Our friendship had given us both a lot of vicarious knowledge. Now he needed help, and so did I.

I met Stevie at Orly. He was pale, thin and down. His hands trembled and he was wired on drugs. For three days he poured out his misery. Ralph had fallen in love with someone else. It was over. Suffering from jet lag, he ate little, slept during the day and paced at night. He popped pills, and I held his hand while he wept. Worried that he might quit eating altogether, I finally forced him to leave the apartment and get some fresh air.

I dragged him like a zombie through the metro and took him to the top of the Eiffel Tower. Where in Paris is there more fresh air? "And where else can you escape the view of this ridiculous structure?" he said, once we got there. During the hair-raising elevator ride to the top, I noticed his face begin to turn green. I began to think this was a mistake. Stevie controlled himself till we reached the platform. There, looking miserable, he sought out an uninhabited spot on the railing.

About the same time, a French woman from the elevator released a naked little Chihuahua dog from underneath her raincoat where she had concealed it next to her bosom during the ascent. As soon as its paws touched the cement, it scampered directly over to Stevie and lifted its leg over one of his shoes. Stevie glanced down at the dog and gagged twice before vomiting all over the impudent little monster who hadn't yet finished urinating. It whimpered and jumped aside while its mistress uttered, "*Mais Monsieur, mon Dieu, Monsieur . . . ,*" knowing all the while that the dog had no business there in the first place.

Taken aback, I watched the exquisite spectacle. As Stevie wiped his mouth with a handkerchief, the French woman fussed over her now untouchable canine that yapped and jumped at her feet, shaking itself violently and imploring to be lifted back into the secure location under her raincoat.

I wondered how she'd get the filthy, smelly beast back down the elevator, but as I approached Stevie, he grinned a smile as wide as the *tricolore* for the first time since his arrival, gestured broadly at the magnificent city below, the Seine underneath, the white Sacre Coeur in the distance, and announced, "That did me good. Vive la France!"

"Are you all right, Stevie?" I asked, as the French dog lover, talking rapidly to herself, threw a malevolent sideways glance in our direction.

"Yes, I'm really much better. Did you know that I hate Chihuahuas? I'd sooner have a mole rat for a house pet. I could run a detention camp for Chihuahuas without the slightest twinge of conscience." For the first time since his arrival, we laughed out loud.

Stevie seemed much better. He said a middle aged gay couldn't afford to grieve too long. His references to aging bothered me. We were both in our early thirties, after all.

That night I dreamt that the Eiffel Tower was actually the Eiffel Well, that Gustave Eiffel had convinced the Parisians that what they needed across from the Trocadero was a tremendous 8-million franc hole in the ground, 300 meters deep so that its bottom could be reached only by elevators. It would house a beautiful underground café and restaurant. Reinforced by an enormous and elaborate iron framework strong enough to withstand natural disasters including earthquakes, it was to be an architectural and engineering wonder destined to attract visitors from all over the world and to become a favorite Parisian landmark. Three elevator platforms at various depths would connect it with the metro, sewer and catacomb tunnels, so that tourists could embark on tours of each of these historic, subterranean worlds of Paris from the Eiffel Well. I woke up feeling better than I had for a long time.

Stevie began to show a renewed interest in life, including a curiosity about my love life. He reminded me that he was an expert in things sexual, having led an extremely promiscuous life for many years in San Francisco, and he urged me to fess up my most intimate secrets. After all, we used to do this all the time. I told him there had been nothing to tell during my married years, but after my divorce from Thomas there had been Andy in Dallas and just now, Alfredo, the magic flutist.

Then I told him of my desire to visit Guido Bonatti from Rome, and the difficulties I had getting through. Stevie said it looked like I was developing an Italian fixation, or maybe I was trying to work out some unconscious thing with my mother. I didn't know about that, but I told him about the incredible affair I'd had with Bonatti during my Göttingen year, and he whistled through his teeth, impressed that I was stalking a European corporate giant. He was dazzled by the idea and immediately said not to worry, he would act as my agent and intermediary and think of a plan. He loved setting up things like this and was good at it. Besides, Italy was a male chauvinist society, and my only hope of making a connection on the telephone was through a man's voice. "Just count on me!" He laughed ironically at his own self-confidence, flexed his muscles like a weight-lifter and at the same time exaggerated the effeminate affectation of his voice. We both fell into a laughing fit over this, but later got down to the serious business of outlining a strategy to get to Guido B.

Stevie pointed out that not only would Bonatti have a busy schedule and be out of town frequently, he would also have a protective bureaucracy that would insulate him from the public. Those secretaries I talked to were part of it. We would have to invent a plausible story to penetrate that protective shield, at least the part that monitored the telephones. We studied the yellow pages to determine which American pharmaceutical companies had branches in Paris.

That was on a Saturday. By Wednesday of the following week, Stevie's plan had obtained results. On Monday he was able to reach Bonatti's personal secretary by pretending to be the American sales representative of the Franklin & Franklin pharmaceutical giant in Atlanta with important, confidential business for Mr. Bonatti. His secretary promised to have Bonatti call Mr. Carpenter or his secretary, Megan Lloyd, at their Paris branch, when he returned from business in Athens on Wednesday. Stevie and I both jumped at 6 PM the following Wednesday when the phone rang.

My palms sweated as I picked up the receiver and answered the way I'd practiced with Stevie: "*Bonjour, Franklin et Franklin, ici Lloyd.*" Within a minute Guido Bonatti had determined I was the American woman who had studied in Göttingen and that this was a setup which he found both charming and provocative. His English was fluent now. He remembered our meeting in Göttingen, but whether or not he could meet me depended on a few things. I must understand he was extremely busy, but that if I would send a recent photo to him—in a manilla envelope marked "personal"—he would consider the possibility and call me back. Then he had to go.

I recounted the conversation to Stevie, who grew wide-eyed with awe. "Wow, a powerful bastard!"

"And an unadulterated male chauvinist," I added.

"Megan, don't be so bourgeois," Stevie chided. "A billionaire corporate president lives in a realm beyond chauvinism; our moral concepts don't apply in his world. Don't be a fool. Go for it! Do you have any pictures of yourself?"

I didn't, so Stevie and I went shopping the next day on the Rue du Faubourg Saint Honoré and spent a ridiculous amount of money on a sexy green silk dress and coiffure in a hair salon. After that he steered me into a photographer's studio which had promised over the phone to develop pictures overnight. The following day we chose the one out of the five shots which was the most sexy and elegant, in which the green of my eyes was brought out to best advantage by my dress. Stevie said I looked fit to kill. He couldn't keep his eyes off of the picture as we took it and a plain manilla envelope to a post office. He said, "If I could have gotten it on with you, Megan, I would have been a heterosexual for life."

The following Monday the phone rang again in my apartment about 5:45 PM. Guido assured me that the picture was stunning, but he wanted to explain that he only afforded himself this particular luxury once a year in some European capital, and would I please write him a letter describing my most intimate erotic desires and fantasies— also in a plain manilla envelope marked "personal." He would call me in another week if he thought a meeting would be desirable, depending upon the effectiveness of my letter.

"God, what a perverted asshole!" Stevie exclaimed, when I told him. "Megan, you don't know how lucky you are. I wish he were gay, damn it!" Then he sat me down with a piece of paper and started dictating a bizarre letter describing all kinds of things I might have found disgusting if it weren't for imagining Guido as the perpetrator of these acts, immune as he was from the laws governing ordinary mortals.

The following week his call came on a Tuesday afternoon, from Lisbon. He was very brief. I was to meet him in Munich in the hotel *Vier Jahreszeiten* the following Wednesday, June the twenty-first, the summer solstice. I was to fly there first class on Swiss Air. He wanted my Paris bank account number so he could deposit expense money into it. I was to wear the green silk dress in the picture and a green scarf, like the one I had worn years ago in Göttingen. I should be sitting in the hotel lobby at 8:45 AM and he would arrive in a Green Mercedes at 9 AM. We would go to the president's suite on the eighth floor together and remain until 3 PM. He had devised a plan for these hours designed to provide the ultimate sexual experience for both of us. Did I agree?

Stevie and I withdrew twelve thousand of the thirty thousand francs which appeared overnight in my Paris account and took a train to Munich a day early. He insisted on coming along to advise me, to be close to the action, to spend a night in a world class hotel and to get a blow by blow description immediately afterwards. He was almost as excited as I was. He proved a good traveling companion, and his own sorrow never surfaced again. We called ahead and rented a room, using my passport number and credit card, with two beds for two days in the *Vier Jahreszeiten* on the seventh floor, one below the penthouse presidential suite on the eighth floor. Stevie and I planned to stay the night after Guido left the hotel following my rendezvous with him.

I slept very poorly on June twentieth in Munich, despite the good bed and elegant room. It grew light already at 4 AM on the longest day of the year. Stevie got up at 7 AM and called room service for breakfast. I nibbled a few bites and then gave up, although Stevie advised I would probably need my strength. He helped me dress and fix my hair like it had been done for the photograph in Paris. He said he wished he could be there to watch, but he'd be back in our room by about noon. Then he wished me much pleasure and took off to wander around Munich for a few hours.

At 8:45 AM I entered the downstairs in the lobby, and the people working behind the reception desk said *"Guten Morgen."* I seated myself in a plush easy chair where I could look down the stairs and see taxis and cars arriving at the entrance. I didn't particularly want the receptionists to notice what I was up to, but they were busy, I reasoned, and in the business of profit, not morality. As I leafed through *Der Spiegel*, a dull green Mercedes appeared outside the entrance where it was taken over by a valet. In an off-white silk suit, dark glasses covering his eyes, Guido entered followed by a porter with a large aluminum suitcase. He was taller than I remembered him and, of course, older. His hair was curly and touched now with a streak of grey over each temple.

He picked me out immediately, but I attributed that more to my photograph than to any real memory from Göttingen. He bent to kiss my hand, pulled me up and took my arm. Then we walked right past the reception desk while a manager in a tuxedo bowed at him and said, "Good morning, Mr. Bonatti. Everything is ready." It flashed through my mind that perhaps he did this every week all over Europe, not just once a year, as he claimed. Why shouldn't he? He could afford to do exactly what he pleased. Some women he remembered, some he didn't, but that didn't matter to the consummate hunter. Bagging the right prey could be an unending process.

We got on the elevator with the porter and his suitcase. On the way up to the eighth floor President's Suite he asked noncommittal questions in English. How was my trip? Was I very tired? Had I seen the Chagall exhibit at the Centre Pompidou? Did I like it? Standing next to him, I became intoxicated by his presence just as surely and intensely as I had many years ago. Whatever reservations I felt about this arrangement vanished altogether between the ground and the eighth floors, and I was weak-kneed with desire as we entered his room.

The suite was enormous and luxurious. The curtains were already drawn shut. The porter set down his bags, hung up our coats and left discreetly without waiting for a tip. The bed covers were pulled down partially, revealing silk sheets. Champagne, raw oysters on ice, caviar, smoked salmon and fruit were spread out on a table. Baroque music played softly from unseen speakers. "Vivaldi," he said, "*Le Quattro Stagioni*, a nice touch, don't you think, *mein Liebchen*?" I expected an embrace now. Instead he opened his suitcase. With his back to me he switched his outdoor sunglasses for a different pair with a wrap-around goggle effect that concealed his eyes. I asked, "Must you wear these strange glasses? I can't see your eyes."

"Ah, but of course, *ma chérie*. Do you not remember that I have composed a plan for this very special day? Of course, I must wear them. And you will trust me, *n'est-ce-pas*, in everything we do? I went to him

"Ah, but of course, *ma chérie*. Do you not remember that I have composed a plan for this very special day? Of course, I must wear them. And you will trust me, *n'est-ce-pas*, in everything we do? I went to him now to put my arms around him. His voice turned me on, and I wanted him to touch me. But he took my hands and held me away. "Not yet, my dear. You must obey the ring master. First the champagne."

He pulled a Louis XIV chair back from the table for me and bade me sit down. He stood at his end while I watched the smooth fingers of his dark hands work the cork back and forth. Then a gentle pop, and without a spill, he poured the opaque vapor followed by the champagne into the two crystal glasses.

"*A votre santé*," he said as he touched his glass to mine. He seemed to look at me, while my blood raced through my veins. He sipped without speaking, each swallow inaudible due to the music. He seemed to become aware of the music and said, "Spring." I must have looked confused, and he added, "The first movement is called 'Spring,' this is *Giunta é la Primavera,* 'Spring's awakening.' You see, the management agreed to pipe it in, at my request. Wonderful service."

"Very nice," I said, for want of anything better.

He smiled and stretched a hand towards me.

I placed my hand in his and he kissed it as well as my arm up to the inside of the elbow joint. Then he pulled me gently out of my chair toward him and embraced me for the first time, kissing me on the lips with great care and deliberation. My adrenalin shot up and my pulse rate soared. Soon our mouths crushed each others' and our hands went on forays, as if for the first time, making discoveries, reveling in every detail. I felt as if my body would melt. I wanted desperately for this man to take me now, and use me to his fullest capacity, and to excite me to the heights of physical pleasure. But again, his hand caught mine before I could touch him between the legs, and he said, "Not yet. It's much too early, the shepherd is sleeping. *Il capraro che dorme.*" He made an elegant gesture with his hand as if to conduct the music in the background, and guided me back to my chair.

We continued to eat and drink champagne for perhaps another hour. It seemed like an eternity, and occasionally Guido kissed or stroked me in some way that left me crazy with desire. How long would this prelude last? At some point the music stopped and did not resume. When I mentioned it, he said that we would hear "Summer," at the high point of the day, between noon and 1 PM. I must be patient, he had composed an extraordinary climax, and I must trust him and

It was effective, this gradual, aesthetic crescendo—the champagne, oysters and caviar. I began to appreciate it as something so unlike my sexual experiences up till now. I sensed that Bonatti's tantalizing game might have the power to push me over some unknown brink.

About 11 AM, Guido announced that it was time for our baths. I watched as he filled one of the sunken marble tubs with water and added one drop of perfume which he retrieved from a tiny bottle, as exquisite in its shape as it was in the scent it gave to the water. He led me back to the bed, undressed me slowly and placed my clothes over a chair. Then without touching me, he circled once around me, like a hawk surveying its prey, and exclaimed that my body was as perfect as the first time, no, that my beauty had increased. Then I had been a girl, now I was a woman.

He guided me by the hand back into the bathroom and directed me to slip into one of the two marble tubs. The warmth and scent were extravagant. He stripped to his black shorts, and I studied him. His body was dark, muscular. A few grey hairs peppered the dark ones on his chest, underarms and pubic area. Middle age had endowed him with a seductive male beauty as well. I had never been so attracted to a body. Only his glasses, these futuristic goggles seemed cold and impenetrable.

He unwrapped a bar of Dior soap from his suitcase, knelt next to my tub and began to wash my left arm, and then the right, massaging every muscle with utmost care. He continued with my legs and feet, lifting them out of the tub towards him one at a time as in a devotional act. I sat up and leaned forward as he massaged my neck and back, each time with the soap that carried the same scent as his perfume— a wild scent as from the *garrigue* during the hunting season. I wanted this bath to never end, yet I was dying for something more.

"Half an hour," he announced, and stepped across the bathroom to turn on the faucets of the other marble bathtub. Then he opened the diminutive perfume bottle again and allowed one drop to fall into the waterfall emerging from the spout. He pulled me up and out of my tub and wrapped me in an enormous, dark green towel. When I was dry, he handed me a new bar of soap to unwrap and instructed me to perform the same devotional for him as he removed his shorts and lowered himself into the water he had drawn for himself. I tried to remember the correct sequence: arms first, legs second, neck and back next, and finally the crotch. When I finally reached the end of the ritual, I urged him to raise his pelvis so that his penis surfaced, and when I saw and touched it for the first time, it was stone hard, engorged with blood and ruby red. I lost myself to the steam, soap, scent and hot water.

Suddenly the music became audible again, and Guido said, "Ah, summer. It must be noon. Come with me, *cara mia*, to bed now."

I collapsed on my back onto the smooth sheets, and Guido arranged my blond hair in twisted strands that curled out over the entire pillow. He smiled as he admired his creation and said, "Ah, your hair. It floats like Botticelli's Venus." I really couldn't stand the waiting any longer, so I took his hand and placed it between my legs, hoping that would finally inspire him to consume me. He climbed over me now and placed his tip so it just touched my entrance. When I tried to push myself against it, he pulled back again. "I'll enter you only on one condition, my sweet," he said now.

"Oh God," I thought, "*Anything*, just name it, but please do it!" I pleaded with him.

He replied, "That I may tie you down on the bed with your legs apart, how do you say? 'Spread eagle,' *n'est-ce-pas*?"

"Why, for heaven's sake?" I asked.

"There's nothing wrong with it, *cara mia*. It's a sexual game called bondage. Have you never tried it? It's truly wonderful, it brings about an exquisite arousal of the senses. It escalates the excitement greatly to make yourself vulnerable to someone—like the thrill of sex when there's a possibility you'll be caught. It heightens the pleasure like nothing else. I have analyzed your letter and I'm sure you will love it. I have nylon cords in my suitcase. Look." He pulled out several white ropes. "We will try just a little bit, and if you don't like it we will stop, but that will be the end of our game. If you do like it, as I predict, you will have to tie me down too, after we are finished with you. And you must abuse me, then, in any way you like. If you do, I'll be yours forever. What do you say, *Geliebte*?"

All inhibitions were gone in me. I made him promise to untie me if I asked, but I was willing to do anything to get him inside me.

He agreed to my condition. "But of course, *ma chère*. I only want us to experience the heights of pleasure together."

Slowly, he tied nylon cords around both my wrists as I lay on the bed on my back with my arms raised over my head. Somewhere, I couldn't see where, he attached the cords to the headboard. "Now if you will spread your legs, *meine Liebe*." With utter devotion he pulled one leg apart from the other and formed a large v with them in the center of the bed. Carefully, he tied one ankle and then the other to the bottom bedposts without impeding my circulation or even pinching my skin. Now I was immobilized in a wide x.

Guido's figure stood wordless at the end of the bed and listened to the peculiar baroque music that filled the suite. His breathing grew heavy as he stared at my helpless body, and I began to writhe in frustration. He accommodated me now for a few seconds by mounting and penetrating me with a couple of powerful thrusts that sent my brain out of my body. But he withdrew just as quickly. I felt devastated, and he smiled triumphantly.

"Why do you stop?" I implored.

"In order to torture you, *ma chérie*, and to give you some champagne," he said softly.

He brought over one of the crystal glasses and held it to my mouth until I emptied it. With his tongue he licked up the drops which spilled down my chin and neck. Then he returned to his silver suitcase and pulled something out of it—a black stocking mask which he pulled over his head. His black goggles protruded out of the eye openings so that his head resembled an executioner from an alien world. He filled the same champagne glass again and held it to his own lips until it was empty. Then he pulled a black leather whip with a smooth, long handle out of his suitcase. He cracked it a couple of times with expert skill before letting it fall lightly on my stomach and trailing it slowly across my body.

"This long snake is going to bite you, my lovely little whore from hell. It will crawl all over your body until it finds the cave where it will strike deep inside." The slither of the whip across my skin made me totally aroused. Suddenly he swung the whip around so that it licked me across the thighs with a sharp crack. I felt no pain, only surprise. Again the whip landed, this time on my belly, a little harder, with a distinct sting. And again. I realized I barely registered the pain in my inital frenzy. But as the strikes continued, the pleasure sank below the rising level of pain, and I told him it was enough. He ignored me and struck again, this time across my shoulder and chest so that it almost hit my face. Once more the whip lashed me across the entire body, this time from the opposite shoulder down to the legs. It was very painful and drew blood, and I cried out loud for him to stop.

Instead, the mood suddenly changed and he commanded me in an angry tone to shut up. From some unknown location, he pulled a short cord, drew it around my neck and began to twist. I felt the strain around my throat and before I could protest again, my breath was cut off. His face black and invisible, my executioner played with the cord around my neck, tightening and loosening it ever so slightly at will, gradually slackening it altogether as I writhed and tugged now at my bonds as fear overwhelmed me. Then he loosened the cord around my neck and held his hand tightly over my mouth so that I still couldn't speak. He was panting audibly while sweat rolled down his body. With one hand he pulled the whip off me and tossed it over his right shoulder. Then he managed to wind it slowly around his own neck two or three times. When he pulled the handle, it tightened around his neck creating such thick folds that his eyes must have bulged behind his goggles. But his own perspiration kept the whip moving, and drops of his sweat fell on my body as he bent over me, our faces less than an arm's length apart. Through my horror I realized how strong his arms must have been as he worked at this. The cord nearly cut the skin, and he could hardly breath, but otherwise he straddled me trembling, gazing down at me. As the pressure became unbearable, I could see his penis jump in his hand as if ready to ejaculate, but at the same moment, the end of the whip pulled off of his neck, revealing red rope burns. He gasped and coughed and drew in a deep breath, as if relieved. Then, still holding one hand over my mouth he said in a gentle, changed tone, almost a whisper, "Don't be afraid, my darling. The opening act is over. If I didn't give you a little surprise like this, you would not reach the same level of excitement. And you will have your turn, too. But first, a short intermission." He released the hand over my mouth, and I was torn between crying out for help, which would have been futile, and remaining silent and waiting for an opportunity to escape.

Perhaps if he would finally just take me in a straightforward way, everything would be under control again. But I had noticed then that my constant writhing had partially loosened the cord around my right wrist. I didn't tell him this, but begged him anew to make love to me.

"Oh yes, my American Gypsy, with the greatest of pleasure. You must excuse me a moment, and when I return, we will make love until the earth quakes. Be patient."

I glanced down at my body and noticed the red welts, some of them oozing blood, streaked across it. I watched his dark figure, still sporting the executioner's mask, turn its back while he sought perhaps another trick in the suitcase. As he searched, he inadvertently turned over an object which looked like a knife. I felt as if my brain had received an electric jolt. Unaware that I had seen anything, he covered it up again with clothes, went into the bathroom and turned on the water.

Twisting my right wrist violently, I somehow wrenched it loose, scraping my skin in the process. With my free hand I struggled to undo the other cord. I suddenly felt absolutely frantic to liberate myself. But the knot was tight and I couldn't see it. My fingers were clumsy. I couldn't turn my body to get in a better position because my legs were still tied down. I forced myself to stay calm. Maybe it *was* just a game, an elaborate sexual ritual or rite of passage, and there was no knife in that suitcase. I concentrated now on the feel of the knot with my fingers, and finally understood its composition. I worked systematically at the loose end—the only possibility for untying it—for what seemed like an eternity, worried that any second my executioner would return. I worked at a feverish pitch.

Suddenly the water stopped running. I froze for a second and listened for Guido's emergence. I was afraid he might see that I had freed myself and try to tie me up again—the bathroom door wasn't closed all the way. I heard him cough and clear his throat. With some further efforts the other wrist was free. In a flash I sat up in bed and untied one leg. "Are you ready, my dear, for the time of your life?" Guido called to me.

As he emerged from the bathroom still wearing his mask and goggles, the cord fell off my other ankle. I sprang up but he caught me and pushed me down on the bed. He said, "Ah, hah, so you've perceived the change in the music. You are a brilliant student. You are introducing the variation at this point—very good, extraordinary! *Mosche e mosconi.*[2] He made another flourish with his hand.

I didn't know what he was talking about. The music was slower, I guessed, but it sounded much the same to me. He said, "The man that hath no music in himself . . . ," but you, my prodigy, must be a musical genius as well! So I'll pass on the baton. Tie me up now and abuse me. He grabbed a cord and started tying his own foot around the ankle. "Here, you tie it to the bedpost." He handed it to me, and I did as he ordered. I tied the other one too, tightly, so as to immobilize his murderous impulses. He held his arms above his head for me, and soon his dark body formed an X on the bed sheet in the same way mine had before. He said, "Very good, my darling. You tie me brutally so my arms and legs cannot breathe. That is good. All of my blood goes to my steed now, for your ride.

---

[2] Flies and bluebottles.

His wine-red organ stuck straight up out of his body demanding me to impale myself on it. My heart pounded like a race horse, the welts stamped on my body burned through my skin towards my core. Although he was temporarily immobilized, my fear continued to rise, and I felt that to play his game was deadly. Yet I felt drawn to my destruction as a moth to a flame. I straddled his body on my knees. My haunches were positioned over his member ready to sink down onto my fate. I was ready to explode into orgasm the instant I would touch his deadly weapon. At the moment I hesitated, the music accelerated again. He whispered, "Excellent, the storm. *Tempo impetuoso d'estate!* Fuck me, my bad little girl! Kiss me, divine whore!"

Without touching him, I slipped off the bed and went to his suitcase. I thrust my hand to the bottom where I found a sheathed instrument with a compass on the end. I pulled off the sheath and opened it. The blade was sharp and gleaming, like the jet's white contrail, like the point of a stiletto leaping forward, high in the Texas sky, breaking it open. . . .

I leapt away from the bed, pulled on my clothes and darted out of the room and down the corridor. As I passed the elevator, the door opened and three odd types emerged, carrying heavy suitcases. They might have come straight out of a Göttingen-Peyote gang meeting, and looked out of place here. I hurried on by and opened the door to the stairwell. I raced down a flight of stairs to the seventh floor and bolted through more empty corridors towards number 719, Stevie's and my room. Around the final corner, I pounded on the door. "Let me in Stevie, it's me, Megan. Please hurry!" A sleepy Stevie opened the door, and I collapsed into his arms.

CHAPTER EIGHT

The Corpse

> . . . I felt myself in air and saw on every side
> nothing but air; only the beast I sat upon
> was there.
>
> Dante

"What happened?" Stevie demanded, seeing the whip marks on my arms. For a long moment I couldn't say anything. "Is that blood on your dress? Damn it! He raped you, the beast!" he concluded. Then he tried to calm me as I became hysterical and inarticulate. I sobbed and sputtered out an incoherent story. When I finished he gave me a valium.

I reasoned I was safe from Guido in Stevie's room. He didn't know about Stevie's existence, let alone that he was in the same hotel. The last place he would look for me now, if he was after me, was in the same hotel. But why would a corporate executive want to kill me?

I tried to reconstruct his facial expressions and tone of voice for clues to his intentions, but it was useless. The more I speculated, the more I came up blank. Why would a businessman go around with a knife in his suitcase?

After a few hours, I sent Stevie down to get himself something to eat, to bring me back some fast food, and to check the garage to see whether or not the green Mercedes was gone. If Guido had already left the hotel, we would probably be safe to leave too. And I didn't want to hang around Munich just for the fun of it. If he hadn't left, we would be safer to spend the night in Stevie's room and wait until the next morning to be sure he was gone.

In less than twenty minutes Stevie was back, his face ashen gray. "I think he's dead," he whispered.

"What do you mean? Who?" I gasped. "Are you crazy?"

"I mean, he *is* dead. Your friend, of course. I've seen a dead body before." He sat down on the bed, shaking visibly. "I mean, I didn't touch him or anything. But, well, see, first I went to the garage, and there was this green Mercedes there. In fact, there were two, but I figured one of them must be his. Then I started walking around to find a restaurant, but I got so curious about that jerk of yours, I came back. I went up to your suite and decided to knock on the door and pretend I had the wrong room." Stevie paused and took a deep breath, and tried to stop trembling. "Maybe it was a stupid thing to do, but I knocked anyway, and the door came open on its own. It wasn't latched shut. Maybe you didn't get it closed when you left."

I didn't know. I shrugged my shoulders.

Stevie continued. "I was worried he might think someone was breaking in, so I called out, "Hi Jill, it's me. Are you there?" so he'd think I was looking for my wife or girlfriend or somebody. But he didn't say anything. In fact the room was silent. So I pushed the door open a little farther and looked inside." He paused again, as if he didn't want to say what came next. "He was lying on the bed on his back. The blankets were pulled up to his armpits and his arms were crossed over his chest as if someone had placed them there. He had marks around his neck and wrists—like scratches or burns. His mouth and eyes were open and he didn't move. Well, I mean . . . he was dead. I know a dead person when I see one."

"Oh my God," I groaned. "Maybe he had a heart attack."

"Well, if he had a heart attack, he certainly arranged himself in an orderly fashion in bed."

"What do you mean?"

"Look, I just doubt if people who die alone prepare by getting into a neat bed, pulling up the covers and crossing their arms over their chests!"

"Christ! Maybe he was only asleep. Are you sure he wasn't asleep Stevie?"

"Do people sleep with their eyes open and rolled back?"

"Were his eyes rolled back? You just said they were open? How do you know they were rolled back? I never saw his eyes. He always wore dark glasses or goggles."

"For Chrissake! I'm just telling you what I saw. I didn't hang around to do an autopsy!"

"Are you sure you had the right room? You said the room was tidied up."

"Didn't you tell me it was 888? Well, I was in 888. That big, fancy suite. And there's a goddamn corpse in the bed!"

"God! What do we do now? This is so weird. We were just making love . . . what am I saying? 'Making love,' it wasn't. He called it bondage. You know about that, don't you, Stevie?"

"Good God, Megan. Don't be naive. Every gay man from San Francisco is an S&M expert. But why don't you ask me about that some other time, OK? At this point I think we ought to be talking about splitting—sooner rather than later, I think."

"But . . . did anybody see you at his door, Stevie?"

"No, the floor was empty."

"Did you lock the door behind you?"

"No, I pulled it back the way it was. Almost shut, but not quite."

I wanted to confirm Stevie's story. "Will you go with me Stevie? I have to see for myself." He read the determination in my voice and agreed.

We climbed up the flight of stairs back to the eighth floor. If we ran into anyone we would keep on walking. The entire hallway was empty. Just as Stevie said, the door to the suite, number 888, was slightly ajar. We pushed it open quietly, entered, and shut it quietly behind ourselves.

I approached the bed, my heart in my throat and my pulse pounding in my brain. Guido lay there just as Stevie had said—motionless, his arms crossed over his chest. For the first time, he wore no glasses. His eyelids were open, but only the whites were showing. The dark hue to his skin had drained away so that his color approached alabaster.

The room was in perfect order. The cords and whip were nowhere to be seen. Nor were any signs of our rendezvous. The bed was made neatly with his body in it. His silver suitcase was open and the things in it ordered. I lifted up the shirts on top and saw the nylon cords that had tied me to the bed wound up now and resting on the bottom. I looked back at Guido. Then I noticed a dark stain soaking through the blanket halfway down the bed. I went back to the body.

I couldn't stand to look at his dead eyes as I tried to pull back the covers. Stevie, who was still frozen with his back to the door whispered, "What are you doing? Are you crazy? Leave him alone!" I ignored Stevie and pried one of Guido's arms away from the blanket they were pinning down.

I placed first one and then the other arm straight out to the sides in cruciform position. Slowly I pulled back the sheet and blanket which had covered him. The body was flawless down to the crotch. But now, in place of his dark red penis was a mess of matted and half dry blood. A knife handle protruded from the spot where the penis should have been. Attached to it was an illegible note finger-painted in blood on white paper.

Twenty minutes later Stevie paid for our room—he had to pay for two nights—and checked us out of the hotel. He explained that our plans had changed unexpectedly. It was 6 PM.

I didn't want to go through the lobby, so I hurried down eight flights of stairs to the basement garage. Not knowing which one belonged to Guido, I shuddered at the sight of two green Mercedes, not far from each other, just as Stevie had said. I followed the exit arrows out to the street, relieved that no one else was in the garage at the moment, but at the driveway an elderly parking attendant addressed me from his booth: "*Ja, woher kommen Sie denn? Suchen Sie Ihren Wagen, gnädige Frau?*" I pretended not to understand: "Sorry, I don't speak German," and kept on walking. "Have you in the hotel an auto, Mrs., please?" he repeated with a thick accent. "No . . . thank you, everything's all right." I kept on walking. "*Na, sowas!*" he exclaimed to himself critically, as I hurried out to the taxi zone on the street where Stevie waited for me.

Inside the train station Stevie dropped our suitcases in front of a departure schedule near the information windows. I couldn't really concentrate on the schedule, and furthermore, I had no idea where we should go. Back to Paris? To California or Texas? To Göttingen? To hell? I hoped Stevie would go with me. I only knew I had to leave Munich and Germany so I could think straight. Stevie figured out that the first train to leave the country for a comfortable distance was departing for Lyon, France in seven minutes. He wanted to leave as badly as I did. He bought second class one-way tickets and dragged me on the run to platform 13–14 where two dreary gray trains were already teaming with people. Students with backpacks clambered onto ours, while dark-skinned men in frayed suits with dirty hands and fingernails— Germany's "guest workers"—boarded the "Athene Express" on the other side. With pockets full of German marks and suitcases tied shut with rope, they were on the way home now to Yugoslavia, Greece and

Turkey to visit their families. I felt a pang of envy for them because they knew where they were going, and for that matter, where they came from.

Stevie and I had difficulty finding a compartment on our train. The only spaces left were in a smoker. As the train pulled out, I asked Stevie for another valium. The sideward glance of a petite dark Mediterranean woman with a kerchief on her head made me wonder if our English was understood. Three young German women in their twenties, probably on their way to vacation in France, smoked and talked in a bored, arrogant way. The peasant woman probably didn't know English, but they easily might have. I realized I wouldn't be able to talk to Stevie openly, if at all.

After the conductor came and went, a vendor shoving a cart of snacks and drinks came by, and I bought us both a beer. From our seats next to the compartment door, the view of the landscape was partially hidden. Eventually the train settled into its normal pace. I began to doze in an upright position, my head falling occasionally from side to side whenever the train lurched or passed over a rough spot. His body immobile, Stevie stared out the window.

As darkness fell southeast of Zurich, I woke to find Stevie gone from the compartment. My heart began to race with irrational fear until I assured myself that both suitcases were still on the overhead racks. Trying to appear calm, I leaned back in my seat. The small dark woman was asleep, and two of the German women played cards while the third read a *Bunte Illustrierte*. She held it in such a way that I couldn't see the cover. Fully awake now, I felt nauseous and got up to go to the rest room. In the corridor Stevie approached me.

"I was just in the dining car," he said. "I got hungry and didn't want to wake you. Are you OK?"

"Yeah, I guess," I said, relieved to see him. Then I thought to myself, "Fool, where could he be, anyway, on a train? He obviously didn't just jump off."

On the john in the rest room, Guido's corpse in the hotel room came back to me in all its horror. I started to retch, but couldn't vomit. My stomach was empty. I sat for a long time trying to breathe deeply and to calm myself down. Twice people knocked at the door and tried the handle, but I ignored them. Finally, the panic subsided as I splashed my face with the nonpotable water which came out of the basin as long as you held your foot down on the floor pedal. I couldn't sort anything out, and wished again I could talk to Stevie—an impossibility in our compartment.

Knowing I ought to force something into my stomach, I went to the second class dining car, got a *Bratwurst* and a piece of dry bread with a dab of mustard. The second bite made me nauseous again, so I gave up on eating and returned to the compartment. At the Bern train station Stevie leaned out the window, bought a *Herald Tribune* from a vendor, and immersed himself in it for the next hour or two, hiding behind the paper from the rest of the world. I resigned myself to a long, uneasy night to Lyon.

Early the next morning we pulled into the huge Lyon station. For a while we wandered aimlessly through its shops, but I was anxious to talk to Stevie. Afraid we might be overheard, we descended back down to a long platform and walked to its deserted far end where we set our bags on the ground and paced back and forth. We crossed in and out of a bright area exposed to the morning sunlight and a section darkened by a shadow cast over the tracks and platform by the station building.

"What do we do now, Stevie? I'm scared."

"I'm not sure, but it feels good to have some distance between us and Munich. I also have the feeling it would be a good thing to be back in California as soon as possible, before this thing heats up, if it's going to."

"I just can't seem to think this thing through. It doesn't make sense to me. I guess you're right. But I'm also not dying to return to the States. Where would I go there?"

"Well you could stay with me at first," he replied, "till you get your bearings, and then you could see. I know a good lawyer in the city. Maybe we should tell him what's happened and get some professional advice, just in case anybody ever tries to pin some kind of rap on you, or us. Anyway, I'd feel a lot better with an ocean and a continent between me and Munich."

We had just missed a train to Paris, and it would be an hour before the next one departed, and a slow one at that. We changed some money, put our bags in lockers, and wandered in and out of shops again, trying in vain to distract ourselves, but mainly just walking, hardly aware of our surroundings. Finally we were ensconced in the interminably slow train to Paris, which stopped in every village in Burgundy. We disembarked at the Gare de Lyon close to 5:30 PM.

In the main hall, the headlines on *Le Monde* stopped us in our tracks. A hawker was calling out something about "Les terroristes d'Allemagne. Chef d'industrie Italien assassiné à Munich!" On the middle of the front page was a photograph of Guido Bonatti and a composite police drawing of a blond American woman, a suspected accomplice of the West German terrorist gang.

I became transfixed in front of the picture which I realized resembled me but wasn't me—an artist's fictional representation of me. It was like looking at a negative of yourself, where what's black should be white, and what's white black, or like seeing for the first time the twin you didn't know you had.

I couldn't look long. Stevie steered me away from the newspaper kiosk and made me keep walking swiftly into the midst of the busy throngs. At the next stand, he positioned me out of view, said, "Don't move," and went back to buy a paper. Coming back, he stashed the newspaper in his shoulder bag and dug out his sunglasses. He told me to put them on, keep my head down, and try to look inconspicuous. He went back into the train station and emerged ten minutes later with a strange hat and a good-sized scarf for me to tie over my hair. Then we crossed the Boulevard de Magenta and sat down in a café where Stevie tried to decipher the front-page story, and I tried to hide behind the business section he handed me.

"What does it say?" I demanded, my heart pounding.

"I don't know for sure, but your name and passport number are here. What *is* your number, anyway?"

I dug my passport out of my shoulder bag. It matched. "Those damn Germans. They're so efficient. How do they do it?" I could answer my own question. "I guess the receptionist got interrogated. They keep track of everything."

"Yeah," said Stevie. "I heard the German government has this huge data bank on everybody. I mean, their own citizens and tourists and everybody who comes through—their finances, politics, sexual behavior—anything they can get. A real big brother kind of thing—the world's best."

"Maybe they have data on me too," I speculated. "I'd like to see what kind of profile they've constructed for me, what kind of person I am." I halfway meant this. "Anyway," I said to Stevie, "What does it say?"

"I don't understand all the French, but it sounds like they think you're part of a German terrorist gang, and that you're to be considered armed and "très dangereuse." Stevie snickered. "Here, you read it."

"Oh, shit, Stevie. Why don't we just get a cab to the airport and get the hell out of here?"

"Hold on Megan. Every good terrorist knows that the airports will be on the lookout for you, your passport number, and your friends."

"Those fucking Nazis! Cut the crap, Stevie. Try to think of something, for God's sake!"

Stevie furrowed his brow. "Well, all kinds of criminals and international terrorists walk the streets of Paris incognito. This may be as good a place as any for the time being until we see what develops. We'll have access to news here, for one thing; and, it's less likely you'll be recognized in a city of five million than in some small provincial village, where every outsider is scrutinized."

"Well then, why don't we go back to my apartment? Maybe we could get our bearings there."

"Megan, don't be an idiot! Think, woman! The minute your landlord reads the news or watches TV, he'll inform the police. That could already have happened. We'd be sitting ducks in your apartment."

"But Stevie, my landlord's a landlady, I mean the concierge, who's the only one I ever talk to, and she's Sicilian. Her French is worse than yours. I doubt if she can read the newspapers."

"But she can watch TV, and she could recognize your face in the composite drawing, now couldn't she? Or your neighbors might talk about it."

I dropped my eyes and blew into my coffee cup. I stared at the ripples this made in my coffee, hoping that in their patterns I could decipher some clue to my situation. But in a second the surface was smooth once again, as placid and meaningless as a cosmic black hole.

We didn't speak for several minutes. Stevie watched the throngs silhouetted against the low afternoon sunlight move by on the broad sidewalk, while I allowed no more than my eyes to appear above the top edge of the business section. A couple of bizarre young freaks with purple, red and yellow hair sticking straight out in a few stiff tufts from their otherwise bare scalps ambled by. In short-legged black baggy clothes, the man had a ring through a nose lobe while his female companion sported fingernails three inches long, covered with rainbow-colored sequins. When they were just beyond the cafe, Stevie bolted out of his chair saying to me, "Stay put!" and rushed to catch up with them. I watched him speak to them in what was obviously less than standard French, pointing at their heads. Finally, they nodded in comprehension and Stevie gave them a pen with which the woman wrote something on the edge of the newspaper Stevie folded open to an interior page. Stevie nodded, patted the man on the shoulder, smiled, thanked them, nodded some more, and came back to the table.

"What was that all about?" I asked.

"Look, I think we ought to disguise you and maybe me too, if we're going to remain anonymous, even in Paris. They gave me the address of their hairdresser. Look—Rue Rambuteau, near the Centre Pompidou."

"What! You expect me to look like them?! You must be nuts."

"Well then, I guess you'd rather look like the drawing plastered all over the front page, or do you have a better idea? I figure, the more outlandish your costume, the less people notice your face. How about it? If we go now, there's a good chance Monsieur le punk Hairdresser won't have seen your picture yet."

"Well . . . fuck! OK. So do you want to flag down a taxi?" I asked him.

"No, I think taxi drivers, especially those waiting for a pickup near a train station, may read newspapers while they wait. Let's take the metro."

"Hey, how many Parisians do you think read the paper on the metro, chump? And you know the other main activity on the metro? It happens to consist of looking at the other people on the metro, studying faces. Have you ever noticed how many interesting faces there are in Paris. In Paris, everybody's face has character. Paris does that for you, if you stay long enough."

"In that case, they also say Paris is a great city for walking."

Stevie removed the identification tags from our luggage handles and returned the bags to lockers in the train station. Then we walked and walked through the city of cities, feeling disconnected and nervous. On the way to the Rue Rambuteau Stevie purchased some baggy pants and coats for us in a clothing store which catered to student tastes, and within another hour we emerged from the punk hair salon transformed and several hundred francs poorer. Stevie no longer had a hairdo. Rather, he was bald except for a laurel wreath around his head with leaves consisting of his own brown hair, sculpted precisely on his scalp by the hair artist of the salon. I, on the other hand, came out with an auburn crew-cut stiffened with gel to keep my short hair combed straight up. It was shaved off evenly on top to form a platform on which you could set a tea cup.

Feeling more anonymous now, we descended into the metro at Les Halles and emerged again as dusk descended at the Boulevard

St. Michel. We wandered around looking for a hotel in the Latin Quarter. In a deserted back street we left our bundle of old clothes next to a sleeping *clochard*, blissfully unaware of his good fortune, on top of a metal grate which covered some subterranean source of warmth.

Spying an appropriately dingy hotel, Stevie went in to try to get a room using only his passport. "We can't go to the Ritz looking like this, after all." I fidgeted nervously around the corner until he returned a few minutes later.

"It worked," he said, smiling. "I told him we'd just come from Marseilles where my girlfriend was mugged and robbed of everything including her passport, and we'd reported it to the police, who advised us to get a new one when we got to Paris. And he bought it, or maybe he didn't understand it all. But he said something like, "*Mon Dieu*," that's the way Marseilles is—uncivilized—and that we could have a room. I told him I'd bring you and our luggage back after dinner. Oh yeah, and we got a room with twin beds, so you don't need to worry about catching anything from me, and a kind of miniature bathroom, *avec douche et bidet*, in a sort of a closet. It's really cute. You'll like it."

I appreciated Stevie's feigned insouciance. In this absurd situation, I had to lean on him. He had problems of his own, and here he was trying to help me, to the extent of endangering himself. I put my hand on his cheek and touched my forehead to his shoulder. "Thanks," I whispered. I suddenly felt drained of all energy.

CHAPTER NINE

Flight

I found myself upon the brink of grief's abysmal valley that collects the thunderings of endless cries. So dark and deep and nebulous it was, try as I might to force my sight below, I could not see the shape of anything. 'Let us descend into the sightless world,' began the poet (his face was deathly pale): 'I will go first, and you will follow me.' And I, aware of his changed color, said: 'But how can I go on if you are frightened? You are my constant strength when I lose heart.'

Dante

I slept the dreamless sleep of the dead and woke up around 8:30 in the morning in the same position in which I'd fallen asleep. No nightmares. But my heart was pounding and my limbs were stiff. I looked over at Stevie, who was lying on his side with his back towards me. The laurel wreath etched with his hair on his otherwise bald scalp startled me, but then I remembered the Rue Rambuteau and our punk hairdos. I touched my hand to my head and felt that my flattop was no longer flat, but clumped together now from the pillow. The covers had slipped halfway down Stevie's bare back. One of his shoulder blades was decorated with an obscene little tattoo of a Hell's Angel with a penis jutting out of his open fly aimed at the unnaturally large buttocks of a second bent-over figure. The tattoo artist had incorporated two adjacent moles on Stevie's back to represent the buttocks in his little creation. I almost laughed out loud. It seemed unlike Stevie, but, of course, he never saw the picture from the perspective of a viewer. I wasn't up-to-date on the details of his personal life as a gay man, and if he were like many of the rest of them, his lifestyle was probably pretty wild. What did seem like Stevie was the fact that his back had a goodly assortment of blemishes and pockmarks; to my mind, this added to rather than detracted from the discrete charm of the taste-less little work of art.

My shower woke Stevie up, and when I emerged in my under-wear he gasped, "God, you look ridiculous!"

"Well, sorry Stevie, but you know, women don't have long dongs and molely buttocks, but that doesn't make them freaks of nature!"

Stevie blushed and pulled his sheets up to his neck. "No, I don't mean your body, I mean your hair. It's sticking straight out to the sides, most of it. Actually, I think women's bodies are aesthetically pleasing. And yours is incredible, if you don't mind a compliment from a gay man." I looked in the mirror hanging on the closet and saw that the steam had melted the gel, and my naturally straight hair stuck out side-ways. Besides, it was the wrong color.

"But you might look at yourself, my dear," I said, "before you start feeling too smug. What do we do when your hair starts growing back in? Hire a French gardener?"

We dressed, left our hotel, and wandered over to the busy Boule-vard St. Michel. We bought three newspapers, including a *Herald Tribune*, and ordered croissants and *café au lait* in a café near the Pan-theon. I hid my face behind the front pages and read in black and white that I was a mysterious American sympathizer with the West German Red Liberators, that I was probably underground in hiding somewhere in southern Germany, and should be considered armed and dangerous. I felt both irritated to be so misrepresented and re-lieved that I wasn't being sought in Paris. But the same composite drawing appeared in *Le Figaro* and *Le Monde*, and it annoyed me more today than it had yesterday. I rationalized that I really didn't look like that, and realized at the same time what an absurd leap my life had suddenly taken. As for practical considerations, there was nothing I could do about my face. My disguise would have to be enough—my ridiculous hair, heavy makeup and large sunglasses. Stevie seemed to be right. When I set my paper down, no one took the slightest notice of me. Maybe Parisians were just like that. But I still let Stevie do the talking to the waiter.

With croissants and coffee in our stomachs, we both felt a little better. "Look Stevie, we've got to make a plan now. We have to think this thing through and figure out what to do. We can't just live in a left bank hotel the rest of our lives."

"Yeah, you're right. Why don't we walk, so we won't be overheard."

The early summer sunshine was warming up the city. The sky was blue, the leaves were green, and strollers of all ages were enjoying the Jardin du Luxembourg, a few blocks from the café. Children, oblivious to Marie de Medici's seventeenth-century residence behind it, sent their model ships into the uncertain waters of the large round pond, imagining them on the treacherous high seas, far from land and civilization, at the mercy of the watery depths. A number of these small vessels met with temporary calamity when they capsized from the breeze or collided with others. Their small captains ran, jumped about and shouted out their defeats and victories, brandishing long sticks and prodding the boats which came within reach of the concrete shore. Adults seated on green metal chairs knitted, read or dozed, their faces towards the sun. Some caressed each other, others watched the children's nautical races and battles or fed the birds. Cultivated flower beds displayed their colors at the edges of the lawns which met the circular path around the pond, and for an instant Stevie and I were transfixed by the idyllic beauty in this best of all possible worlds. In another minute, however, we were back in the dark predicament of our lives, and as we walked the length of the tree-lined paths towards the Boulevard du Montparnasse, the grace of our surroundings dissolved in worries.

There seemed to be few options. To try to fly back to the United States was impossible without showing my passport. In fact, crossing any border was probably out of the question now. Stevie's name hadn't appeared in the newspapers, at least not yet. I suggested that he could leave—he was free to go back home—at the same time I hoped he wouldn't. I was relieved when he refused, saying there was nothing for him there now—without Ralph. It was all too sad, and he'd rather have "an adventure" with me in Europe than face life at home. After all, he wasn't a suspect at this point, so even if the authorities caught up with him, he hadn't done anything. "Except aid and abet me," I reminded him. "But *you* didn't kill him, remember?" answered

Stevie. "Maybe those weirdos, those punks in the hotel did it. What were they doing in a fancy place like that, anyway?"

"It's strange, but somewhere I feel guilty, Stevie. Can you imagine that? It's like when I was a little girl and I didn't want to go to school, I'd tell my mother in the morning that I had a stomachache or a sore throat or something, and pretend to be sick. And she'd always let me stay home and bring me something special, like a comic book, from the store. And during the day, as I played the role of the sick kid, I actually felt sick."

"But that's just the role," Stevie said. Then he snickered at a new thought. "Well maybe you should feel guilty that you engaged in some pretty kinky sex with the poor bastard. For that they would have burned you at the stake in Salem." Then he got serious. "They would have burned me too, I guess, for all the things I've done. I don't know which is less forgivable—to be born a woman and to express your needs and desires, or to be born a homosexual man and threaten the power structure by sometimes behaving like a woman."

We wandered around Paris for two days and devoured papers for news of the terrorist murder in Munich. But a PLO bombing in the EL AL Airline office near the Paris opera upstaged it in the French headlines. In the hopes that things might cool down for us, we relaxed and almost began to enjoy Paris again.

Late one afternoon we sat outside at Chez Francis just across the Pont de l'Alma on the right bank in the wealthy eighth arrondissement. A great people-watching spot, and it also has the best view of the Eiffel Tower. Stevie ordered a Pernod and I had coffee while we buried our heads in the *Tribune* and *Le Monde*, respectively. While I read I became aware of a familiar tobacco aroma—and looked around to spy Mr. Dickerson, my old poetry teacher from Berkeley, as he extinguished his pipe in an ashtray a couple of tables away from us and then stood up to leave the café. He hadn't seen me, or if he had, he didn't recognize me. Probably he wouldn't even remember me. But as he left the café and headed up the Avenue Montaigne, I was seized by an uncontrollable urge to contact the kindly man who had represented for me the love of poetry—something that seemed so remote from my current predicament and therefore so terribly important. If I didn't move now, he would be gone.

I rattled Stevie's newspaper, pointed at the disappearing figure, excitedly told him who it was and that I had to talk to him. I told Stevie to stay there in the café. I would come back and pick him up after

I'd made contact with Mr. Dickerson. Stevie tried to protest, but I gave him no chance. I hurried out of the café, passed the newspaper kiosk and started up the street. I could just make out Mr. Dickerson's figure opposite the Theatre Champs Élysées, and I extended my pace almost to a trot. I didn't want to actually run, as I feared it would draw attention to me.

By the time I was opposite the theater, Mr. Dickerson was already in the next block that was parked full of limousines, some with their chauffeurs waiting for wealthy employers who were staying at the *Plaza Athené*. I gained on him gradually, and by the time I rushed by the hotel doormen, Mr. Dickerson began to turn left onto Rue Clément Marot. I called out his name just before he rounded the corner, but he must not have heard. Once he was out of sight, I began to run. I didn't want to lose him. I rounded the corner at a fast clip and just about tripped over one of two French poodles on a line. I think my foot grazed the beast in the head and it yapped at me as I shot by. Both animals wore dog coats color-coded to the same mauve dress, lipstick and fingernails of their mistress. She began to complain in French, but I didn't break stride. I just smiled. The threesome fit perfectly into this elegant neighborhood with its wrought-iron balconies and the heavy wooden entrance doors with their polished brass fixtures.

Mr. Dickerson was crossing to the left side of the street where the short one-way Rue Chambiges meets the Rue Clément Marot. I crossed over immediately in order to beat several approaching cars and called out his name again—louder this time. He heard it, as did several pedestrians who looked at me. He paused and turned around. I waved, trotted towards him and called out, "Mr. Dickerson, wait a minute, please!"

He waited for me at the corner of Clément Marot and the Rue de la Trémoille, trying to figure out who I was. I was a little winded when I reached him and he looked quizzical as I extended my hand to shake it. He still looked puzzled when I said, "It's me, Megan Lloyd. Your old student from Berkeley." Then I remembered my punk hairdo and my strange appearance. "I look different now, don't I?"

He shook my hand lightly, but in the middle of the shake sort of cut it short and let it drop, as if I might contaminate him with a germ or something. He said in a whisper, "Wait a minute. Aren't you the fugitive Megan Lloyd?"

I whispered too. "No, I mean yes, but I didn't do it. This thing is a bizarre mistake. I've got to talk to you. Please!"

Mr. Dickerson looked around, as if to see if anyone was watching us. "How did you find me?"

"I saw you leave the café down by the Place de l'Alma and followed you."

"Did anyone else see you?"

"No." I didn't want to tell him about Stevie until I was sure he would talk to me.

He hesitated and then said, "All right. My apartment's across the street from the post office," glancing in that direction. He indicated I should come with him, so we quickly crossed the street, ducked behind a large door and walked up three flights of stairs in a poorly lit stairwell. Mr. Dickerson said nothing to me until he had opened his door, ushered me in and locked it behind him. He still didn't speak as we walked into his living room—very French with high stucco ceilings, an ornate marble mantel around a fireplace that probably was never used and long white sheer curtains over the windows that led to his narrow balcony with its iron railings. He didn't seem to know how to treat me—whether to tell me to sit, to offer me a drink or what. He closed the heavy drapes to cover the sheers, and it made the room so dark, he had to turn on the light. He decided to pour us both a sherry. He nervously downed his entire glass and poured himself another. Then he lit up his pipe and puffed furiously.

He had to clear his throat several times and repeated my name, as if it were difficult to pronounce. "Ms. Lloyd. . . ," he finally managed to say. He addressed me first, as if he were about to tell me something, but he stopped short. I thought then that I should say something. After all, I had pursued him. But I suddenly didn't know what it was that I wanted to tell him—that I was innocent? That he should protect or hide me? That he should explain my case to the police? Nothing seemed realistic from a man who represented for me only some abstract humanistic notions. He didn't really know me. I didn't know him. What did I expect of a coincidental meeting precipitated by the aroma of a pipe? Where should I begin?

He interrupted my mental confusion by posing the first questions—how had I known he was in Paris? I hadn't known it. I just happened to notice him in the café—sheer coincidence. Was I absolutely certain no one had followed me here? I was sure. I was a stranger in Paris, and besides no one could recognize me because of my disguise.

He looked skeptical and said I seemed to be playing a dangerous game. Then he explained that he had just arrived in Paris five days ago. He wasn't quite settled yet. He was just beginning a half-year research sabbatical. Did I know he had a professorship at Princeton now? He seemed to relax as he talked about himself. His wife would be joining him the following week. She was in the Outer Hebrides visiting distant relatives and investigating her family history—a very gentile pursuit, he thought. He was very busy trying to get the apartment ready before she arrived. And they would be very busy once she did arrive. I realized that he didn't really want to deal with me. The more he talked, the more he relied on an anachronistic professor-student relationship to keep me at a distance.

Suddenly I interrupted him by saying, "I'm desperate, Mr. Dickerson." At this I saw his body stiffen. He turned his back to me and looked into the mirror over the mantel. His shoulders raised as he seemed to take a breath before deciding to turn around and face me. Now he took complete control of the situation. Within a minute I was dispossessed of my sherry glass and standing near the front door. I heard him advise me to continue my writing—I had shown definite talent at Berkeley—and admonish me to tell the truth to the authorities. That was my best possible course. They were professionals with my best interests at heart. I even found myself shaking his hand and returning a faint smile. I agreed never to mention this visit to anyone else and thanked him for his time before he ushered me out, closed the door and locked it behind me.

Absurd! And so much for the true, the good, the beautiful. I descended the stairs. I walked back to Chez Francis, cutting through the Rue Chambiges where a truck stopped in the middle of the block had brought all traffic behind it to a stop. Cars were backing up in both directions in the Rue du Boccador and horns were blaring and drivers leaving their vehicles. Tempers flared as they began to argue with each other over this affront to their civil rights and right of way. I overheard one man say to another he was *désespéré et capable de tout*. I repeated these words to myself several times on the way back to the café and to Stevie.

I told Stevie about the encounter. He was nervous and upset that I would abandon him like that and said, "I could have told you so." He emphasized that I ought to consult him before doing anything rash again. After all, he, Stevie, *was* actually looking out for my best interests, crazy as it seemed. It was true. Furthermore, he convinced me that Dickerson might call the authorities and thereby make Paris a little less safe for us. We decided we'd better buy some different clothes to improve our disguises.

Late the next morning we took the metro to go shopping. At Port Royal I watched a girl, perhaps twelve years old and her father, who had a tight grip on her hand, get off and vanish into the nearest *correspondance* tunnel. Stevie and I got off at Denfert Rochereau. In a clothing store on the Boulevard Général Leclerc I chose two pair of pants and a jacket while Stevie waited patiently and advised me what suited me best, or worst, for that matter. I was ready to leave, but the saleslady was implacable in a rather charming way. *"Oh oui! Ça vous va très bien! Parfait,"* she exclaimed at everything I tried on. She helped with zippers and buttons, but when I showed a slight irritation at her zealous attention, she vanished for several minutes, before returning with renewed enthusiasm and an armful of new clothes to try. She assured me she would make me a very special deal; her store happened to have the clothes which were perfect for Madame; she understood her physique and her tastes. She would be very satisfied. My patience was beginning to wear thin. Even Stevie was yawning and fidgeting. *"C'est tout, madame,"* I insisted. *"Nous voudrions payer maintenant, s'il vous plaît."*

"Mais, Madame, ce n'est pas fini. Il faut essayer d'autres vêtements." It suddenly struck me that the saleswoman was stalling. Stevie and I took my items to the cash register and reverted to English. "Now we want to pay," I demanded emphatically.

The saleslady slowed down, visibly. *"Ah, c'est vraiment dommage,"* she exclaimed. *"Un moment, s'il vous plaît."* She took the clothes from the counter and over to another woman in the back of the store where they spoke in low voices. Irritated, Stevie went over to them and said, "Come on now. Do you want to make a sale or not? We don't have all day!" Waiting at the cash register, I began to feel nervous. I had the uncanny feeling that someone was watching us. I glanced out the store window towards the wide boulevard in time to see two blue-uniformed gendarmes jaywalking rapidly across the street in the direction of the store. For an instant I experienced a kind of hot flash—neither fear nor panic, but a sudden rise in temperature as if my blood were about to boil through its vessels. I surveyed the back of the long narrow store, hurried over to Stevie and said in a low hiss, "Let's get out of here. The police are coming. Come on!" I grabbed him by the arm and pulled him away from the protesting salesladies who immediately started to call out, "*Voleurs! Terroristes!*"

"Holy Jeeesus!" said Stevie as we darted in and out of clothes racks towards a back door I had spied as our only possible escape route. As if made for us, the door opened into a dark little storage room strewn with boxes and clothing racks. We could hear the questions and exclamations of the police mixed in with the rising hysterical voices of the saleswomen as we plunged through the locked corner door of the storage room that Stevie had to kick open with his heel. He did this with impressive alacrity. "Karate," he remarked.

"Terrific," I said, and we found ourselves running pell-mell through a dingy passageway between buildings, which had the advantage at least of being outdoors. I gasped as we ran as fast as we could, now able to hear the police calling somewhere behind us, "*Arrêtez! Police! Arrêtez immédiatement!*" We burst around a corner into an alley, one direction of which led back to the Boulevard Général Leclerc. There people went about their business as if the world were in perfect order. Without hesitating we ran for it, on the assumption that we were safer in a crowd. Apparently acting on the opposite assumption, the agents on our trail lost a few seconds, so by the time we regained the boulevard, Stevie and I had a half-block lead heading back towards the Place Denfert-Rochereau.

Darting in and out of pedestrians, I exclaimed, "If we can just make it back into the metro!" "We can't do that!" countered Stevie. "What if we have to wait for a train?

"Oh shit," I gasped, as panic started to rise in my throat. "I'm not a long-distance sprinter, you know."

"Well, you better keep going till we think of something better."

We accelerated up the broad sidewalk, knocking and shoving shoppers aside. The police seemed to be out of earshot, and as we neared the metro entrance we skidded to a halt at the main intersection and turned around, out of breath. No sooner had we stopped than we saw the blue caps of the police bobbing towards us, and on the cross street behind us, even closer, two more approached on the run.

Stevie barely had to touch my elbow, and we bolted into the fast-moving traffic of the boulevard towards a large line-up of people on the other side. Renault and Peugeot drivers, conditioned to deal with the unexpected, swerved and braked skillfully, gesticulated, and maneuvered their vehicles past us as we darted towards the safe shore of the other sidewalk. I felt no particular fear of the deadly vehicles compared to the uniformed figures on my tail. Stevie yelled "Olé!" as he leapt onto the curb, and I thought to myself, if those had been German drivers, we'd be hamburger meat by now.

We cut our way into the crowd of people, mostly foreign tourists, that moved slowly towards some kind of entrance. "What's going on here?" Stevie asked.

"I think it's the entrance to the catacombs."

"Can we get lost in them?" Stevie wanted to know.

"I hope so!" I yelled. We pushed and shoved through the crush towards the entrance.

"Goddamn punks," uttered an American voice.

We quit talking and concentrated on pushing. As we squeezed through the main entrance, a pair of police voices was audible at the back of the pack, "*Arrêtez, police!*" To the protests of the other tourists, we surged towards the ticket booth in a barred lane which was no longer quite so crowded, monitored as it was by the catacomb guards. Beyond the ticket booth, the guards allowed only a few at a time to enter the stairway which descended into the bowels of the earth. If we could get that far, we could descend into the Hades of Paris.

Saying, "*Excusez-moi, pardonnez-moi, s'il vous plaît, excusez-moi, Monsieur, Madame!*" Stevie yanked me forward, to the annoyance of the queued tourists, shoved a hundred franc bill under the grate of the ticket booth and grabbed two tickets which the grey-haired ticket-seller had just set down for someone else. "*Excusez-moi,*" Stevie said, and pulled me forward, not waiting for change, pushed aside the frail old guard who was about to make us wait at the top of the stairs, and bounded crazily down the stone stairs five steps at a time.

While we descended the police would be fighting their way through a stickier, protesting crowd towards the head of the queue. Everyone in line probably felt self-righteously mistreated and insulted by this disturbance. Confirmed in their natural reluctance to spend money on this particular attraction, the claustrophobes among them would have persuaded their partners that they had told them so, that something was bound to go wrong with such a visit.

The stairs spiraled interminably downward. There were no windows or other points of orientation, and my head swirled from dizziness. I repeatedly pushed a hand against the hard wall to keep my balance. But at least I'd caught some breath, and thank God, we encountered only a few people, whom Stevie bullied past with "*Ex-*

cusez-moi!" I scraped a hand against a wall to keep steady, but stumbled nevertheless and twisted my right ankle before I caught myself. "Damn!" I swore under my breath. Stevie heard the stumble and turned around. "Be careful, for Chrissake!" I suppressed the pain which shot through my foot and kept going. My knees trembled and I wondered whether it was really necessary to bury bones this deep underground.

All of a sudden, the last step shot us into a series of small rooms with pictures to orient the tourists. Then came a long narrow tunnel carved out of stone like a mine. The walls were damp and slimy with occasional trickles of water. Here and there the ceiling dripped and small pools formed on the ground. The odor was dank and moldy. An occasional weak electric light bulb reduced the darkness but failed to make the strange environment bright or inviting.

Stevie and I no longer heard police voices, and were soon relieved to realize there was no guided tour we were expected to join. We pressed on past the first clumps of visitors. Some held flashlights as they checked their information pamphlets. After a number of empty tunnels we came to the first dimly lit ossuary room where bones were stacked by the thousands and arranged according to type—arm, leg, pelvis, skull—in a symmetry as perfect as a French garden. Stevie exclaimed, "Jeeesus!" I shuddered at the penetrating dank odor and the overwhelming presence of death.

"It's sort of like a wine cellar, with all the barrels arranged and stacked up neatly," I suggested.

"No, it's too wet for that here. The humidity would ruin the corks in no time," observed Stevie.

In the next room three young people with Scandinavian accents were taking close-up shots of each other as they played up to skulls and crossed arm bones from the Cimetière de la Trinité.

"What now?" I asked Stevie as our breathing slowed to normal and we proceeded more slowly through the masses of human remains of several centuries. The long corridors left us no choice but to continue along with the curious tourists from one morbid treasure to the next. "I wish we had a map of this place," said Stevie.

Eventually we entered a tunnel which descended further into the earth and led to a stone sculpture of a fortress carved in the wall. A bearded man behind a tripod and klieg lights was peering through his camera at the miniature scene. Stevie nudged me and pointed to the items the man had propped up on the gravel floor of the narrow tunnel. As we passed by, he stooped down and picked up the flashlight and brochure that were lying next to the man's backpack. Then he ushered me into the next area, past a deep clear-water well, and into a large chamber of bones, at the end of which stood an open door supported by two stone pillars. Above the door was an inscription carved in marble: *"Arrête! C'est ici l'empire de la mort."*

CHAPTER TEN

L'Empire de la Mort

Abandon every hope, All you who enter.
Dante

Stevie and I crept through labyrinthine galleries of bones, all neatly stacked, labeled and dated—from the cemeteries of Saint-Laurent, Saint-Jacques-du-Haut-Pas, Saint-Leu—past crypts, altars, poems and inscriptions, all devoted to the meaning of life and death. An artful display of shin-bones reminded me that my ankle was beginning to throb with pain. As we continued, I tried to suppress the nausea that rose high in my abdomen whenever the image of Guido's corpse came to me. I imagined his dismembered organ piled up here along with these bones.

At the end of one large wall of femurs stratified with three different layers of skulls was an iron gate leading into another unlit tunnel forbidden to the public. A wire was twisted around the rod of the door and its post, but it wasn't locked. Ropes and warning signs of "Defense d'entrer" marked it off. Tools, heavy equipment, debris, rock piles and wooden beams lay on the ground beyond the ropes and suggested some kind of construction zone, perhaps excavation or reinforcement work.

We paused, safe from pursuit for a few moments. We occupied ourselves with the femurs and skulls until a group of Spaniards was safely past us. Then we ducked under the ropes, untwisted the wire secured to the gate, opened it and shut it again behind us. We tiptoed into the darkness to get beyond the range of the weak electric lighting. About fifty feet away, another tunnel led off at a right angle. Having turned the corner, we felt safer still. Peeking back, we watched several sets of visitors pass by the forbidden ropes, then we proceeded deeper into the uncharted tunnel where Stevie turned on the flashlight, once he was convinced its light wouldn't be seen anymore from the roped-off entry way. We walked through two more rooms of bones, similar to those on the official tour, but without poems or inscriptions. The flashlight beam illuminated still wetter and shinier walls. Finally we came to a low ledge of bones about a meter high where we sat down on its uneven surface and rested.

I adjusted my hips between the bumps as well as possible, stretched out both legs, and took hold of my right ankle which was swollen to the touch. I pulled down my sock and rubbed it. The skin was hot, and I felt my pulse throb in my leg. It felt good to take my weight off of it. Stevie settled down next to me, dangled his legs over the edge and pulled the brochure he had stolen from the photographer out of his hip pocket. The front cover read: "Les Catacombes de Paris."

"Here, hold the flashlight so I can read this," he said, and handed it to me. He flipped through several pages before coming to a map and legend of the contorted walkway which led through the official tour area of the ossuary. The legend listed the various attractions—the tombs, wells, plaques and bones on the route. "Look, this must be where we came in," Stevie said, pointing to the "Entrée de l'Ossuaire," at the corner of the Rue Hallé and the Avenue René. "And this is the exit at the Rue Rémy Dumoncel. So it's not a circle. But, of course, the police will be waiting for us at both ends. That's probably why they didn't bother to follow us while other tourists are in here."

"Does it show any other entrances or exits?" I inquired.

"Not on this map. Remember it's just for tourists, not fugitives."

"If the catacombs are anything like the sewers, there are bound to be other ways out," I offered. "The sewers are supposed to have something like twenty to thirty thousand different openings to the outside all over the city."

"Well, that might help us if the catacombs connect up with the sewers." Stevie flipped through the pages looking for more information and then read a few sentences in an impossible accent: "'l'Ossuaire a été aménagé dans des vides d'anciennes carrières de pierre à bâtir. . . . ' What does that mean?" he asked and handed me the text.

I tried to translate as best I could in the beam of the flashlight. "It means that the bones have been placed in what used to be underground quarries. They lie in four hundred meters of chalk or limestone or something like that. Let's see what else there is . . . something about the geology of the city . . . a lot of cave-ins over the years. It says about a twelfth of Paris' total area is situated over underground cavities—like the catacombs, the metro, the sewers . . . about three hundred kilometers of underground passageways. . . . Uh, let's see, lots of abandoned quarries, some have been filled up by landslides or by hand." Stevie listened intently to my translation of the pamphlet in the hopes it would give us some clue as to how to get out unobserved. But its information was elusive. Eventually he suggested we turn off the flashlight to conserve the batteries and just rest and think a bit. I was tired, so I agreed. I stretched out on the uncomfortable bed of bones. Despite the impossibly rough surface, the last thing of which I was consciously aware were Stevie's motions as he shifted around in an attempt to find a comfortable position to rest.

All of a sudden, he was shaking me. "Let's go Megan! The police are coming!" Stevie's whisper was urgent. I was aware of being very cold, and couldn't understand why I couldn't see. I thought I had opened my eyes, but I saw only pitch black. As I sat up, the shooting pain in my ankle brought back the desperation of our situation. I wondered how long we had napped. It could have been minutes or hours. In the underground darkness there were no clues as to the time of day.

Stevie pulled on my arm. "Come on," he whispered again. "Can't you hear them?" Now I became aware of the faint voices of French men that came from somewhere, as if from outer space. I couldn't make out what they said, but it was obvious from their tone that their mission had nothing to do with tourism. "Maybe, they're just workmen," I offered to Stevie.

"Do you want to ask them?" he replied as he dragged me off the bed of bones and pulled me farther into the tunnel. My ankle throbbed sharply with each step. At the same time I tried to tread as quietly as possible. Stevie lit the path with the flashlight. We came to another fork in the tunnel and I asked, "Which way?" to which he replied, "As far away as we can get," and pulled me to the left.

"How do we remember how to get back?" I inquired.

"Why on earth would you want to get back? he retorted. "Are you planning to befriend a French policeman, or what?" Stevie sounded exasperated. I guessed I was still more afraid of the police than the

Parisian underworld, so I kept quiet and tried to forget the pain in my foot. The thought of getting lost must have bothered Stevie too. He suggested we turn right, then left, and then right again, alternately, whenever we had a choice. In that way we would move in a more or less diagonal direction away from the tour area, and, at the same time, if we needed to, we would be able to retrace our steps by reversing the procedure.

As we moved forward almost noiselessly, my ankle lost a little of the stiffness it had taken on during sleep, but the hurt was still there in a dull way. "What time is it Stevie?" I murmured.

"About 7 PM," he said, without breaking his stride. For some reason I wanted this confirmed and asked him to shine the flashlight on my watch. I saw it for myself and said, "I guess the catacomb tour would be closed for the day by now."

"Yeah, probably a couple of hours ago."

Suddenly a voice called out distinctly, "Arrêtez! Arrêtez! Police!" and then again in accented English, "Stop! Here the police!" We froze while we heard our pulse race through our veins.

It was hard to tell from which direction the voice came. Several more voices joined in with the original one, and we could now hear running footsteps. Stevie switched off the flashlight and stuck it under his belt. He took me by the left hand and touched the clammy wall with his right. "Come on," he muttered under his breath, and pulled me as fast as he could, guiding our forward motion with nothing more than his hand on the wall.

We were less careful about the noise of our footsteps now. Those of our pursuers, who obviously outnumbered us, drowned out ours. At the next fork Stevie made another right turn and continued down another tunnel, thinking it better, I guessed, to maintain a safe distance, even at the expense of the directional strategy. I was relieved it was a tunnel, and not a big room of bones without a clearly marked wall to follow. It seemed to continue farther than usual in one direction, and we were grateful now for the level ground, even if it was wetter and full of puddles. The darkness didn't bother us too much, as long as we felt we were making progress. We seemed to be leaving our pursuers behind as the sounds they made faded. At least they had quit shouting for us to stop, but unintelligible voices and footsteps were still audible.

Suddenly Stevie stopped and turned on the flashlight. His right hand and fingers, scratched and wet from the rough quarry walls, groped thin air. Now the beam of light illuminated a large room which seemed to contain several small anti-chambers placed like chapels in the apse of a cathedral. Two main exits led from the room, one to the right and one to the left, but it was impossible to know how they might branch out in this underground labyrinth. Stevie whispered that if the passageways were truly complex and wide-spread, once this small group of followers had passed, they would most likely not return for a while, at least not until a major search party was launched. If we could shake them now, we would gain time plus the possibility to search for an escape route—into the sewers or the metro tunnels and from there into the open. The small group of police would probably stick together; they must have had some kind of central map and hoped they would find us by sheer good luck. If that failed, they would have to plan a better-organized attack, proba-bly for the next day, maybe with dogs.

We continued through the room and took the right exit which opened up into another large room much like the others, filled with neatly stacked bones. Then we proceeded into another long tunnel where Stevie again switched off the light. He put his hand up in front of himself on the wall while I held onto the back of his leather jacket. We proceeded in this manner for several minutes until suddenly Ste-vie cried out, "Ow! Oh shit!" and stopped.

"Jesus, what's the matter?" I asked.

Stevie turned on the flashlight swearing, "Damn it! Shit, that hurts!" and shone it on his right hand and wrist. Blood was oozing from around the joint.

"I cut myself," he said. He pointed the flashlight up at the wall now, and we saw a sharp metal rod sticking out between the stones at the level he had been feeling the surface.

"Here, give me the flashlight," I insisted. I took it from him and focussed it again on his hand. A nasty gash had opened up about an inch of skin at the bottom of his life line where it meets the joint be-tween hand and wrist. I directed the light at my purse and found some crumpled kleenex. When I tried to lay the wad of tissues on the torn wrist, Stevie yanked it away from my hand.

"Don't touch me!" he hissed. The blood-soaked tissue fell in a puddle at our feet.

"Jesus, I only wanted to help you stop the bleeding. Look, its dripping right off your arm."

Stevie turned his back to me and raised his shoulders as if to sob. Why was he so touchy about this cut? It couldn't hurt that much. I told him to turn around, and I pointed the flashlight at his wound. The blood continued to run down his hand and drip off his fingers.

"Do you have a handkerchief or scarf or something?" he asked.

"I'm afraid not. I didn't exactly come prepared for this today."

"Well, maybe I could take off my shirt and tie it around like a bandage."

"No, you need your shirt against the cold down here," I said. "If you don't mind, I'll give you my underpants. They'll do if we twist them around."

"Well, I could use my own."

"No, don't bother," I said. "Hold onto your wrist. You'd get blood all over your clothes."

I gave him the flashlight, turned aside and braced one hand against the wall. I pulled one pant leg and then the other over my shoes, careful not to let my pants fall on the wet ground. Then I pulled the panties out of the pants and stepped back into my long pants.

Stevie aimed the light on the panties and managed a feeble joke: "Those are cute, Megan. I'll bet you'd rather be taking them off for some other man in some other room."

"Try them, you'll like them," I said.

He would never be able to tie a knot without my help so I said, "Here, you hold the flashlight with your good hand, and I'll tie the bandage."

"No, there's too much blood," he argued.

"I'm not afraid of a little blood," I countered. I ordered him now to hold the flashlight in his good hand, stretch out his wounded arm and pull back his sleeve.

"Maybe you should be," he remarked, cryptically.

"OK,OK, already." I twisted the panties into as long a piece as possible and tied them over the wound, avoiding contact with his precious blood.

"There. No sweat. Hold your hand up over your head for a while."

We started walking again, deeper into the subterranean empire. If we followed in the tracks of the police, we didn't know it. We no longer heard nor saw any trace of them. We abandoned our strategy of alternating right and left turns. Concerned about the batteries, Stevie only flashed a beam down each new corridor. If the passage was relatively straight and free of obstacles, he switched off the light and gave it to me to carry. Then he placed his good hand gingerly on the surface of the wall and guided me until his instincts told him to have another look. The darkness was complete and heavy. I held onto the tail of his leather jacket, so silky smooth to the touch. We groped on in blindness for several hours.

We examined each new room and corner for signs of exits or connections to the sewers or subways, but so far the labyrinth appeared to be a network of its own. Eventually fatigue overcame us. And with the immediate stress of the chase behind, we also became aware of how hungry we were. We realized we would have to rest. Time in the dark underground world was irrelevant, yet our watches indicated 11 PM.

We stopped in a room which contained a stack of wooden planks and beams. We selected out a few and arranged them on the wet gravel, constructing for ourselves a hard but at least dry bed where we intended to rest a few hours. Now that we had stopped moving, the dank cold of the underground began to penetrate through our street clothes. Stevie switched off the flashlight and set it down. Then we lay down close to each other.

Stevie's plank bent a bit more under his weight than mine did, and I was bothered by this unevenness, stretched out as on a torture rack. We shifted around, holding onto each other for warmth, trying to find a position comfortable enough for sleep. We would try to hold still for a while, but then either he or I would twitch or jerk, and we'd start shifting around all over again. "This is how I imagine marriage," Stevie joked.

"Oh, it's not always that bad," I said, without really thinking.

"Come on, Megan. Everybody knows it's the pits. With your track record you're a great one to defend *that* institution. Did I ever tell you about my grandparents?"

"No, I don't think so. Why?"

"Well, let me tell you now. It makes a good bedtime story," he said.

"OK, why not?"

We shifted around once again. He turned on his side in a fetal position and I snuggled up to his back. I held one arm over his head and the other around his waist and chest to provide him with as much of my warmth as possible.

"Now try to hold still," he admonished. "And pay attention."

"OK,OK! I'm all ears. I'm not going anywhere!"

He finally began. "It's about my paternal grandparents."

"Got it," I said. "On your father's side."

"Right. He—I mean my grandfather—was a sort of fiery little Irishman and my grandmother was supposed to have been delicate and refined, from Wales. At least that's how the story goes. I never knew them, because they died before I was born.

"That's logical," I exclaimed.

Stevie pinched my thigh to punish my sarcasm. Then he proceeded. "Anyway, they both emigrated to Canada when they were teenagers. I don't know why. And they met in the dead of winter outside of Edmonton when he discovered her wagon stuck in a snowdrift and helped her get it free."

"Very gallant," I remarked. "Just like you!"

"Right!" Stevie laughed. "Good genes. Anyway, she moved into his log-cabin homestead, and they had nine children, but five of them died."

"So you're lucky to be here," I noted.

"Lucky to be *here*, for sure." He emphasized the irony. "They spent their last years in a two-story house in town."

"How do you know, if you never met them?" I asked.

"Well, this is an important part of the story, or the family legend or whatever—that it was a two-story house. You see, what happened was that when my grandfather was eighty and my grandmother seventy, the old bastard decided they had nothing more to say to each other, so he moved all his things upstairs and ordered her to live downstairs and not bother him anymore. He hired a maid who did the cleaning and cooked for them. And since they quit talking to each other—I mean, *he refused to talk to my grandmother*—the maid had to carry messages up and down the stairs between them. Apparently, every day for ten years my grandfather asked the maid how my grandmother was feeling, and my grandmother in turn asked the maid about his health. The maid also had to tell my grandmother who my grandfather wanted her to vote for in elections. The maid was always happy when someone dropped by to visit them, because the visitor got to carry some messages up and down the stairs.

"That's absurd!" I said.

"Very perceptive. But that's not all," said Stevie. "My grandmother died on her eightieth birthday, which was also their sixtieth wedding anniversary. He was almost ninety when it happened. And believe it or not, the *maid* had to tell my grandfather that his wife had died, and *she*—the maid—had to make the funeral arrangements. Then, and this is the killer, the old fart went out of his mind with grief, and he also drove the maid crazy complaining how lonely he was until he finally died three years later!"

I guess I burst out laughing first, and then Stevie caught on. I held tighter to him as we shook the planks and our laughter reverberated through the darkness.

Soon Stevie was asleep in my arms. I held him gently without moving. I couldn't sleep at first myself, for thinking about him. How could he manage to tell me this funny story in our crazy situation? How could he continue to do things that made me feel better? What really motivated him to stay with me?

For some reason he seemed to see things more clearly, to understand people and to face life squarely. I realized I no longer knew what to make of the relations between men and women. Both sexes lived in the worlds of their own brains. In intelligence we were equals, but something had brought about a frightening asymmetry in our emotions and our concepts of humanity. Were these differences biological or cultural? Were we condemned ineluctably to war?

The concepts that were supposed to work—trust, honesty, kindness—didn't seem to hold in most relationships. I was aware, however, that for the first time in my life I had a strong urge to get to know a particular man, that is, this unusual man. I wanted to talk to him. He seemed to hold the key to something important about life. Was it love? I had come to think that love was just another male construct for manipulating situations in a particular direction, but this rule didn't seem to apply with Stevie. And there was something else with Stevie . . . was it courage?

I resolved to open up to him at the first opportunity, since I sensed that he might open a doorway for me. I held Stevie tighter as sleep finally overcame me. I felt close. . . .

Somewhere, far in the distance, on a white sandy plain, my dark, dark lover moved toward me on a magnificent silver horse whose eyes were covered by a black hood. The speck that they created on the horizon under the wide sky enlarged as they slowly came closer. Despite the distance, I could see in great detail that the horse galloped at full speed straight into its own blindness, muscles bulging, shanks lathered, foamy spray flying from its mouth. It strained forward in a supreme effort for the sake of its dark master who whipped its flanks and spurred its belly without mercy. Blood, which oozed from the lash marks and the spur pricks, flew with the foam onto the white sand where it pearled in glistening droplets. It left a track for anyone who might trace the rider's path back to his point of departure, like bread crumbs in a fairy tale. The more frantically my lover urged the steed, the slower their progress toward my naked body, stretched out in the sand under the scorching sunlight. Through the distorting heat waves which separated me from man and beast, I could clearly see the animal's veins swollen all over its body. Sand clouds billowed up around the pair. I waited for them.

Suddenly, they were in front of me. As the dark rider dismounted, the masked horse fell on its side and rolled in the sand. It heaved furiously, legs twitching, and expired its last breath.

Now my lover stood over my glistening body, shading the sun behind his head, which would otherwise have blinded my upward gaze. The halo of light obscured his face, and for an instant I feared this was not really my lover, but his twin, whom I hated as passionately as I loved my lover. I closed my eyes again as he lowered his weight onto me and caressed me with his hands. With the moisture of his body he massaged my skin to protect me from the desert sands. Then he made love to me at first with slow deliberation, and I opened my depths willingly to his surging member and to the noonday heat which subsided during the long afternoon hours as he ravaged my body.

Flies buzzed around the horse's corpse, and the distinct scent of death filled the air. As the sun descended behind the mountain peak near the horizon whence they had come, and before it sank into the ocean beyond the plain, the man finally retracted his smooth penis. He stood up in the same spot from which he had lowered himself earlier. As he held his sex organ in his hand, a wine red fountain sprang from it and arced into my mouth. But the dead taste of the drops made me realize my error.

From the oasis not far away my true lover began to wail piteously as he watched the culmination of the scene, having arrived too late. I still lay on my back in the sand while the brother stood over me. I turned my head toward my lover in time to see him fall directly from his horse to his knees and sink the sharp blade of his own long penis deep into his abdomen, as if in one long motion. The force of the thrust cut off his cry abruptly and held his figure motionless, suspended for an instant. Then, both hands clutching his bloody middle torso, he fell forward on his face in the sand. . . .

CHAPTER ELEVEN

Quicksand

He steered for me . . . and thus a subtle bond
had been created, of which I only became
aware when it was suddenly broken. And
the intimate profundity of that look he gave
me when he received his hurt remains to this
day in my memory—like a claim of distant
kinship affirmed in a supreme moment.

Joseph Conrad

I woke up when Stevie moved. "You're awake?" I said.

"Yeah, I had to move. I was getting stiff."

"What time is it?" I asked, opening my eyes. The darkness was
total with eyes opened or closed. I shut them again to avoid the unpleasant sensation with lids open that I had lost my vision.

"I'm trying to find the flashlight. I'll tell you in a minute." Stevie
felt around next to the planks in the wet gravel. Finally he located the
cold metal cylinder and flipped the switch. A welcome patch of light
fell on the stony wall next to us—a minor miracle in our dungeon. I
wanted to put my hands over the inviting beam, as if it might warm
them. Stevie looked at his watch.

"My God. It's a quarter to eight!" he exclaimed. "We actually
slept the whole night. Here," he said, handing me the flashlight,
"check yours out too."

I looked at my watch. "I have seventeen to eight," I announced, as if greater precision might somehow help our situation. "We must have slept better than we thought. No wonder we feel stiff. We must not have moved all night. I'm amazed the cold didn't wake us up."

"Me too," said Stevie. I guess we were more exhausted than we realized. And, of course, a hot bed partner is always a good soporific, don't you think?"

The hotel room in Munich came slowly back to me. It all seemed like centuries ago, as if from a previous lifetime which had faded into oblivion and which I could drag out of the dark recesses of my memory only with great difficulty. I tried to grope my way back to the strange drama that preceded the death of my Italian lover, but it didn't make any sense. Maybe it would help to go over the details again with Stevie at some later point. But now we had other problems to deal with.

"Well, how about some breakfast?" I asked, trying to sound cheerful. I sat up and pulled my knees to my chest. A sharp pain shot through my sprained ankle. "Damn," I swore, and clutched it with my hands. It was still swollen, but not any worse than before. I figured I'd forget it when we started walking. "How's your wrist?"

"Oh, it's probably OK. It stopped bleeding."

I shone the light on it. Blood was crusted around it and had turned brown on my white panties. "Do you want your underwear back?" Stevie asked.

"No thank you!" "Why don't you keep them as a souvenir of your visit to Paris. You're probably not the first man from San Francisco to appropriate a pair of women's panties in this city. But the circumstances are unique, you must admit. Maybe they'll add our story to the tourist brochure of the catacombs someday. Besides, we shouldn't disturb the wound."

"OK. Well, *allons-y!*" Stevie said in his inimitable French. Why don't we visit the Café de la Paix this morning. It's near the opera, probably not too far from here. I want to mingle with elegant people today. And I'm dying to sink my teeth into a soft croissant. And café noir would be perfect after such a great night's sleep. The weather's so nice, let's sit outside and watch the world go by. *D'accord?*"

"*Mais oui, monsieur.*" I realized that Stevie would be having the same thoughts as I did about the police search with the dogs. It was probably already underway, so we should make use of whatever time we had. Stevie helped pull me up off the boards. He took charge when

I was indecisive, he organized things and kept up our spirits. I was glad to follow, because I truly didn't know what we should do—whether or not we would be better off giving ourselves up to the authorities—that is, *I* should give *myself* up since Stevie had nothing to do with it all, and explain my plight and rely on my innocence to set me free. But I buried this thought every time it entered my head. A powerful survival instinct told me not to get caught any more by anyone who wanted to limit my movements.

We started out, resuming the method of the last night whereby Stevie led. He groped the walls of the passageways with his good hand, and turned on the flashlight when it was necessary to reorient. I held the back of his black leather jacket in one hand. My fingers marvelled again at its fine quality—as smooth as foreskin. As we walked, I thought of questions I wanted to ask him later. Was he terribly lonely without Ralph or just emotionally numb? Was he trying to keep his mind off himself? Did he enjoy this wild adventure? Was he a chivalric knight trying to save a damsel in distress or the ancient ferry man guiding dead souls across the river Styx?

We had traversed perhaps three or four new rooms and passageways when Stevie whispered excitedly, "I think I see light ahead." I opened my eyes, and seeing nothing at first said, "Point the flashlight at it."

"No, stupid! Think a minute. If I point the light at it, we won't be able to see it. Look!" He pulled me next to him in the dark, placed his hands next to the sides of my head like blinders and pointed it toward the sliver of light he had perceived. "Look straight ahead." Then he whispered, "What light is breaking through yonder window? Do you see it?"

"Yeah, now I do!" A rush of hope ran through my body. "What do you think it is? Let's go closer."

"OK, but don't say anything." We proceeded with caution, treading as gingerly as possible on the coarse path towards the faint source of light. It gradually grew brighter the closer we came, and our eyes adjusted to it. It seemed to have the whiteness of natural daylight. I dropped Stevie's jacket, which I no longer needed for guidance, and walked beside him. Unaided by the flashlight, we could see that our long corridor opened into a large room or cave. The light emanated from beyond it. We both breathed faster now, and my pulse accelerated. We paused several times as we approached the room and listened for any sounds, but everything remained dead still.

The chamber was different from anything we had yet encountered underground. It was more like a naturally-formed cave, not a man-hewn room. From its entrance, we saw that the light came from another passageway that led off at a right angle at the far end, about forty feet away. We still couldn't tell exactly what kind of light it was, but our eyes welcomed it. The chamber had a high, symmetrical, bell-shaped ceiling from which water occasionally dripped down into the middle of a large pond that covered the entire floor area. It was impossible to know how deep the water was, and where the floor began. Stevie turned on the flashlight to augment the light, but this ancient indoor pool refused to reveal its secret to us. The water was silty and opaque. We had no choice. The only way to the tunnel and the light on the other side was through the water. We didn't need to discuss it.

"Well, we can hope it's not too deep, but if it is, you can swim, can't you?" Stevie whispered.

"Of course! Don't *you* be stupid. I'm a Californian. Have you forgotten all those summers at the beach and all those swimming pools we grew up with? This is shorter than most of them. But you know, I still hate cold water," I added.

"Well, I'll go first and warm it up for you."

I gave up whispering and said, "Come on. Hurry up, or I'll push you in." My voice echoed slightly just the way it would in an indoor swimming pool.

Stevie took off his shoes and socks, stuck the socks back into the shoes, and hurled them one by one across the water. The first fell short, splashed in the water and sank about eight feet from the edge; the second did the same. Wordlessly, we watched them go under. Stevie looked at me and shrugged his shoulders. Then he rolled his pants above his knees and took three careful steps into the water. It came up to his ankles, but with the fifth and sixth step, it rose to his knees. He turned back as if he'd forgotten something and handed me the flashlight saying, "Water's great. You'll love it. But hold onto this so it doesn't get wet, just in case it gets deeper and I have to swim. You can throw it to me when I reach the other side."

"Good thinking, Stevie, and bon voyage!" I said, excited.

Stevie stepped back into the water and waded in the direction of the center. "The bottom is soft and muddy," he reported. About three or four yards out he was in to his knees again, trying to pull his pant legs up further. A few more steps and he gave up as the water continued to rise. Almost in the middle of the chamber, the water was up to his crotch and Stevie came to a halt. Suddenly I had an idea. "Hey, why don't you walk to the edge next to the wall; maybe it's not so deep."

"Yeah, good idea. But first I've got to pick up my right foot. This mud is incredibly sticky, like molasses."

"That must feel good, oozing through your toes," I echoed back. We didn't bother to lower our voices anymore.

"That would be OK, if it didn't slow you down." He tried to get going but was prevented as if by magnetic boots. "Shit! I can't pull my right foot out." He jerked his body now and leaned back towards his left foot which was behind the right one. "Damn it. I'm sinking, Megan! I don't believe this! My feet are sinking into the damn mud!" He twisted his torso around towards me, as if facing in the solid direction from which he came would somehow improve his predicament.

I saw his sudden panic. The water was approaching his waist and rising slowly. Stevie began to paddle with his arms at it, as if swimming motions might be powerful enough to pull him away from that spot. He flayed, beat at it and splashed wildly. "Holy Jesus, Megan! I'm sinking! Megan!"

A flash of horror bolted through my brain. But I said almost automatically, as if to an accident victim, "Calm down, Stevie, don't panic. Don't move so much. You'll make it worse. Your arms are free. Try to lift one leg out with your arms. They're strong. If you can pull out one leg, you're home free."

"OK," he gasped. His back to me once again, he reached down towards his right side and bent his torso so that his head almost touched the water. He seemed to sink even further.

"No. Try the left one, it's not in so deep, is it?" I cried, as if talking louder would help him.

"But I can't reach it either. It's too far behind me. I don't have as much leverage." Stevie started to sob and curse and flail at the water again, churning up a turbulence on the surface.

"Stand up," I commanded. "Don't lose your balance!" I could see that the water was already half way up his chest. As fast as I could, I took off my shoes and socks and pulled off my pants and waded into the water towards Stevie, carrying my pants. The mud was silky soft to my bare feet. "Stevie, I'm going to pull you out," I called to him. He twisted his upper body towards me and stopped flaying and cursing as I came closer, naked from the waist down.

"But you'll sink too," he sputtered, in utter terror.

"No I won't. You were OK out this far." I was out about seven feet, and I could feel the mud beginning to stick with a mild suction. Holding one pant leg I threw the other out towards him like a fly caster and commanded, "Grab my pants." It fell short of Stevie's outstretched arms. I took another step forward with one foot into deeper mud and tried again. This time Stevie caught the leg on the surface of the water with his left hand. He gasped as in relief and pulled on it forcefully. I had to lean backwards to counteract his weight, but this had the tendency of forcing my heels deeper into the quicksand. I realized from its texture that with another step or two I could easily reach the area where semi-solid turned into cool molten, and there would be no more resistance against my feet to help either of us.

Now I pulled with all my strength on Stevie's lifeline as the water rose up to his armpits, his imploring arms stretched towards me. Choked with fear, he began to whimper. The taut tension in the pants remained constant and told us that it was hopeless. The power of the quicksand was irrevocable, and it had already claimed too much of Stevie's body to give it up.

My shoulders felt like they would come out of their sockets through the force of the terrible slow vortex. Suddenly Stevie screamed, "Pull, Megan! Pull harder, God damn it! Why can't you pull?" He was salivating at the mouth, and as he screamed at me, he spit and slobbered into the water as it rose toward his chin. Then, just as suddenly, he stopped and began to sob. He looked straight at me now and whimpered like a still-breathing animal struck by a car. The opaque sandy water rose into his mouth. He spat it out furiously, blew bubbles and made terrible sounds as he tried to shout something to me. Then he tilted his nose back, so it could catch his last breaths of air. Fixed on me, his eyes were crazed. His mouth under water, he hung onto the pant leg with undiminished strength, and as his nose filled up and bubbled, he began to shake his head back and forth, creating smaller and smaller waves. His eyes remained open always fixed on my own, even as he sank underneath the surface. Not until his forehead began to disappear, did the pressure on my pants give way all at once. The last thing I saw of Stevie was the top of his head. The laurel leaves created by the punk hairdresser turned around in a slow half circle before they disappeared.

I released my pant leg with a shudder, as if I had been forced to hold a repulsive reptile and now was free to let it go. It floated briefly on the surface before sinking.

Although deeper in the silt now, my feet were not hopelessly stuck. With some effort I lifted my left leg out of its gluey depression with the help of my arms and set it behind me. Then I shifted my weight backwards as much as possible, careful to maintain my balance, and twisted and gradually pulled my right leg out of its trap. Now I retreated slowly back to my safe haven at the entrance to the chamber. I accidentally stepped on the flashlight, which I must have set down on the threshold before my wading expedition. I picked it up and shined it over the surface of the pool. It was as still and calm and murky as we had found it, as if undisturbed for centuries. As I stared, a drop of water fell into its center from the bell-shaped ceiling and sent a perfect configuration of concentric rings vibrating out toward the walls.

I don't know how many hours passed before I heard the barking of German shepherds and the voices of the police.

∘ ∘ ∘

Gordon:

Ever since I first read her account of these infernal incidents, a bad dream has pursued me: I am down there in the Parisian catacombs with them, and I hold onto Megan's blond hair as she slowly sinks into the quicksand herself, pulled down by Stevie. She stares at me as she goes under after him.

I always wake up perspiring and exhausted with my own voice echoing in my ears: "Let go of him, Megan. I'll save you!" I fear that this nightmare will recur for the last time at the hour of my death.

You will understand that these sections on her European odyssey finally brought me back face to face with myself and my role in Megan's fate. Up until this point in her writings, I was able to look elsewhere for explanations, to rationalize, speculate and to hope that I had placed too much importance on our incestuous encounter. But as my daughter's tragedy unfolded, it was, ironically, the totality of her confusion in relation to her crime against her lover that convinced me she committed it . . . and that I was the cause of it. I finally understood something about her terrible gaze so long ago. She was not simply looking through me. Rather, she was obliterating me and my deed from her conscious mind. She eradicated her own crime in the Munich hotel in the same way, and this mental surgery left a tragic blind spot at the center of her being. Why she made this fatal pact with her psyche, I will never know. I can only assume it was because of my threat to kill her—how could she know I didn't mean it, that I only wanted to ensure her silence? Or could it be that my crime was so heinous that she had no capacity to inscribe it in her memory in the first place? At any rate, the psychic damage was done. Was it a form of cowardice on her part? Or the only survival strategy available to her?

I am sure she was not a member of a German terrorist gang, but I am also sure that the German scene provided her with a kind of stage to act out fantasies of violence in the name of setting wrongs right, far from the place of her most intimate struggles.

I am to blame for it all—for Bonatti's death, Stevie Carpenter's and hers. Her actions were only the answer to my crime against nature, which had set in motion a chain of events that could never be reversed. I had launched the deadly space ship. And once it left our solar system, it couldn't be stopped. Too late, I know that to force someone to do something against her will in that most intimate area of life, the area closest to one's soul, one's sense of security, happiness and life itself, is the worst transgression you can commit, short of murder.

Finally, I am left with the unbearable recognition of the cruelty of her fate as opposed to mine, the incommensurable, undeserved advantage I have had over her. While life has granted me the opportunity to know and confess the truth, my daughter died in darkness.

It was a long time before I could admit the truth of these insights to myself, Gordon. In the meantime, I pushed on relentlessly with my investigations. The last significant person to see and speak with Megan while she was still in full command of herself, was this Professor Dickerson, her former poetry teacher.

I telephoned him at Princeton University disguised as my alias, George Cooke, senior editor for a large publishing house. I described the diaries, memoirs, fantasies, notes and stories written by his former student that had come into the possession of my publishing house and the course they must have taken from California to Europe. The French authorities had confiscated some of the documents from her Paris apartment and the rest directly from her. My publishing house had negotiated for the rights.

I told Professor Dickerson about the research I was doing on Megan Lloyd's life and my contacts in Europe and America. I said that I was struck by the disparity of opinions among these people who had known her, by the lack of agreement or consensus that had emerged to suggest a personality made up of contradictory facets held together only by her name. Thus, I concocted some rather elementary questions about her: Who was she, really? Was she a terrorist or not? What motivated her?

I let him know that I had not edited or censored the fragments. I had only put them into chronological order. Then I asked him if he would be willing to perform the job of literary sleuth. I was motivated by two desires. For one thing, I wanted him to help me trace every step of Megan's life and to illuminate any mysteries I might have overlooked in her story. For another, I wanted him to help me memorialize my daughter and her suffering.

He agreed, so I sent him a copy of the same fragments I am giving to you—minus, of course, any comments of mine. In due time I received the following letter from him on Princeton University letterhead. I thought about shortening his incredible reply for you, but I decided not to, since it throws quite another light on things. Although I hate admitting it, his letter ultimately helped me come to grips with myself and my relationship to Megan.

❊   ❊   ❊

Dear Mr. Cooke,

Since our phone conversation of a few months ago, I've had a chance to peruse the writings of Megan Lloyd that you sent me. My heavy research commitments would normally prevent me from responding in detail, but her surprise visit in Paris and her subsequent notoriety intrigued me sufficiently to devote some time to her material. To think that an infamous "terrorist" sat in my poetry class in Berkeley in the late sixties!

You asked if I, as her former teacher, had any insights into her character, and, whether her writings had literary value. On the first score, it would probably be too harsh to say that Ms. Lloyd deserved the fate that she suffered. Later on I explain why I doubt that she was actually a political terrorist. Yet, somewhere I believe in the notion of karma, and that one should therefore be very careful about the choices one makes in life and the people with whom one associates. At any rate, Ms. Lloyd took my American poetry class in 1969–70, and university records show she received a grade of "C." As I recall, she spent more time protesting than studying her poetry. These fragments also confirm my grave reservations about her character, and, frankly, they provided me with more information than I ever wanted to know about her.

As for the literary value of her writing, I jotted down notes and observations as I read them in much the same way I would for an English composition or fiction writing course. In fact, I've tried to read this manuscript as if it were the rough draft or outline for an eventual novel or film script. Surely, this is what you, as a publisher, have in mind. I've tried to critique the potential of the text on this assumption.

If it were a novel, the first installment about her childhood suggested to me a kind of female *Bildungsroman* with a female *picaro* (*"picara"*?) hero, or perhaps an autobiographical sketch concerning sexual awakening. The move from Beverly Hills to the wild canyon must have precipitated some fundamental conflicts between Megan's parents, but the child may well have been shielded from them. This conflict over the use of wealth overlaps with deeper male-female conflicts.

Lloyd understands her world to be one dominated by men and "male" activities while she fails to appreciate the cultivated, aesthetic aspects of her domestic environment. Probably as an expression of penis envy, she tends to deviate early on from the interior female sphere of the household. She recalls in detail her first sexual intimations, and some confusion regarding heterosexuality. The sexual focus, however, precludes the emergence of clues to any latent terrorist penchants.

A drastic change of tone takes place in the second episode. We are suddenly confronted by an angry, rebellious student. "Chapter One" clearly constitutes an attempt at polished fiction. This piece about Berkeley, on the other hand (including her feeble excuse for a research paper—this satirical, even misanthropic attack on the male sex is very apt in this context), indicates a fundamental shift. The spoiled daughter of the upper class has become a student rebel with an obnoxious reportage style to match. Her anger without focus—and lacking all *raison d'etre* on a deeper, more enduring level—is that of a woman, who "had it coming," to put it in the vernacular. Parenthetically, to return to her alleged terrorist mentality, it does not surprise me that such a twisted personality would be attracted to the uncivilized subcultural milieu of illicit sex and anarchical politics.

I suspect that her stay in Göttingen encouraged Ms. Lloyd's anarchical tendencies by providing ideological focus for her frustrations. But fortunately, this Thomas, whom she marries, proved to be a veritable *deus ex machina,* at least for a time. He always appears at the right time and place to save her from her own tendencies to stray from the straight and narrow pathways of life (what a tragedy for her that they parted). At this point, he must have known or suspected she was involved with the German terrorists, and when he read about the assassination, he took the first plane for Germany to whisk her out of danger.

The next section, devoted to Ms. Lloyd's married years in California, contrasts with both the Berkeley and Göttingen sections. Its smoother writing style would suggest a better period in Lloyd's life when she enjoyed the advantages of a calm (aside from the fire incident), suburban existence and the protection of a loving husband. The smooth style may be deceptive, however, since these fragments actually have very little to do with the protagonist's marriage relationship. Whereas she had the perfect opportunity to explore the most important relationship in her adult life in depth—that to her husband—Thomas is hardly described and thereby trivialized. He remains a static background figure, at times even a source of irritation. She is clearly incapable of love, although she seems to have enjoyed a healthy measure of it in her childhood. (Probably this character flaw figured in the eventual breakup of her marriage. Her near total avoidance of marital and divorce issues in this and the next chapter make me suspect this was the case). In fact, the main piece from her marriage relates their chance entrapment in the middle of a Malibu fire! Nature plays the major role here, as it suddenly and randomly wrenches its human pawns out of their social context and places them at the mercy of much stronger elemental forces. Perhaps catastrophic random events, so much a part of contemporary life, resonate in the collective American character—if the idea of a national character may be given any credence.

I was certainly taken aback by the next installment about her trip to Dallas, Texas. Don't you think she's pulling everyone's leg here? I would bet that she wrote a satire on TV soap opera rather than a diary about an episode of her life. Pardon my pun, but one might title it "Phallas, Texas," replete as this chapter is with phallic references.

If I am wrong and this is in actuality, fact and not fantasy, then our "heroine" engages in a rather unsavory affair and an equally repulsive dream, and then has the incredibly bad taste to drag "Romeo and Juliette" into it! She seems to harbor some repressed or innate propensities for perverted sexuality. In indulging in these tendencies she seems to be taking a rather sick revenge on her poor ex-husband. Some might consider this "liberated," but to tell the truth, it's just one more form of submission she does not understand. A Freudian analyst would have had a field day with her, and she would have done better to spend her money on a psychiatrist's couch rather than on a fancy French meal in Texas, of all places.

The fantasy piece on the German *Autobahn* is the only bit of her writing I could relate to in a positive way. I attended a conference several years ago at the University in Freiburg. Innocents that we were, my wife and I rented a car at the Munich airport and drove to Freiburg, but never again! It was a truly hair-raising experience, and I can understand how a woman alone must have felt trying to navigate in her little Opel on the German freeways with their aggressive, speeding Mercedes trying to run her off the road. (Perhaps Ms. Lloyd should have specialized in surrealist writing to escape, at least on the level of fiction, her unspeakable life).

Amusing as this piece may be in itself, it only adds to that chaotic mix of styles and genres that reflects the fatal fractures in her personality. There is no organic growth to her life and no cohesion to her story. Where would responsibility be instilled in such a rootless drifter? Where would the moral core be centered in such random happenings? Her life is characterized only by disjuncture, much as a television movie is by commercial interruptions. The epic voice is dead.

The next sections, dealing with the murder of the Italian industrialist, Bonatti, only add to this impression of disjuncture. I assure you, I read all the Paris newspapers about this supposed terrorist assassination with interest, even before Ms. Lloyd ran into me there. Although I was and am no fan of hers, reading her version has confirmed my suspicions that the media and the authorities were off the mark in this case. What she describes suggests that she became a victim of chance, circumstance and impulse, not that she was a terrorist *engagé*. I would daresay that she was one of those radical adventurers of the mind so typical of the socially less constructive members of her generation. There is nothing in her life's story to motivate the horrendous act attributed to her. Most women survive a few negative experiences with men (like hers with Professor Bilsky, if she is not making *that* up) without wanting to castrate them, much less carrying out the desire! In other words, if I read the clues correctly, I think the police pursued the wrong person; the true terrorists—probably the strange types she saw in the Munich hotel—covered up their tracks and let her take the blame. Yet, there exists a kind of guilt by association, a culpability caused by the kind of company she kept, the friends she made. Therein lay her error.

To be fair, I should point out one nice artifice in this installment that stimulated my fancy. The bondage episode, with its serpent-like whips and ropes, brings to mind the mythical Trojan priest, Laocoon, who, along with his sons, was killed by a serpent sent by Athena or Apollo. I am particularly reminded of the statue of late Greek antiquity, described so brilliantly by the German art historian, Winkelmann, in which the artist has suspended the three horrified figures at the moment before the serpent strikes and kills them. The sculptor captures and freezes this most pregnant instant which precedes the fulfillment of the tragedy. Here too, the suggestion of violence has been made, and the action is cut off at a suspenseful moment by the end of the chapter—a good touch. But the ungodly space between fantasy and reality that characterizes Ms. Lloyd's life and writing in general does not open these historical allusions to clear and unequivocal moral insights.

It is disturbing to see myself appear again in the ninth "chapter" of this story when she attempts to elude the authorities in Paris—a time when I thought I was safely ensconced in my sabbatical. Needless to say, her rendition of our meeting distorts and downplays the degree to which I put myself in jeopardy for her, risked my own interests and engaged sympathetically in her plight. She obviously never learned the meaning of the word "gratitude"!

As for the later disturbing chapters in the dark nether world of Paris, if what she tries to suggest here is a "female cave of refuge," then, as a culture, we should never have left Plato's cave with its promise of light and insight! I prefer the light of rationality and serenity, to paraphrase the German poet Friedrich Schiller, and would leave the murky waters behind and below. Her life's story emphasizes the dark, violent undercurrents of western culture, particularly the American variant thereof.

My worst suspicions come to fruition at the end, when the narrative stops abruptly without explaining the loose ends. The entire story seems to revolve around a dark center, but nothing clarifying emanates from it, no explanatory event, no enlightening constellation of circumstances. Ultimately, we don't know whether the murder was committed by a terrorist gang, by Lloyd or perhaps by this Stevie character. Personally, I don't believe Berkeley created any true revolutionaries, let alone terrorists, during the sixties and seventies. The thoroughly bourgeois students of Ms. Lloyd's generation had nothing in common with the working class. Youthful idealists and reformers, perhaps. But Ms. Lloyd's involvement in German terrorism would only have been peripheral, not essential to her random, violence-marked life, in my opinion. But, as often happens in life, she was, by her own choice, in the wrong place at the wrong time, and could do nothing to stop the ineluctable unrolling of absurd, tragic but inevitable consequences.

Summa summarum, the protagonist is as passive, and therefore unsatisfying a heroine as one could imagine. She continually reacts rather than initiates or creates. She becomes a victim and finally, an animal bent on self-preservation—but to what purpose? She loses in the process the only tool which might have allowed her to comprehend or cope with her situation—her memory and thus her intellectual functioning. Amnesia becomes her last escape, this time from human society. This is a radical way of saying that nothing adds up, there is nothing to be learned or gained either from experience or reflection. Her life story becomes a kind of anti-*Bildungsroman* of gradual diminution and self-cancellation, valorizing nothing. If I had to give these fragments a title, I would call them "The Chronicles of a Life without Meaning."

I usually ask for a consulting fee when reading manuscripts for a publisher, but in this case I'll make an exception. I don't know if this has helped you, but more I cannot do for you.

Sincerely,
Paul Dickerson,
Professor of English

°   °   °

Gordon:

I cannot tell you how much Professor Dickerson's letter infuriated me—the insult that Megan's life had been meaningless. In fact, I found almost everything he said insufferable, and at first I tried to dismiss him and his letter. But they gnawed away at me. They kept me awake nights. Finally, I sat down and formulated a reply to refute the insult and to demonstrate that the grid of his academic mind was only capable of processing what it itself had produced. I wanted to devastate him, but I found my words inadequate. So I discarded them and started a new letter. Then another and another. Soon it became a daily habit. I wrote reams to him, but I continually tore up the pages as I produced them and drafted new beginnings. I wanted to convince him that Megan Lloyd's writings could not be taken at face value or used to spin an in-group yarn that he labeled a literary critique. I wanted him to accept her as a person, not reduce her to a fictive "heroine" or "protagonist," and to see that the tragedy of her personal fate was inextricably linked to violence, sex, and finally to her place as a woman in this world. I almost drove myself mad in this exercise. I think I was trying to give Megan back the voice that I myself had silenced long ago.

Absurd though it was, I continued to attack this professor on stationary that I never sent. I criticized his devotion to humanities, claiming he lacked insight into human beings. I accused him of a narrow professionalism and a cowardly retreat into Ivory Tower academese. I attacked his blind male chauvinism, sensing at the same time I was powerless to affect it.

I became addicted to my inconsequential battle with this Dickerson. Week after week I stayed up late nights at my typewriter tearing apart each paragraph of his letter with long dissertations of my own. I became as glued to my typewriter as a teenager to his video games. I explained that what she wrote was only a partial representation of the truth and criticized him for having overlooked her most important lines, in reference to her life in Berkeley: ". . . what you write isn't necessarily honest—you always choose what to put in and what to leave out." I argued that what spoke loudest all the time was what she left out of her text—her anger and hurt at the outrages she experienced and saw all around her. I made feminist arguments—for example, that society expects women to suppress negative feelings and to cultivate nothing but positive, nurturing, loving emotions, while men let out their hostilities on the world. I vied against him on pages I was too cowardly to send, but somewhere I was waging a war with myself. I argued that whatever exploded in Megan Lloyd in a context where she feared for her life was ultimately the result of male sexuality and violence. I came very close to the truth, but remained silent about my own part in it.

The sheets of paper I put into my typewriter became my voodoo dolls. The black words I pounded so vehemently onto those white pages were the pins I stuck into this antagonist. To complete my revenge I also had to enlighten him about his own blindness, saying that I feared it most, since he represented, even with his intellectual armor, what society as a whole continually hides from itself—its Rambo-like love of power, dominance and aggression. I told him that he, more than she, made me believe we were doomed to eternal cycles of darkness and violence. That if we persisted in remaining as blind as he was, we were ultimately just as culpable, or more so.

I became transfixed for a long time by my own secret game and absurdly compulsive behavior. But finally, an inherent solipsism in its structure brought me back to myself. I had gone so far as to draft an entire letter to Professor Dickerson out of all the arguments I had formulated and rejected along the way. But I could no sooner mail this letter than any of the preceding fragments. When I realized I hadn't the strength to take this last step, I burned this final, definitive letter, so that the entire evidence of this obsession was transformed into a heap of ashes in my fireplace. The sight of these ashes convinced me of the futility of berating this stranger. After all, I had deceived him and withheld information that would have enabled him to see things differently. So I dropped the notion of ever sending him a reply. At the same time I made the sacred vow that I would reveal the truth to you and engage your help in vindicating Megan's life.

CHAPTER TWELVE

Dear Gordon,

I still have a vivid recollection of the day you drove me to LAX and delivered me to the Air France terminal. We sat side by side in your car and uttered only a few perfunctory remarks, each immersed in his own world. You were doing me a favor, but I felt as if you were delivering me to my execution. While the other passengers eagerly anticipated their arrival in Paris, for me the flight was a nightmare. I wished the entire jumbo jet would plunge into the waters, disintegrate into a million pieces and sink out of sight forever.

A taxi took me straight from Orly to the prison hospital. Before reaching its gates, I turned off my feelings as much as possible and erected a protective wall around me. Otherwise, I could not have gone through with that visit. I entered the room where Megan was lying, and in the hours that followed it was as if we both were caught in an absurd drama—we only had to play out the scenes and speak the distorted and unfamiliar lines. They had shorn her head, and I was plagued by the illusion that she was a newborn who had yet to grow her first hair. After the initial visit, I slowly tried to open up and reach out to her, but at each attempt, she was not there, and I reached right through an apparition. It froze me to the core.

In a frantic attempt to help her, I talked with her psychiatrist and therapists and consulted attorneys and people who knew her— the Paris police, her concierge. I took a side trip to Germany and talked with the management in the Munich hotel where Mr. Bonatti *was murdered. I didn't know at that point how useless my attempts would be for my daughter, nor that they would mark the beginning of a quest that would control me to this day. My European trip was cut short by news of Gina's illness, and before I could return to see Megan again, my daughter was dead.*

✿ ✿ ✿

September 22, 1982

They tell me I've been in the hospital for five weeks now. Why am I here? How did I get here? I can't remember where I came from or what my name is. They tell me it's Megan Lloyd and that I'm an American from California. They speak to me in French and sometimes English. I understand most of their French. How did I learn French? They tell me to write a diary every day and to try to remember my past. I have terrible headaches and I prefer to sleep. It tires me to write.

October 16, 1982

They removed the bandages from my head today. They say the wound is healing and the stitches are dissolving. They gave me a mirror. My head is shorn and I did not know I looked so strange. I stare at the mirror a lot. I imagine myself with shoulder-length hair. I saw Dr. Duval again today. He is a psychiatrist. He and the nurses tell me I suffered a bad head injury. They don't tell me how. They tell me it's important that I remember at my own pace as my health improves. They think I will improve and gradually regain my memory. Dr. Duval encourages me to write whenever I feel like it. My headaches are a little less severe. They give me medication which helps the pain, but it makes me sleep most of the time. I have no desire to be awake.

November 1, 1982

One of the nurses, Greta, who says she is half German, has been taking me on walks through the hospital and the grounds. German comes easier to me than French. I asked her why so many windows have bars, why the closed courtyard, and why the barbed wire around the wall. She told me that this is a prison infirmary. She refused to tell me why I'm kept here. I am angry sometimes and worried almost all the time. I demanded to see Dr. Duval. He cannot see me again until next week.

My headaches are better. I can get by on aspirins and I'm awake more, but I don't feel like doing anything. They have given me a pile of travel books on European countries and the United States. They tell me I'm from California. I stare at the pictures of beaches. I sit here in this cell with bars, and I can't seem to make contact with these pictures. I am drawn to them, but they pull back. The more I try, the more they seem to retreat beyond my grasp. I don't enjoy looking at the pictures of Germany or France either, so I look at places like Spain, England, Holland. I have no feelings about them. Who lives there? Have I been in these countries? They tell me I have not. So I can relax about these pictures, because nobody asks me to relate them to anything. No effort required.

November 9, 1982

I talked with Dr. Duval and demanded to know why I'm in a hospital with bars. He tells me I have been arrested for a crime and must stand trial when I am well. He refuses to tell me any details. He insists that the amnesia must run its course, and it is important not to prejudice my memory of events. I might not believe them if he told me, anyway, he claims—not until I recall them on my own. He does tell me that my head was injured six weeks after my imprisonment when some other inmates attacked me with a fire extinguisher in the dining hall. He tells me I was lucky not to have been killed. The common criminals have little sympathy for my type of crime. They have had to separate me from the others for my own safety. I try to imagine what type of crime I might have committed, but I come up against a wall in my mind.

I asked Dr. Duval what happened during the first six weeks of my captivity, before this blank period set in. What did I do? He said I wrote a great deal—stories, apparently about my life.

He tells me my brother will be here in three weeks to see me. He says that my father was also here, after I came out of my coma. My family has been in touch with the American Embassy and the other authorities involved in my case. I was puzzled to hear I have a family, but Dr. Duval says that my mother is not well, so my father could not stay longer, and that I have two brothers, and that this is a normal situation. The one who plans to visit is named Christopher, a pilot. I cannot imagine how I will react to him. Will I suddenly remember him and everything else? Will he look like me? It makes me nervous.

"Why does he come?" I ask Dr. Duval. He tells me my family is doing everything it can to help me. He doubts that his visit will improve my amnesia, but he has no reason to prevent it.

One day is like the other. They're trying to teach me a card game. I like learning the rules. They say it's good therapy for people who lose their memory. I enjoy the logic of it, the control it provides me. I can remember the rules as long as we play, but then I forget them in between times, and they have to explain them to me all over again the next time. It frustrates me and I cry.

December 2, 1982

I met with my brother Christopher for about two hours today. (They said it was my brother). It made no difference to me. He was not familiar to me and I didn't like it to have a stranger hug me like he did. He's a tall, good-looking type with wavy black hair and steady brown eyes. He sat facing me in a private room across a table which the prison provided for this visit. But I imagine they were probably observing us. He wore a light blue shirt and jacket. On his lapel was a small silver-white airplane pin with folded back wings. It's sharp nose pointed towards his heart.

He told me about our family in California. My mother was in poor health and my father was taking care of her. They were very upset about my situation and were trying to do what they could for me. Our brother is well and has a new baby with his third wife. For a long time he asked me questions about my situation—how I got here, what I had done, didn't I remember anything? If I could remember anything at all, maybe they could help me in preparing a defense. They had engaged a French lawyer to take my case. I didn't know what to say. I guess he meant well and had gone to a lot of trouble to come here, but I told him maybe he should talk to Dr. Duval, who seemed to know more about me than I did. When he left, he cried, so I let him hug me again. He made me promise to write as soon as I remembered anything at all. It seemed like he'd gone to a lot of effort for nothing.

December 21, 1982

I quit writing my journal for a long time because I got depressed. They tried letting me eat again with some of the less violent inmates and taking my daily exercise with them, but it went badly. For one thing, I couldn't communicate very well with the other women. Most of them avoided me and one of them threatened me. And what's worse, part of my memory returned one week. I began recalling my childhood in California, my marriage to Thomas and our divorce before I set out for Texas. I remembered my brothers, including Chris, and felt bad that I didn't recognize him when he was here. Why I was in Europe, I couldn't remember, but some of the prisoners referred to me as a "terroriste." I still seem to block out whatever terrible deeds I'm supposed to have done. It drives me crazy not to know what they are. Dr. Duval put me back on medications—this time anti-depressants—after I started talking about suicide. And he's started to talk to me about my childhood. But he's an urbane Parisian who's never been to California, and when I try to explain the expensive scotch, classical music and the property strewn with junk in the hills of Los Angeles, he just shakes his head. He's also told me that I may soon be extradited to Germany. Since my childhood memory has returned, they expect the rest to follow in due course. I have had to talk to my French attorney who tries to explain to me the complexities of my case, but I can't retain what he says. My mind still has troubles with new information, and so much of my past seems like an unfathomable black hole.

June 21, 1983

I have been in a mental asylum in Stuttgart, Germany, for about three months, since they extradited me here. I still don't know why I was arrested. That is, I "know" because both the French and German authorities eventually told me what I'd done (or allegedly done), and they gave me newspaper articles to read about the murder in the Munich hotel and about the West German terrorist gang of which I was apparently a member, hoping it would jolt my memory after I failed over time to respond to therapy. I still read and reread the articles thinking they will unlock my memory, but they only make me feel even more isolated in myself. I never get the sense that they are talking about me. I try to imagine what it was like to commit that murder in the Munich hotel, but it sounds more like something perpetrated by a backward Bulgarian peasant or a decadent French count, far away from polite society. That crucial period of my life has become like a smooth, polished silver ball. Everything surrounding this ball is reflected in its shining surface, but no matter how I turn it, it doesn't seem to have an inside, or if it does, there's no way of penetrating to it. I think of that ride at Disneyland that enters into a snow flake. You go deeper and deeper into its transparent molecular structure, which looks soft and lace-like, until you approach the center. Then you see this pulsating red ball which forms its core. All of its power is enclosed in it, seemingly unreachable. Sometimes I turn my search outward, away from myself, and then I have the suspicion that I'm being framed by some person or group.

Anyway, it seems I don't belong in prison because I am not medically sound enough to stand trial, and the German doctors find no reason to keep me in a normal hospital either, since I've recovered my physical strength and ability to express myself. Dr. Duval certified that I'm not insane, but my hoped-for total recovery from amnesia has not taken place. He says perhaps my brain lesions are too severe, after all. I don't fit very well into the European health care or penal system. I'm still technically innocent as long as I don't stand trial and am proven guilty, but I'm also medically incapable of standing trial even though I'm not insane. So here I sit. They won't let me out on bail, because I'm considered too dangerous, and the only safe place to retain me seems to be this place with its bars everywhere. I see a therapist once a week—Claudia, a social worker. She's about thirty years old with short black hair, brown eyes, a slightly crooked nose—attractive. She's slim and soft-spoken, but her chain-smoking bothers me.

July 4, 1983

Claudia did something nice today. She gave me a blue narcissus and a small American flag of the sort you might find sticking in the chunk of pineapple in a rum punch. She said red, white and blue were nice colors. It was her form of Independence Day celebration for me. I cried and she touched my forearm.

July 26, 1983

Time passes. Being aware but not knowing is the worst torture—why am I here? Did I really do it? If I had these answers, I could at least admit my guilt and accept my fate. The life of an imprisoned terrorist would surely be preferable to this, because there would be a reason for it.

The only pleasure I have here is the one hour once a week with Claudia. Last week, however, she called off our appointment and I got worried. All the other workers, the nurses, the warden and the guards handle me as if they were embarrassed to admit to themselves that I'm not insane. They are used to crazy people, and not one of them talks to me in a natural way. But then again, I suppose they all assume I'm the terrorist the newspapers describe, and maybe they also think that I'm hiding behind my amnesia.

I follow my case in the newspapers—whatever little there is left of it. None of the terrorists have been caught, except for me, as they say. They are thought to be underground (I've always thought of gophers and snakes in connection with that term, and animals that hibernate—I mean, how do you live "underground"?), and I am pretty much forgotten. There is no trace of the male accomplice with whom I fled into the Paris catacombs the day before my capture. It's like reading biographical sketches of someone else's life. In letters I try to reassure Chris and my family in California, but I don't tell them my doubts.

Chris mailed me the paperback volumes of Dante's *Divine Comedy* which he said had been my favorite reading during my college days. I found some good lines in one of them:

> "I saw it, I'm sure, and I seem to see it still:
> a body with no head that moved along,
> moving no differently from all the rest; he
> held his severed head up by its hair, swing-
> ing it in one hand just like a lantern, and as
> it looked at us it said: 'Alas!' "

August 15, 1983

I have been sleeping later every morning and also taking naps during the day. Sleep covers my mind and blankets my body. Last night I was awake for hours. I stared into the dark and out at the dim lights from a distant street. I don't really want to get out of bed, but they make me get up and eat and exercise. I have to force myself. I have lost my appetite and some weight—I can tell because my clothes are looser. Today Claudia came to my cell since I told Anton, the guard who takes me to my appointment, that I was sick. She told Anton to leave her alone with me, so he locked her into my cell. It was the first time that anyone else has been in my room with me. She sat on the chair next to the table, and I sat up in bed, my back against the wall. I pulled the covers over my shoulders, since I had nothing on. She seemed nervous and smoked a cigarette, even though she knew I didn't like it. She got up to flick her ashes periodically into my toilet in the corner of my cubicle. I didn't protest. She wanted to know what was wrong, but I had nothing to tell her. There wasn't anything more wrong than there always was, being incarcerated in a German mental hospital. She tried to talk to me, but she couldn't get much more than one-word answers out of me. I wasn't trying to be stubborn. I just couldn't think of anything to say. It surprised me when she asked if I were mad at her. I told her no, that I liked her and was grateful to her for trying to help me. She said that she liked me too, but she was worried about me. I couldn't understand why she was worried about me, but I didn't ask because I began to cry. She got up, threw her cigarette into the toilet and came and sat next to me on the bed. She put her arm around my shoulders, pulled my head toward her and stroked my hair where it covered my wound. It was so strange to be physically close to someone, and in this room, to have an arm around me. Who was the last person to touch me with any affection? I cried and I trembled. She said, "I don't believe you are guilty," pronouncing each syllable slowly and with deliberation.

I was afraid to move, for fear she would take back what she said or that she would stop. But instead, she moved her hands to the back of my neck and massaged my neck and shoulders. I turned my back to her touch, and the blankets slid off my body. The fingers of an angel rubbed my shoulder blades, my spine, the small of my back. I sank down onto my stomach and she rubbed my legs and feet too for a short eternity, resurrecting me from the dead. Too soon, Claudia whispered that our time was almost up, and that Anton would be back to get her. I hated to hear this news, and I didn't move from my prone position when she stood up, hoping to better retain the last touch of the warmth she had infused in me. Before Anton came a minute later, Claudia leaned back down to stroke my hair, and for a fleeting moment, I could feel her soft breath near my neck.

August 16, 1983

I stayed awake for hours. It was a rare clear night, and from my bed I could see the Big Dipper. With my eyes I traced an invisible path from it to the North Star, which seemed to rest on the ledge of my window sill. I fixed my gaze on that star by which navigators had charted the first voyages around the earth.

I thought about Claudia's hands on my back, how they felt. In the night I had a dream. It began in black and white with the grey walls of my cell. They were pockmarked with hundreds of small, ugly blotches—maybe letters or swastikas. I had been sitting in this cubicle for a hundred years trying to decipher the meaning of these marks. I had a long white pony tail which grew only out of the scar tissue on my scalp. Otherwise I was bald. Black mold grew on the concrete floor and spread out gradually. It crept up the walls towards the ceiling, devouring the unintelligible blotches.

The walls began to move slowly towards me as I sat on the bed, shrinking the size of the room. I sat and waited as the walls pressed against and began to deform the mattress. Then a crack appeared in the wall in front of me, and a tiny violet flower on a red shoot pushed its way inside where it began to grow and its petals open up. The walls stopped moving and the crack opened wider. More red shoots, curled tendrils and finally clusters of dark red grapes entered. With them came sunlight, fresh air and all the colors of the outside world.

August 22, 1983—morning

This morning I awoke at the first rays of dawn, with poetry in my brain. " . . . what light through yonder window breaks?/ It is the east, and Claudia is the sun! Arise, fair sun, and kill the envious moon,/ Who is already sick and pale with grief. . . ."

This is the day for my appointment with Claudia. I'll get dressed early to be ready. I'm going to jot down some lines from Dante's *Divine Comedy*. I want to show them to her:

> "As he who sees things in a dream and
> wakes to feel the passion of the dream still
> there although no part of it remains in
> mind, just such am I: my vision fades and
> all but ceases, yet the sweetness born of it I
> still can feel distilling in my heart. . . ."

August 22, 1983—evening

My heart was pounding when I entered the office. She was not there. A Herr Feister greeted me and informed me that Frau

Martin-Breuer had been transferred unexpectedly to another position in Bremen—a better job, an advance in her career. He would be seeing me from now on.

❁   ❁   ❁

From the *Los Angeles Times* of August 26, 1983:

> "Yesterday, Megan Lloyd, 34, a former resident of Brentwood, California, and the alleged murderer of the Italian pharmaceutical magnate, Guido Bonatti, was found dead, hanging by the neck from a light fixture in her room in the Stachelheim Mental Hospital in Stuttgart, West Germany, where she has been held awaiting trial since March 23 of this year due to amnesia. She is alleged to have been the American member of the West German terrorist gang, the 'Red Liberators,' that is also suspected in the conspiracy kidnapping and murder of the former West German Minister of Culture, Ludwig Reichhardt in 1970. German authorities reported that Ms. Lloyd committed suicide by using bed sheets to hang herself. The body was found at approximately 10 AM Thursday. An autopsy will be performed."

Epilogue

Gordon:

The days of my life are numbered now. Things begin to fall away from me one by one—unimportant things. But one idea has seized me and takes on sharper contours as the daylight yields to the dusk.

What if an artist were to create a crucifixion of a woman—a sculpture or painting of a woman, crucified on the cross?

It would be a "cruci-fiction," to borrow the term of the extraordinary surrealist, Herlinde, since it would constitute a thing which has never existed and never could be tolerated—a tortured, mutilated woman, hanging from a cross—perhaps even with a pregnant belly? You will notice how sacrilegious it is to even entertain this thought in the privacy of your own mind.

A female nailed to the cross with a crown of thorns, wounded in her side, bleeding—to many this would seem an outrage. The Vatican would denounce it and the international media would buzz with the controversy. If an artist had conceived such an image in the sixteenth century, he would have been promptly burned at the stake, his ashes swept away from the village square by a cold wind.

But what if a contemporary artist created a crucified woman, thus challenging the myth of a solely male creator and a male Trinity, the claim that masculinity alone is divine? It would be branded obscene or trivialized and ignored by the powers, political and religious, that are interested in the perpetuation of this myth.

What if an artist created a crucified woman as tragic as the Grünewald altar in Colmar? As gnarled as Dürer, as rosy as Rubens, as perverse as Dali? It would be deemed pornographic—kin to the cheap pulp magazine or the sleazy sex shop, and more harmful than slasher books and snuff films in which fictional and real women are

173

dismembered for the amusement of their audiences and the profits of their producers. Who is outraged by the latter? Who says NO to them? But if an artist were to depict a woman hanging from the cross. . . . And yet, it would give lie to the claim that men have suffered more in this world than women.

What if an artist were moved to create a female crucifixion? What if there were a Corpus Sarah or corpus Elisabeth, Shulamith, Carmen . . . or Megan?

What if the central myth of western culture and the path to the highest spiritual transformation were not the symbolic cannibalism of a male's body, but rather transubstantiation of a female body, the partaking of her flesh and blood, her body? It would be rejected in the western world. Because it would suggest that a woman's body, soul and suffering were equivalent to those of a man. It would mean that we could no longer burn her as a witch and we'd have to burn ourselves.

I nailed the body of my daughter, Megan Lloyd, to the cross. I am male violence. I am not the savior, but the executioner.

✿　✿　✿

Late one afternoon Gordon Sheridan turned right off of Sunset Boulevard and proceeded up Mandeville Canyon Road. After several miles he turned off the main street and wound around for a while before reaching the gravel driveway of his old friend, J. Arthur Lloyd. Arthur was dying and Gordon had come to see him and to pick up a manuscript. He had promised Arthur not to read it until after his death. Only then would he show it to his friends in the publishing houses.

The sun was beginning to set in the Pacific when Gordon embraced Arthur and left him to the care of his nurse. He carried a cardboard box containing a typed manuscript under one arm as he walked down the steps to his white Lincoln Continental town car waiting in the driveway. As he lowered himself into the driver's seat he set down the box, which was fastened with tape and string, onto the plush leather next to him. He glanced up at Arthur's expansive home and wiped his eyes and blew his nose before turning on the ignition. The large car sprang to life and he drove it slowly around and out of the crescent driveway and down the hill back to Mandeville Canyon Road. When he came to Sunset Boulevard he turned left, and ten minutes later he reached the interchange of the San Diego and Santa Monica freeways where he headed east toward the skyscrapers of the sprawling metropolis that rose hazy gold and brown out of the early evening smog.